The Revenge Playbook

ALSO BY RACHAEL ALLEN

17 First Kisses

The Revenge Playbook

RACHAEL ALLEN

HARPER TEEN

An Imprint of HarperCollinsPublishers

HarperTeen is an imprint of HarperCollins Publishers.

The Revenge Playbook
Copyright © 2015 by Rachael Allen
All rights reserved. Printed in the United States of America. No part of this book may be used or reproduced in any manner whatsoever without written permission except in the case of brief quotations embodied in critical articles and reviews. For information address HarperCollins Children's Books, a division of HarperCollins Publishers, 195 Broadway, New York, NY 10007.
www.epicreads.com

Library of Congress Control Number: 2014946550
ISBN 978-0-06-228136-4 (pbk.)

Typography by Ellice M. Lee
15 16 17 18 19   PC/RRDH   10 9 8 7 6 5 4 3 2 1
❖
First Edition

To all my best girls,

because the best ones are like sisters.

RANBURNE PANTHER
SCAVENGER HUNT

You will complete the following 14 dares—one for every game the Panther football team won last year. All dares must be photo documented in order to count. The entire team must be present for each dare even if it doesn't take the entire team to complete the dare. If and only if you complete every dare on the list, you may proceed to Catcalls in Slocomb where you can exchange the completed dare list for the Football of '76. Ask for Destiny. Should you fail to retrieve the football before Catcalls closes at 3:00 a.m., you will be walking onto the field naked at Homecoming. Good luck.

In Ranburne:

1. Fill a condom up with water. Draw a face on it. Put it on Principal Corso's doormat, and ding-dong ditch. (One person)
2. The egg-on-a-string trick. Hang an egg from a power line by a string and watch a car run into it. (Everyone)
3. Paint the David Bowie statue at Old Lady Howard's corn maze. (Everyone)
4. Chair race through Walmart. (Everyone)
5. Get a picture of the team with the Ranburne Panther. (Everyone)

6. Go to the Dawsonville football field. Find that stupid rock they touch before their games. Pee on it. (Everyone)

In Nashville:

7. Visit the illustrious Delta Tau Beta fraternity at Vanderbilt. Have a beer with Panther alum TJ McNeil and take a picture of the legendary scar he got during a game-winning play against Dawsonville. (One person)

8. Go to LP Field and reenact the "Music City Miracle." (Everyone)

9. Go to Centennial Park and jump in the pond behind the Parthenon. (Everyone)

10. Go to The Jackrabbit Saloon. Walk to the very middle of the dance floor and attempt to do the worm. (One person)

11. Go up to a girl who is totally out of your league, get down on your knees, and ask her to marry you. (One person)

12. Go up to a fat girl and tell her "You're so beautiful . . . for a fat chick." Bonus points if she throws her drink on you. (One person)

13. Hug a biker. Bonus points if he has a mullet. (One person)

14. Get a girl to give you her thong. (One person)

5:30 P.M.

MELANIE JANE

My hands grip the paper tight like it might evaporate. This is it. The Ranburne Panther Scavenger Hunt dare list. Our best and last chance at revenge.

Every kid in this town has been hearing about the hunt since before middle school, back when the idea of the high school boys doing an annual tear-up-the-town scavenger hunt seemed like the coolest thing you can imagine. Now that I am actually in high school with them, the football team has lost their heroic shine. But the hunt? It's mythical.

"I still can't believe I got her to give us the list," says Ana.

"Do you really think we can beat them?" asks Peyton.

"I want to read it next!" squeals Liv.

"Here." I smack the list down on the console in Ana's car where everyone can see it. "It's not going to be easy."

It really isn't, but after weeks of planning, we are so close I can taste it. I picture us holding that precious football, Weston having to walk onto the field naked at Homecoming, and I grin.

The hunt is football players only—a rite of passage the older Varsity players put the rookies through. Unless you count Destiny, the grizzled stripper who has apparently played the part of list keeper since the beginning of time, no girl has ever held this list before. That's why it's extra important that we beat them.

"I think we have a shot." I read over the dares one more time. "But we're going to need to plan this really carefully. I think we should go back to Ranburne. We can talk strategy on the way."

The three of them nod in agreement.

Ana checks the clock on the dashboard. "It's five thirty. Do you think the boys have already started? I can have us in Ranburne by six o'clock, maybe sooner."

She shakes her black hair out of her eyes so she can check for oncoming traffic before pulling out of the parking lot across from Catcalls.

I frown at the list. "Actually, you know what? Let's go to Dawsonville first. We can get the Walmart chair races out of the way and pick up all the stuff we're going to need for the rest of the dares."

Liv points to dare number six. "Oh! And we can go to Dawsonville's football field while we're there."

"Uh-huh." I feel my face tighten. There is no way I am peeing in public. On camera. I can't think of anything less ladylike.

Ana grimaces as she changes lanes. "Some of those dares are really disgusting."

"Right?" I'm so glad I'm not the only one who is freaked out over this peeing business.

"I mean, telling a girl she's pretty for a fat chick? Getting a thong? I wonder if there's any way we can modify them and still have it count."

Yes. Modify them. Excellent idea! And let's modify the one about the peeing while we're at it.

"Some of those dares are going to be easier for us," says Peyton. "Liv, you're out of my league. I could totally ask you to marry me. And it's going to be way easier for us to get a thong."

"I wonder if she'd think that was cheating," says Liv. "Maybe we should ask a boy to marry us instead of a girl."

Ana snorts. "Yeah, but how are we supposed to find a boy wearing a thong?"

Yeah, that's not going to happen. Especially in Nashville. "Maybe instead we get a boy to wear a thong? And, like, dance around in it or something?"

The girls all start cackling.

"That I could get on board with," says Ana. "I have a feeling Destiny would be okay with it too."

"Hey, how did you get her to agree to this anyway?" asks Liv. "When she told us no back there, I thought we were done for. What did you say to her?"

The atmosphere in the car changes. I had been wanting to know the same thing, but wasn't sure how to ask.

"Oh, um." Ana's knuckles tighten on the steering wheel. "I just— We understand each other, that's all. I was able to make her see why this is so important."

Well, that was the vaguest answer in the history of the universe. None of us press her on it though. Something in her voice says not to.

"So, we still haven't figured out what to do about the fat chick one."

Ana. Always the master of changing the subject.

The car goes quiet again. Not in an uncomfortable way. Thinking quiet. We're unable to come up with a way to put our own non-evil spin on this one, but we can figure it out later. I put the scavenger hunt locations into my phone, so I can maximize our efficiency. Luckily, everywhere we need to go in Nashville is only five to ten minutes apart.

And then Ana pulls into the Dawsonville Walmart, and I start barking orders like a drill sergeant. "Okay. Let's get the supplies first in case they kick us out after the chair races. Peyton, you get the paint. You're so innocent looking, no one would suspect you of vandalism. Does anyone mind buying condoms?"

"I can do that," says Liv.

"Awesome. I'll get some flashlights." I grin. "And a thong. That leaves string and eggs. Ana, can you get those?"

"Sure."

The second the car comes to a complete stop, we scatter. Run to the entrance. Grab baskets. Like sweeping through Walmart in every direction as part of a covert mission is something we do every day.

We need to fly through these dares because I have no idea how far ahead the boys might be. One major advantage (other than our inherent awesomeness): the boys don't know they have competition. The rookies do the hunt as one group, not competing against each other. It's supposed to enhance team unity or something. Because I guess slapping each other on the butt all the time isn't enough.

I throw four flashlights in my basket and rush to the underwear section. Granny panties, boy shorts, crazy lace contraptions. Thongs! There they are. I grab the most ridiculous one I can find, pink with lacy ruffles, and sprint to the front of the store. I hope I'm first. Not that it's a race.

Except it is. Because Ana and I burst out of the aisles at exactly the same time, and there is one and only one checkout counter open. Our eyes meet, and we both know this is a showdown, and we go for it. I slap my basket on the counter just in front of hers, and she rolls her eyes like she wasn't competing too. Victory is sweet. We laugh uncontrollably while the Walmart lady rings up our items and stares at us like we are mentally deranged.

Ana and I walk our "groceries" to the car, and Liv joins us a minute later. We have to wait a little bit for Peyton.

"Sorry," she says. "There was one thing I had trouble finding."

Um, I thought she was just getting paint, but whatever. We throw everything in the trunk, and then it's back inside for chair races.

"The office supplies are at the back!" yells Liv.

A few shoppers turn to watch the crazy girls run past. We

each grab a rolling desk chair, and Ana turns on her video camera.

"We're going from here to the housewares aisle." She barely gives us time to get into position before she shouts, "Ready. Set. Go!"

I kick off hard and pump my legs. Liv is my real competition. Peyton's spindly legs were not designed for chair races, but Liv's got some quads on her. Ana's more concerned about getting good footage of the race than trying to win, so I think I've got this. Housewares is coming up soon. Just a few more kicks.

Liv puts on a burst of speed and passes me just as we reach the finish line, aka a selection of laundry baskets. Her chair keeps rolling as she pumps her fists in the air.

Peyton's chair putters to a stop just past the finish line. "Maybe we should get out of here. Like, before they catch us?" She checks over her shoulder for authority figures.

"It's too late," says Liv, reversing her chair and kicking toward Peyton. "You're already in trouble."

"What?" Her brown eyes dart around the store.

Then Liv crashes into her, bumper-cars style, and they both fall apart laughing. Thankfully, no one seems to be able to recover from our weirdness fast enough to arrest us, so we're able to get back to the car without so much as a lecture. The other girls are checking the list again, but I don't have to. I know what's next. And I am dreading it.

I pull a small pack of baby wipes from my purse. That was way too much physical activity for my sweat glands to handle, and now I feel positively gross. I wipe myself down while my friends crack jokes about my obsession with looking polished at all times. *Friends*. If you had told me two months ago that the four of us would be sitting in this car together, I never would have believed you.

1

Friday, August 7 (Seven weeks earlier)

PEYTON

*N*o one here knows you're a loser. Take a deep breath. Stand up straight. Smile.

And no one has to know.

I wait my turn for dance team sign-ins with dozens of other girls and try to ignore the feeling of being in a cattle line. If I can get through another day of auditions without passing out from fear, I will consider it a raging success.

The two girls in front of me were in my geography class last year. I should totally say hi to them. It would be easy. I'm going to do it, like, right now. Well, maybe in a minute. After the heart palpitations stop.

"Hi," I finally say. I tuck a sheet of light brown hair behind my ear out of habit, then pull it out again so it won't get a wrinkle.

They either don't hear me or pretend they don't. Awesome. I am off to an awesome start.

"Can you believe the routine from yesterday?" I say it a little louder, plowing through the jitters. "The choreography at the end was really intense."

This time one of the girls glances at me over her shoulder before turning back to her friend. She can hear me—I just don't have enough cool points to be worthy of her attention. This is the part of dance team tryouts I hate. The awkward-small-talk-during-breaks, all-the-other-girls-safely-in-their-cliques part. I sigh. Sometimes I feel like there's this extra layer to the world of social interaction that's invisible to shy people, and if I could only see it, I'd be able to make friends.

The summer before eighth grade, I did the thing from the teen movies where you have a summer transformation—the braces came off, I bought new clothes, I even learned how to use a flatiron. It didn't work out the way it does in the movies though. It wasn't like everyone suddenly noticed me. Well, Karl noticed me. This is the first thing I've tried to do for myself since I broke up with him. And I know it's just making the dance team, but sometimes it feels like a test. If I fail it, I fail at being on my own.

It's my turn to sign in, so I write *Peyton Reed* in my neat, clear handwriting and sit down on a patch of grass to stretch while I wait for the good part of tryouts—the dancing.

"We're going to run through yesterday's routine again," yells Coach Tanner. "Make sure you're where you can see one of the veterans, and remember, we're just practicing right now. There's no need to be anxious."

Yeah, right. If you're dancing and the coaches are watching, it's part of the audition. I know they want to see how fast we learn, and I'm not going to disappoint. I hurry to join Liv Lambros's group—she's the only sophomore veteran leading her own practice group. She's also the best dancer on the team.

"Hey! Are you guys psyched about how awesome this dance is? Because I am psyched!" Liv bounces up and down a little as she talks, her blonde curls fighting their elastic.

There is some awkward smiling/mumbling/head nodding.

"I am going to pretend that means you are all REALLY PSYCHED!"

I giggle, and she smiles at me. Score!

Then the music starts, and we're all in the zone. Liv rattles off the eight count while she goes through yesterday's steps. She has this amazing spark when she dances—she commands your attention even though some of the other girls on the team are better technical dancers. I pray the spark is contagious.

Yesterday, we mostly worked without the music, doing the steps at half-time until we had them perfect. Today we are at full speed. You never appreciate how fast a Beyoncé song is until you're expected to do two double pirouettes during the first verse.

The crazy thing is, at ballet class last week I was cranking out triple pirouettes no problem, but it's different now because my feet have to be parallel instead of turned out. Plus, with hip-hop everything's off center instead of straight up and down, so my center of gravity pretty much hates me right now. I try to keep up and do a pretty good job considering how long it's been. I need to rebuild my stamina, though. Ballet doesn't push me in the same way. By the second time through the song, I am panting like crazy. By the third, I decide Beyoncé is a sadist.

When the song ends for the third time, the coaches signal a water break, and I take the opportunity to flop on the ground. This would be a whole lot easier if I was still taking my other dance class. If I hadn't cut hip-hop out of my life two years ago. I saw a documentary about phantom limbs once. Someone loses an arm or a leg, and even though it's gone, they still feel the pain of it, haunting them. Well, hip-hop is my phantom limb. I think about it. I dream about it. I pop sassy moves into my ballet routines without even meaning to, and if I hear more than a few beats of bass, I'm busting out spontaneous choreography.

And ballet is great, don't get me wrong. But all I am is straight-laced and predictable and controlled. Hip-hop was my one outlet to be something else. To feel something different. So I'm worse than the phantom-limb people. Because if they had a chance to have their limb back, you know they'd take it in a heartbeat. And I've been living without a piece of myself for the past year because other people made me feel ashamed of it.

When the music starts again, I don't worry about keeping up. I don't worry about anything. I let myself go and maybe, just maybe, reclaim a little piece of what I lost. I can't stop grinning. I forgot how much fun this could be. I feel a burst of energy I didn't have before—there is more air in my leaps, more booty in my shake. When I get to the end of the song, I realize I may have gotten through the entire thing mistake-free. The best part: I don't know because I was having so much fun I forgot to count my mistakes.

Liv bumps me with her hip. "Nice job, rookie."

"Hey, thanks!"

She noticed! I am giddy for the rest of practice.

When we finish, I walk to the parking lot to wait for my mom. She won't be off work for at least half an hour. I picture what Karl would say if he saw the way I danced at tryouts today. The things he said to me last year when I called him crying after the lock-in and told him I was having second thoughts about dance team tryouts replay in my head.

They dance like how strippers dance. I can't believe that's even something you would want.

I'm just trying to protect you. Women who do stuff like that are one step above whores. I don't want people thinking about you that way.

You're so shy—do you really think they'd pick you anyway?

I sigh because that last thought still gets me. Even though Karl and I are over, he's haunting me. He is the voice in the back of my mind that whispers I can't do it.

I sit on the curb and try to ignore the cold feeling that has slipped into my stomach. If what the voice says is true, that brilliant moment of life-reclaiming I had at tryouts today? I can kiss it good-bye.

Friday, August 7
LIV

ackle hugs are kind of my thing. I know a lot of people *say* *tacklehug* like in texts or on the internet or whatever, but most people have never actually tried to simultaneously tackle and hug another human being. Most people are missing out. There is a special kind of joy that radiates through you when your arms and legs are wrapped around another person and for a split second you have no idea whether you're both about to end up on the ground or not. I can't just put something like that into words.

It's why I'm tucked behind the bleachers right now waiting for my boyfriend, Trevor, who I estimate is twenty yards away. Timing is a critical ingredient in a good tackle hug. I poke my head out for one more peek and have to jerk back quickly. Yep, he's close. He and some friends from the football team stroll past the bleacher next to mine, decked out in their practice gear. They're so close I can hear their voices. I flex my leg muscles like a runner in the starting box, waiting for my first glimpse of Trevor's blond head so I can pounce. And then they stop walking. Right in front of my bleacher.

Huh. Well, creeping in the shadows wasn't exactly what I had planned. I'm debating whether to go for the running leap–tackle hug combo when I hear a voice say, "Hey, have you broken up with Liv yet?"

I feel like I just took a punch to the gut. Did I really hear that right? The words are there, in my head, wounding me, but they don't make sense. There's got to be some other interpretation that I'm not getting because Trevor wouldn't. I mean. He loves me.

"Oh, um," I hear Trevor say.

Another voice, one I recognize, cuts him off. It's Chad MacAllistair, senior, football captain, star receiver, and therefore king of the universe. "That's a no. Dude, we've been talking about this for weeks. You gotta man up already."

Weeks. They've been talking about this for *weeks.* Were they talking about it five weeks ago when Trevor and I stayed up until 8:00 in the morning talking on Skype? Or two weeks ago when we went out to dinner for our ten-month anniversary? Or maybe last night when Trevor kissed me on my forehead and nose and mouth and told me he couldn't imagine being with any other girl but me?

He finally pipes up, but his voice is feeble. "She's a pretty cool girl."

"I'm sure she is. I'm sure she's a lot of fun," says the first voice. The guys all laugh, and I feel like something must have happened that I can't see.

"Hey, I've seen the way she dances. I get it," says Chad. "But what have we been telling you? She's toxic."

"But—"

"Calm down, man. There's plenty of other girls at this school," says someone who isn't Chad or Trevor. Other voices chime in, and I can't tell who's saying what or who they're directing it at.

"Yeah. Girls who aren't skanks."

Somebody laughs. "That's cold."

"What? You've seen her. She's a straight-up slut."

"I bet she puts out after the first date."

"I bet she puts out after no date."

"She's probably banged at least twelve guys."

"Dude, that's a Tuesday for her."

I wait for the part where Trevor speaks up and defends me. And then I wait some more. He knows it's not true. He knows he was my first, and even if he wasn't, he's not the kind of guy who talks about girls like that. I keep waiting while the sobs form in my chest like a hurricane working its way to a Category 5. But he never says a damn thing—not in my defense, not even just to say, "Hey, man, it's gross to talk about girls like that."

"Guys, guys," says Chad. "We all know Liv Lambros is a gigantic whore. What we need to know is when our man Trevor is going to do something about it." He lowers his voice. "I don't want this to get ugly."

"Today, okay?" Trevor sounds exasperated. "I'll do it today."

"You better. I want you to be a free man for Casey's party next weekend. Text me after you do it, okay, brah?"

"Yeah, okay."

The tiny hope that Trevor would come to his senses and tell

them no was the only thing keeping the tears at bay, and now they come crashing down. And because I am crying so hard I can't see, I don't realize that Trevor is barreling around the corner until he has already crashed into me. He wraps his arm around my back to keep us both standing, and we have this split second of vertigo when I think we might both end up on the ground before he pulls away.

"I'm so sorry, sugar. I didn't see you there." His easy smile dies on his face. "Hey, what's wrong? Did you—? I mean, did you hear—?"

I stand there with my fists clenched, trying to keep the storm inside even though I'm already falling apart. "It's fine, Trevor. I already know what you're going to say."

"But—" He reaches out to touch my cheek, something he always does when I'm sad.

"No." I catch his fingers before they graze my face. And if it were possible to take everything those guys said about me and everything Trevor didn't say and forge my hurt into a weapon that I could plunge into his stomach making him feel everything I feel—that is what I'd do. He lets out a small gasp like he felt my imaginary stab wound, or maybe he's just gearing up for another attempt at apologizing. "I have to go."

I point my chin in the air and walk away from him with as much grace as I can manage.

"Liv," he calls after me.

I turn. His face tells me there is so much he wants to say to me right now, but I shake my head sadly. "Don't ever talk to me again."

I force myself to keep putting one foot in front of the other, even though it hurts. With every step comes a flash of a perfect, wonderful moment with Trevor—the time he kissed me in front of the duck pond, the day we came back from Chickasaw Trace Park soaked to the skin because a summer storm crept up on us, the baby rhino picture he emailed me last week because I was at my dad's house and feeling sad. I stomp those memories to pieces. When I reach the parking lot, I'm lost. I really don't want to be alone right now. Marley already left, and because this is a time of crisis, of course her phone is dead. A couple of other girls from dance team are sitting in one of their cars listening to music, but they're both kind of dramatic, and I don't think I can handle that. I decide I'll just sit on the curb and wait for my mom to pick me up.

There's a rustling beside me. "Hey, um, are you okay?"

I jump. I thought I was the only one here, but there's a girl from tryouts looking at me with the widest, most innocent eyes I've ever seen. I swear if she didn't look like Bambi, I wouldn't be spilling my guts to a total stranger, but I find myself trusting her. "My b-boyfriend just broke up with me."

"Oh." She frowns, and her giant eyes look genuinely sad on my behalf. "We could walk to Jake's and get ice cream?"

Ice cream. That's what you're supposed to do when you get

dumped, isn't it? I'm not sure how eating my weight in dairy is going fix the colossal hole in my heart, but it does seem like a pretty good idea. I realize the girl has already turned away from me like she's not expecting an answer.

"Ice cream sounds good," I say. Now if I can just get through this without ugly-crying in public.

Friday, August 7
ANA

could have forgiven them for the drops of melted ice cream dotting the end tables. And for the cups and spoons they didn't throw away but instead left on the coffee table arranged in the shape of a giant penis. And yes, even for the M&M's I keep finding in every corner and under *every* chair and between *every last freaking* set of couch cushions, probably the result of failed attempts to toss them into each other's mouths. But this, this is unforgivable.

I peel the chocolate-soaked napkin away from the cover with an acute sense of dread. *The Once and Future King* by T. H. White. *Merda.* Those stupid, primeval JV pissants! Don't they understand this book is life-changing?! And magical! I scrub at the cover with a clean napkin, but it is sticky with a chocolate sauce stain that is never coming out. And worse, the napkin does that fragment-y thing where pieces cling to the chocolate like cheap toilet paper. I take the book back to the main room where the front counter is because we keep hand towels near the register, and maybe if I use some warm water, I *might* be able to fix this.

Jake's isn't like other ice-cream places—it is the best ice-cream shop in the whole world. It's a converted house, and the main room is about what you would expect with the round tables and the register and the display freezer that looks like a child's watercolor palette with its colorful tubs of ice cream. But there are all these other smaller rooms with squishy chairs, tons of board games, and antique floor-to-ceiling bookcases. Most people are pretty cool about taking care of the games and books, but some people, well, some people suck.

The bells attached to the front door let out a happy jingle, and just when I think today can't get any worse, Melanie Jane Montgomery walks in dragging her boyfriend, Weston, behind her.

Everyone else thinks Melanie Jane is the most perfect girl in the entire state of Tennessee. I know better. She's not perfect, and she's terrified people will find out and she'll fall from her castle in the sky so fast she'll get whiplash. I may very well be the only one in school who knows her secret: Melanie Jane is missing part of a finger. Not like a big part or anything, just the tip of one of her pinkies—like, if you hold out your hand and cover up your pinkynail, that is what her hand looks like. She was born that way—she told me in eighth grade, back when we were still BFFs. The reason no one else knows is she's completely OCD about positioning her fingers so the top of that pinky never shows.

It's not even a big deal or anything. She's the most gorgeous girl I've ever seen. But it is the chink in her armor of perfection, so of course it drives her absolutely batshit crazy. I can't believe I was ever friends with someone who cares more about appearances than actual important stuff. Like *the truth*.

Melanie Jane paces back and forth in front of the glass case. "Can I try the Chocolate Slap Yo Mama?"

"Sure."

I scoop some up with a tiny plastic spoon and hand it over. It's one of our biggest sellers—a chocolate ice-cream base with chocolate syrup, mini-chocolate chips, and finely ground fudge-covered Oreos—and it's so freaking good it could make you, well, slap yo mama. I realize Melanie Jane is grimacing at me.

"Can I try something else?" She winces.

I sigh. "Sure. What'll it be?"

She flips her so-brown-it-is-almost-black hair over her shoulder.

"Mmm . . . the Cinnamon Apple Piescream?"

This time when I hand it to her I purposely stare directly at The Finger. I don't mean to seem like an ogre, but the girl is as fake as the prosthetic fingertip she wears during pageant competitions. She always leads the singing at the Friday morning church-group-before-school thing, and she always acts like she's soooo holy, even though if you really love God you're supposed to forgive people when they mess up, and also it bothers me that she's always preaching virginity when you know she screws Weston six ways from Sunday.

Anyway. Weston gets a Chocotella Dream, and Melanie Jane orders a Brown Sugah Vanilla like she always does because I think she can tell I am going to leap over the counter at her if she asks to try another flavor. He follows her to a table by the window, and even though I'm trying to concentrate on cleaning the book, they're the only people sitting in the main room, so

I can't help but overhear, especially now that Weston's voice is getting louder. I've gotten the book about as clean as it's going to get when Weston says something about sex. I make an effort not to glance in their direction, pretend that wiping down the counters is an all-consuming task, but he won't stop talking about it.

"We could compromise. Just let me tell the guys we've had sex," he says. "There's so much pressure on me."

And I stand corrected. Apparently, Melanie Jane practices what she preaches after all.

"I told you what to do about that," she says, unconcerned. "If they ask, just say, 'A gentleman never talks.' And they'll assume what they want, and you're off the hook." She checks the purple polish on one of her thumbnails.

"Yeah, and that was enough. When I was on JV. But I'm on Varsity now. There are all these expectations. I need to be able to say we've had sex. Or at least that we're getting close."

She shakes her head. "Being vague is one thing, but I'm not okay with you making stuff up."

"Yeah, I'm not either. All the guys are really honest with each other. I'm part of a brotherhood. I can't lie to these guys." He is so serious about this brotherhood business that I'd laugh if it weren't so tragic, but she doesn't seem to notice.

She rolls her eyes. "Okay. Then tell them we don't have sex."

"I don't want to."

"Okaaay. So don't tell them we don't have sex. That's what

you're already doing. Why are we even having this argument?"

She is eating her ice cream like it is the most important thing in the world. He rakes a hand through his hair. "I don't think you're hearing me. I want to be able to tell them I'm having sex with my girlfriend because I'm actually dating a girl who wants to have sex with me."

"Wait." She finally sets her spoon down for one freaking second and looks him in the eyes, and what she sees makes all the color drain from her face. "Are you breaking up with me?" She checks to see if I'm listening and lowers her voice. "Are you?"

"It doesn't have to be that way."

Holy crap, I can't believe Melanie Jane Montgomery is getting dumped, and in public no less. This is probably the worst thing that has ever happened to her.

"You just said you want to be dating a girl who has sex with you."

"You could be that girl."

"No. I couldn't. You *know* that."

He gives her a look like he's the one being dumped. "I want you to be."

"Don't you make that face at me. You are breaking up with me because I won't have sex with you. You don't get to make that face."

"That's not why I'm breaking up with you."

"It isn't?" Her voice has a dangerous edge now, but Weston is no Hermione Granger so he misses it.

"No."

She stands and saunters toward him, running her fingers along the tabletop and then up his arm. She crawls into his lap and nuzzles her head against his neck, and I think . . . ew! I think she just nipped his earlobe.

"So, what if we went into that bathroom over there and did it right now?" she asks, her voice a purr I can barely hear.

"H-here? At Jake's?"

"Mmm-hmm. I think I want to after all. If we did that, do you think we could work something out? Stay together?"

Boy, if you say yes, you are every bit as dumb as I've always thought. I practically lean over the counter to hear his response.

"I mean . . . yeah. Of course. I love you. I don't want to break up. But are you sure you want to do it *here*?"

She gets up off his lap. "So you *are* breaking up with me because I won't have sex with you."

Oh, she is good.

Weston needs a little more time to make sense of his impending doom. "Wait, what?"

"I want to remain a *virgin* until my wedding night. Do you really think I'd lose it in a bathroom? What is wrong with you?! No, you know what, don't answer that. We're done here. Get. Out."

"But how are you going to get home?"

"I'll figure something out. Just go. Don't act like you give a shit."

"I thought you said God doesn't like it when we swear."

Wrong. Wrong thing to say.

She fixes him with a glare that could singe your eyebrows. "God makes exceptions for asshats like you."

Friday, August 7
MELANIE JANE

I am in shock. I do believe this is the first time I have ever been dumped. I. Just. Got. Dumped. I am the reigning Mule Day Queen of Ranburne, Tennessee. You don't dump me! And in front of Ana Cardoso. This is kind of the worst thing that has ever happened to me.

It's not that I was over-the-moon, going-to-marry-him in love with Weston. I never get that close to any of the guys I date. They're fun and sweet and distracting, but whenever I feel us getting to a point I'm not ready for, I think of a reason to break up with them. It sounds awful, but when I go into a relationship knowing there's an expiration date, there are a lot less hurt feelings involved. For me anyway.

Weston's expiration date was next month, but *I* was supposed to dump *him*, and did he have to do it in front of Ana of all people? I know she was listening. She pretty much has no moral standards whatsoever, so I don't know why I'm surprised. Plus, she's always so angry and hipster-y, and she wears the weirdest clothes like the vintage blue-and-yellow-print dress she has on today that could actually be kind of cute except that she paired it with canary-yellow chucks. *Gross.*

And I saw her looking at my finger!

When I glance up, Ana is headed my way. She doesn't meet my eyes as she clears the empty ice-cream bowls and sets a new bowl in front of me. "Extra scoop. On the house," she says.

"Thanks." I blink. That was unexpectedly nice of her.

She hovers over the table.

And hovers.

Oh. Oh, *gosh*. Is she going to try to talk to me about it? Oh, please, no.

Before anything catastrophically awkward can happen, the bell rings, and Ana has to scurry back behind the counter, and we are saved. A couple girls who I think are on the dance team walk in, one of them crying while the other hesitantly pats her shoulder. They scope out the selection—I'd bet my Tiffany bracelet they're getting post-breakup ice cream.

Post-breakup ice cream. I poke at my sympathy scoop with my spoon. I guess that's what I'm eating now too.

I scroll through my phone, trying to decide who would be best to call to pick me up. Definitely not my parents. I groan just thinking about them. They loved Weston—they'd gotten really attached to this one. I'm sure my mother will never let me hear the end of it—she's always getting onto me for "chasing off perfectly good men."

The dance team girls take their ice cream to a little room near my table and curl up on an eggplant-colored fainting couch. I have a clear view of them because the doorway between the two rooms is so wide, and I'm compelled to listen in because, (A) it helps take my mind off my own breakup problems for a minute, and (B) I have to know everything about everyone. (No, for real.

Perez Hilton is my spirit animal.)

The girl who got dumped, Liv—we had English together last year—is ranting about being called a slut while her friend makes sympathetic noises at all the right places.

"And just so you know, I'm nothing like those guys were saying. I've only ever been with Trevor," says Liv, her shoulders slightly hunched like what happened today has made her ashamed of even that.

Her friend moves like she wants to touch her hand but turns it into a roundabout swoop for her ice-cream spoon. "It's okay— you don't have to explain yourself to me. Why do you think they went after you like that?"

She shakes her curly blonde head. "I don't know. Aubrey Peterson has had sex with lots of guys, and no one ever calls her a slut."

And at this point, I can't stay out of their conversation any longer because I totally know why they call her a slut, and I could totally help her, so I rush over to their table and pull up a chair.

"It's the Cyrus-Swift Phenomenon," I say.

They look at me like I am a lunatic. "The what?"

"The Cyrus-Swift Phenomenon. Taylor Swift has had, like, eighteen boyfriends, but everyone still thinks she's really classy because she's just so poised and sweet and *appropriate*-looking. Meanwhile, Miley Cyrus was with the same guy for practically forever, and people are always calling her a slut. And I'm not saying we should be calling T. Swift a slut instead—even if you do date a lot of guys, you don't deserve that. What I'm saying is, when it comes to popular opinion, it's all about the persona. And sweetie, I hate to be the one to tell you, but you're the Miley in this scenario."

Liv's eyebrows crinkle in genuine confusion. "Why am I the Miley?"

I exchange an uncomfortable look with her friend. I think her name is Peyton, and I think she goes to my church, but I've never really talked to her before. Actually, I can't remember hearing her speak before today, period. Guess this is on me.

"It might have something to do with . . . for example . . ." How to be diplomatic about this? "The amount of cleavage you show."

Her mouth falls open in a little O shape. "Wait, I show a lot of cleavage?"

We blink at her, neither of us quite sure how to respond. She looks down at the workout top she's wearing.

"But this isn't cleavage, right? Okay, maybe it is, but it's, like, church cleavage."

I snort. "The fact that you think there is such a thing as 'church cleavage' proves my point."

"That is ridiculous. Miley and I don't deserve to be treated like this! So what if I like to wear sexy tops? Or make out with my boyfriend without feeling properly ashamed of it? I'm not going to pretend to be someone I'm not just to keep people from talking."

"Oh, I'm not saying they're right. I'm not saying you should change either. It's a completely screwed-up way of thinking. All I'm saying is that it happens." I bite at the inside of my cheek. "Is that really why your boyfriend broke up with you?"

She sighs. "Kind of. I mean, I got the feeling he didn't really want to, but he just made Varsity and the guys, well, they kind of made him."

She rehashes a story that makes me want to hunt down every Varsity football player, especially Chad. I can just picture him tearing down Liv with that smug smile of his. His grin is the reason why Germany invented the word *backpfeifengesicht*—a face that desperately needs to get punched.

"That is the biggest bunch of crap I've ever heard of!" I slam my hand down on the table. Liv and Peyton jump. "Sorry, I just, do you know I just got dumped by the football team too?" I explain what happened minutes before they walked in. "I'm so sick of it. Those guys think they own this town. They say and do whatever they want. They loogey the freshman boys. They haze the crap out of the new guys. They treat women like objects. They cheat in all their classes, if they even bother to do the work at all."

"Yeah," says Liv. "And they throw crazy parties with tons of alcohol and egg people's houses and drag-race out at Crooked Oaks and have you ever seen *any* of them get arrested?"

"Preach. They never get in trouble for any of it because half the men in this town used to play football, and the teachers just look the other way."

"Like with Charlotte Fisher," says Peyton in a voice that is almost a whisper.

The three of us stare at our laps the way anyone with a conscience does whenever someone mentions Charlotte.

Charlotte Fisher was a sophomore last year when we were freshmen. All she ever did as far as I could tell is break up with her football player boyfriend and start dating a guy in the next town over. But since that guy played for a rival football team, this was a sin of an unpardonable degree. One Friday, Big Tom, her ex, cornered her after class and started to rip her a new one. I was coming out of French two doors down, and I had never in my life heard someone yell at another person like that. I don't think Charlotte had either because she wet herself right there in the middle of the hallway. A crowd of people started gathering, and I know there were a couple of teachers because when Big Tom slammed her into that locker, one of them *walked away*. I don't know what really happened that weekend—some people say the football team went on a campaign to flat out massacre her; some people say she tried to kill herself—but I do know that Charlotte Fisher doesn't live in our county anymore. And that nothing ever happened to Big Tom.

"I'm over it," I say. "I really am. I'm not going to put up with it anymore."

Liv shakes her head. "What are you going to do? Move to another town?"

"No. I'm going to make them pay. I don't know how yet, but I'll figure it out."

"*We,*" says Liv. "We are going to make them pay."

"I'm in too," says Peyton, and then as if she feels the need to explain herself, "I know I didn't just get dumped, but it isn't right how they treated y'all. How they treat everybody. So, yeah, I'm in."

"Me too," says a voice from the doorway, and we all turn to see Ana standing there, her mouth a hard line.

My jaw practically hits the floor. I didn't realize she had been listening in. I try not to make a face at her, but I'm pretty sure I'm failing. "Why would you want to help us?"

Her shoulders tense and her eyes get this sad, faraway look. "Maybe I have my own reasons for not liking the football team."

RANBURNE PANTHER SCAVENGER HUNT

In Ranburne:

1. Fill a condom up with water. Draw a face on it. Put it on Principal Corso's doormat, and ding-dong ditch. (One person)

2. The egg-on-a-string trick. Hang an egg from a power line by a string and watch a car run into it. (Everyone)

3. Paint the David Bowie statue at Old Lady Howard's corn maze. (Everyone)

4. ~~Chair race through Walmart. (Everyone)~~

5. Get a picture of the team with the Ranburne Panther. (Everyone)

6. Go to the Dawsonville football field. Find that stupid rock they touch before their games. Pee on it. (Everyone)

In Nashville:

7. Visit the illustrious Delta Tau Beta fraternity at Vanderbilt. Have a beer with Panther alum TJ McNeil and take a picture of the legendary scar he got during a game-winning play against Dawsonville. (One person)

8. Go to LP Field and reenact the "Music City Miracle." (Everyone)

9. Go to Centennial Park and jump into the pond behind the Parthenon. (Everyone)

10. Go to The Jackrabbit Saloon. Walk to the very middle of the dance floor and attempt to do the worm. (One person)

11. Go up to a girl who is totally out of your league, get down on your knees, and ask her to marry you. (One person)

12. Go up to a fat girl and tell her "You're so beautiful . . . for a fat chick." Bonus points if she throws her drink on you. (One person)

13. Hug a biker. Bonus points if he has a mullet. (One person)

14. Get a girl to give you her thong. (One person)

DARES REMAINING: 13

6:45 P.M.

MELANIE JANE

The sun is beginning to drop behind the concrete stadium seating that flanks one side of the Dawsonville football field. It's a reminder of exactly how much time we don't have.

"Melanie Jane, you have to. The list says everyone. If you don't do it, nothing else we do tonight will matter, and we'll never get that football."

Ana is not willing to let up. Not even a little bit.

My hands fly to my hips. "I. Am. A. Lady. Acting silly in Walmart is one thing, but urinating in public? I just can't."

The argument has been going on like this for minutes that feel like hours, our sentences chasing each other in the same circles.

"Look. We'll all go stand way over there." Ana points toward the twenty-yard line. "I'll take the picture from really far away. It'll be blurry. No one will ever know."

Peyton puts a tentative hand on my shoulder. She and Liv have mostly been watching up until now. "Please, Mel-Jay? We can't do this without you."

I think of all the work we've put in. All the weeks of scheming. And Weston. It always helps to think of Weston.

"Fine," I say through clenched teeth. "No one tells a soul."

The girls hold up scout's honor signs and back away before

I change my mind. I drag my feet with each step. The rock is waiting, challenging me. It sits waist high, black as sin, with one side polished and etched with the words DAWSONVILLE KNIGHTS. It glistens in the fading light. Ugh. I can smell the urine. I'm the last one, and the boys were here before us—we could tell because it was already wet. I shudder. Poor Destiny. She is going to be looking at a lot of penis pics.

I turn my back to the rock. Pull down the new pair of panties I just got at the Victoria's Secret outlet. This is so humiliating. At least my skirt covers everything important.

"I don't even have to go!" I yell.

"Just try!" shouts Ana.

"Think about waterfalls!" yells Liv.

Peyton turns her head, too embarrassed for me to watch. They call that *pena ajena* in Mexico—humiliation by proxy.

I close my eyes. Try to relax. Do you know how impossible it is to relax when your legs are shaking and the slightest misstep could send you tumbling into a pee-covered rock? Finally, the tiniest trickle comes out. I wipe with a baby wipe, get my clothes in order, and stand up. Thank goodness it's over.

You'd think I was a hero or something by the way the girls are jumping all over the place. I shake my head. This hero is never going to feel clean again. That stupid football better be worth it.

2

"So, how do we do it?" I ask.

"Do what?" says Melanie Jane.

Given that she was the one who came over here and started all this, I was kind of expecting her to know what to do next.

"Get revenge. Shake them up. Whatever the crap it is we're doing."

"It has to be something big," says Ana. "Something that will really hurt." The intensity in her eyes is a little scary.

"We have to think like football players." Melanie Jane

shudders at the thought. "What is it they really care about?"

"Sports."

"Beer."

"Getting laid."

"That stupid football," says Peyton, and then when she realizes we are all staring at her, "What?"

"That's it. The football," I say.

Melanie Jane practically cackles with glee. "The Football of '76. They'd lose their minds!"

If football is a cult in Ranburne, Tennessee, the game ball of '76 is their most holy of artifacts. Touching it before each game is a sacred rite. It's what they've done every single season since that fateful game in 1976 when the Panthers took State for the very first time. Which means that with ninety players on a football team and thirty-eight years of championships, approximately 3,420 smelly teenage boys have touched that football over the years. And that doesn't even count water boys and coaches and stuff. I'm pretty sure the football has herpes.

Peyton doesn't seem as excited, even though it was her idea. "Don't they keep it locked up? How are we going to get to it?"

"Well, they take it out for every game," says Melanie Jane. "We'll just have to do some recon first."

A jolt of electricity shoots through me. "Recon! Do I get to wear all black? I can buy night vision goggles!"

She gives me a wry smile. "You are entirely too excited for someone who has just been dumped."

I wince. I had managed to forget about the dumping for four whole minutes.

"Sorry," she says. "I didn't mean to—"

"It's okay," I say.

But it gets me thinking about the horrible things the guys said about me. And about what Melanie Jane said earlier. About the Cyrus-Swift Phenomenon. Really, how come I don't get to be the Taylor Swift? We have practically identical hair!

But the thing is, I do kind of know why people call me a slut. Nice girls aren't supposed to wear short skirts or dare everyone to jump in the lake naked because the water is exactly the perfect temperature. And they aren't supposed to kiss their boyfriends the way I do. You know how people get when they've had a few drinks and suddenly everything seems like a good idea? Well, that's what it feels like to be me ALL THE TIME. I'm energetic. And impulsive. And passionate. But just because I'm all those things doesn't mean I give my body away like free samples at the perfume counter. I wish I could make people understand that.

Ana's voice brings me back to reality. "So when do we start?"

"The football team is having their back-to-school party next weekend," I say.

Melanie Jane grins. "Perfect. I always go to that anyway."

"We'll go too." I gesture to myself and Peyton, whose eyes get a little big.

Ana's lip curls. "There is no way I'm going to a football party.

I'll do my own football recon that weekend," she adds when she sees the question marks in our eyes.

After that, my mom calls to tell me she's outside, and we all throw away our trash and go our separate ways, and it's weirdly anticlimactic. I get in the car and stare out the window, and that's when the full, crushing weight of the breakup starts to hit. My boyfriend, the guy I love, the guy I lost my virginity to, broke up with me, and it didn't even seem like he wanted to. I pull out my phone—Trevor called and texted about a dozen times while I was at Jake's, but I ignored him. Now I need to know. I start with the texts first.

I'm so sorry. Please don't hate me.

I need to talk to you. Will you please call me?

Just five minutes so I can explain. Please?

What if I come by your house later tonight?

I'm sorry you overheard the guys like that. It must have been awful. I understand why you don't want to talk to me.

I'm going to leave you alone now so you don't think I'm creepy, but call me when you're ready?

None of them say what I'm hoping for: *This isn't what you think. I know we can work this out.* So I delete all of them. Just as I'm about to start in on the voice mails, another text comes through.

I love you.

I burst into tears.

"What's the matter, cutie?" Mom manages to stroke my hair even though she's driving.

"Trevor. He—he broke up with me. And. All these guys at school were saying stuff about me." I can't tell her what. It's too horrible.

"Trevor made you cry?" asks my six-year-old sister from the backseat in a voice like someone just told her all the candy in the world had disappeared.

"I like Trevor!" says my four-year-old brother.

"Well, we don't like him anymore!" says my sister.

I laugh a little as I wipe away the tears. "We sure don't."

We pull into the driveway, and I want my mom to ask me more about it, but we're already trapped in the frenzy of our evening routine with dinner-making and my brother spilling most of a bag of dog food on the floor in an attempt to "help." Then my mom hurries to change clothes for the restaurant, and I hand her her dinner in a Tupperware, and that's all the time we have. It's hard with her being so busy, but I know I'm lucky. Lots of kids have parents who don't even care, and I know my mom loves us. She loves us so much she works two jobs and then cries at the dinner table after she thinks we're all asleep.

"Hey." She runs a hand along my cheek. "We'll talk about this when I get home. I'll see if I can get off early, okay?"

I force myself to smile so she won't worry. "Okay."

Friday, August 7

MELANIE JANE

n the end I call Aubrey. She's the biggest gossip on the cheerleading squad and my current closest friend, and I need to put my own spin on this breakup fast. Telling her goes better than I thought, but that doesn't keep me from feeling any less sick when we get to my house because now I have to tell someone much worse. My parents.

They are on me the moment I open the front door.

"Where have you been?" Mama calls from the kitchen. "Cheerleading practice ended over an hour ago."

I find her making homemade salad dressing. (Hers is so much tastier than store-bought.) Daddy is on the back deck manning the grill, but he comes inside when he sees me.

"Hey, princess."

"Hey." I give him a hug. "Weston and I were at Jake's getting ice cream," I tell Mama.

"You ate ice cream? Miss Nashville is right around the corner."

I roll my eyes. "Mama, it's still weeks away. One bowl of ice cream isn't going to ruin my chances."

She shakes her head, her glossy black hair reflecting the light. "That's the kind of attitude that gets you first runner-up. The judges expect perfection."

"Mama, I—"

"That reminds me, your pageant coach is coming over tomorrow, so make sure to come home right after practice."

I wrinkle my nose where she can't see. I hate meeting with my pageant coach. She's always trying to make me memorize canned answers to questions on current events (um, hi, unlike all those other girls you coach, I have strong opinions about things like global economics and the state of our education system, so you can peddle world peace somewhere else), or worse, find ways to help me capitalize on the fact that I'm 25 percent Cherokee, which makes me feel 100 percent gross. "*Mama.*"

"And when was the last time we deep conditioned your hair? It's looking a little damaged."

"*Mom.*"

"I'll set up an appointment with Charmaine." She squints at my forehead. "I think you're getting a breakout. You should—"

"Weston dumped me!"

My parents stare at me in shock. "He did?"

I nod pitifully. "In front of Ana Cardoso."

Mama makes a clucking sound with her tongue. "That girl dresses like a heathen, bless her heart."

I feel deflated. I pull up a bar stool and slump into it, my perfect posture shot all to hell. "It was awful."

"Why would anyone ever dump you?" says Daddy.

"He always seemed like the nicest boy. I can't believe he would do something like that," says Mama.

"That boy is obviously a dumbass," says Daddy. me to kill him?"

I shake my head, but it makes me smile because ..., never hurt anyone. Mama, on the other hand . . .

"What happened?" she asks.

I can't tell them the real reason. Talking about sex with your parents is worse than Chinese water torture. "Um."

Daddy puts his hand on my shoulder. "Are you okay, princess?"

"Um." And then for the first time today, tears fill my eyes.

Daddy runs to get a glass from the cabinet. "Do you want some water?"

"You need to drink something," says Mama.

"Do you want some tea?"

"I have some that I made with agave nectar," she says. "There's hardly any calories."

"How about some juice?"

"Juice has too much sugar."

I cry harder.

Mama makes her solving-a-problem face, probably because I've never cried this much over a boy. Not since that thing that happened last year with Ana anyway. "What's wrong? Did you do something?"

I stare at her, my mouth wide open. *Seriously?*

"What? What did you do?"

And then I explode. "Of course you think I did something.

Of course you think it's all my fault because you could never believe a sweet Southern gentleman like Weston could do anything wrong. Well, he is not as sweet as you think. And this is not my fault." Daddy still hovers with the glass, now filled with tea. "And I don't want anything to drink!"

I flounce upstairs to my room, really unleashing my inner pageant diva with foot stomps and door slams. It feels good. Not quite as cathartic as going off on my parents, but good. I flop onto my four-poster bed and bury my face in my pillow. I wonder if the boys I dumped felt this bad when I dumped them. A few minutes later, I hear a quiet knock at the door.

"Mel Belle?" says Daddy. "Can I come in?"

I lift my head just long enough to say, "Not now, okay?" before letting it squish back into my pillow.

"I'm just going to leave a tray outside for you, then."

After I hear him go back downstairs, I open the door, and my heart melts. There is a glass of tea, a plate with some Tagalongs (my most favorite of Girl Scout cookies—how he has managed to hide them from Mama's sugar purges, I'll never know), and a note, smiley face included.

I'm sorry we upset you. Please come down to dinner soon. Love, Dad
P.S. That boy really is a dumbass. ☺

Daddy's note gets me crying all over again. My parents really are sweet in their own suffocating way. I pull the tray inside and drink the tea and eat the cookies. Just two though. I don't want to have to worry about *Kummerspeck* on top of everything else. (Side note: whoever it was in Germany that thought up a word that (A) means the weight you gain from emotional bingeing and (B) literally translates to "grief bacon" is a genius.) The tears trickle off, because really, who can cry when they're thinking about bacon?

I stand in front of the mirror, taking in my puffy eyes and red nose. *Do you see how hideous crying makes you look? Don't do it! Especially not over Weston.* He had an eight-month expiration date—he is totally not worth a Scarlett O'Hara tomorrow-is-another-day scene.

Scarlett had that part of it right though. Tomorrow *is* another day. And I will go to that party next weekend and pick out another boyfriend, and then I will find a way to steal that stupid football and make Weston sorry he ever dumped me for a bunch of sweaty guys.

Wednesday, August 12
PEYTON

The list is up. People have been stalking the bulletin board all day, but the coaches waited until the very last bell so as not to interfere with any learning. Because you totally learn a lot on the first day of school. Now the first day is over, and I can see the white sheet of paper flapping in the school's subzero air-conditioning. Girls on either side of it are jumping up and down and squealing. Or crying.

I stare at the list from across the hall and work up the courage to walk to the bulletin board. If I were still with Karl, I wouldn't have to make the walk by myself. I miss having someone to be here with me. I don't miss what came along with it. Sometimes you think someone is holding your hand when really they're holding you back.

"I can do it myself," I whisper, but my heartbeat disagrees. As I walk through the sea of girls surrounding the list, I assess the butterflies in my stomach. Today's feel like monarchs.

I approach the list. Search for my name.

PEYTON REED.

There it is! I touch my index finger beside it just to make sure it's real. As I turn around, a huge grin plasters itself across my face. You know, the kind that makes you look goofy when you're trying to appear calm and sophisticated? That's the one. I am a Ranburne High Pink Panther. And I made three new friends this week. Not that that was the only reason I agreed to be part of the football team revenge plot. I mean, it was part of it, for sure. Ever since Candace moved away, I've been hoping to find that kind of friendship again. But I really do think things are screwed up at our school, and I really do love the idea of being part of something that could change that. This week is everything I wanted but never thought I could have. My grin gets, if possible, even bigger and goofier.

And then I am on the floor.

From a hug—at least I think this was meant to be a hug. It could also be a mauling.

"You made the dance team! I am so excited! You were the best in my group!" Liv squeals all of this rapid fire into my ear. It feels awesome.

"I can't even believe it," I say as I untangle the two of us and help her up.

"You'll believe it when Coach Tanner kicks your butt at practice tomorrow."

I grin, excited at the prospect of getting my butt kicked by dance.

But something's off. I feel him watching me before I see him, almost like my body is programmed to be on edge whenever he's within a thirty-foot radius. I search the hallways and, sure enough, Karl is standing by the double doors leading to the parking lot.

"I better go," I tell Liv. "I'll see you tomorrow?"

"Okay! And you have to come over to my house this Friday

to get ready for the party, okay? My friend Marley's coming, and I really want you both to be friends too!" says Liv, bouncing forward on the balls of her feet.

"Definitely." I can't help but smile even though Karl is still waiting for me.

I pace over to him, hoping we're far enough away that none of the dance team girls will hear us if things get ugly.

"Hi," I say, for some reason feeling the need to stretch to my absolute tallest.

"Looks like you made the dance team." It sounds like an accusation.

His hard blue eyes won't let go of me, and I start to splinter into familiar pieces. I feel an overwhelming need to defend my choices. To apologize. To beg for scraps of approval like a half-starved dog.

I force my mouth to form short, strong words. "Yes. I did."

Karl sways a little on his feet like I pushed him. He recovers quickly. "Good for you." His voice says he thinks it is anything but good. And then he's standing right next to me, and there's no breath in my lungs. So close I can feel him even though he hasn't touched me yet. "Do you want a ride home?" His lips hover dangerously close to my ear.

"No. My mom's picking me up." *I don't need you anymore.* "Bye, Karl."

I turn and don't let myself look back. I'm breathing like a gazelle that just outran a tiger, but I walk away feeling stronger with every step. Each day, more of the invisible strings between us snap. When I get to the turnaround at the front of the school, I sit down on a planter and pull my knees to my chest. I'm shaking, but I'm smiling.

I did it.

And I think I sounded kind of tough too.

I stare out at the bumper-to-bumper pickup traffic and my mind replays the conversation I just had with Karl and that gets me thinking about my name on the dance team list which gives me chill bumps even though it's 92 degrees outside and humid but also takes me back to last year's dance team tryouts and the reason I didn't audition.

It started at this youth group lock-in, the summer before ninth grade. Fifty-seven middle schoolers packed into a church gym, hopped up on Mountain Dew and hormones. The boys were mostly playing basketball. Not, like, a real game, just trying to hit threes and goofy trick shots. Leaving their arms hanging in the air a second too long after they made it and checking over their shoulders to see if any girls were watching. There were people playing air hockey and listening to music, and a few of the sixth graders had already passed out in their sleeping bags in the room set aside for lock-in wimps. Some of the chaperones played alongside us, but most of them had more important things to tend to. Chiefly among them:

1. Keeping Jimmy Ferraro from breaking any more church windows and/or bones.

2. Drinking coffee and looking very tired.

3. Making sure none of the couples disappeared because if two teenagers of the opposite sex were left alone in a room for more than five minutes, God would surely smite us all.

A few of us girls practiced cheerleading jumps and dance moves on the carpet behind one of the basketball goals.

"Your toe-touches are really good," said one of the girls, Mandy, who was captain of the eighth-grade cheerleading squad.

I blushed. "Aw, thanks. I stretch, like, every day."

"She choreographs her own dances too!" said Candace. "Show them the one you showed me yesterday!"

"Okay!" I squealed, partly because I was excited and partly because Candace and I had just split a Nerds Rope.

A pop song blared over the gym speakers. It was a little bouncy for this dance, but fast enough that it would still work.

I took a deep breath and bobbed my head to the music for a second. I knew this dance cold, I made the thing up, but Mandy was about the coolest person who had ever talked to me, so I didn't want to screw it up in front of her. And then I was flying through the steps, pumping my fists and shaking my hips, and the leaps—oh, the leaps in this dance. By the time I finished, Mandy's mouth was open, and she was all, "That was awesome!" And there were boys hollering things at me from the basketball court. I was grinning like crazy.

Until a hand clamped down on my shoulder.

"You need to come with me," said Mrs. Bellcamp, one of the unhappier-looking chaperones.

And it's not like she dragged me off by my ear or anything, but that's sure what it felt like. She got me alone in the kitchen, and man, did she ever start in on me. The way I was dancing was wrong, did I know that? I was sinning, and I was causing all those boys watching me to sin too. If she had just asked me not to do any more dancing at the lock-in, I would have listened. But the things she was saying, I had to fight back. At first, anyway. It was like she was telling me I was morally deficient, and she wouldn't be satisfied until I agreed with her. We weren't arguing about dancing anymore but about my value as a person. And I wasn't a bad person. I knew it. But when I talked to Karl about it the next day, he had all these reasons, and they seemed like good ones. And somehow I ended up feeling bad enough that I stopped dancing.

I'm doing everything I'm supposed to. I already had a snack, I've got my rain-forest sounds playing, and I'm sitting at my desk with my homework notebook open and my laptop and phone stowed safely downstairs. But so far, all I've accomplished is turning to the correct page of my textbook and reading the first problem of tonight's geometry homework approximately eighty-seven times. Between Karl and dance team, I was doomed before I started.

I sigh and begin attempt number eighty-eight.

1. State whether the figure is a line, a ray, or a segment.

Finally, *finally*, I am able to block out the dog barking next door and my conversation with Karl and the annoying way my sleeves brush against my wrists whenever I move my arms. A ray! The point on one side and the little arrow on the other means it's a ray! I write *ray* beside the figure and then I get to thinking about this guy I saw at youth group last week who I think is named Ray only maybe it's spelled Rey and I wonder if it means anything different when it's spelled with an *e* and I wonder if he was really smiling at me or some hot girl I couldn't see but assume was hovering nearby and—

"Peyton?" I hear the door close downstairs and know my mom is home. "I've got dinner."

I realize my hand is still holding my pencil, and I've only written the letters *R A*. I roll my eyes and add a *Y* before I clomp downstairs.

"What'd you get?" I ask.

"I went to that little Greek place in Dawsonville," she replies, setting two plates with gyro sandwiches on the kitchen table.

She's already changed out of her work clothes and is currently wearing my red halter top, but I let it slide because there's baklava.

I slather tzatziki sauce onto my sandwich. "I can't wait to see what we do at practice tomorrow. I'm so excited!"

The corners of Mama's mouth turn upward in a sly smile. "You might have mentioned that."

I blush. "Sorry."

I've been like this since she picked me up from practice. She'll say something, and I'll respond with some completely unrelated piece of information about the dance team.

I'm thinking of dyeing my hair red. Dance team!

I can't believe how hot it's been this summer. Dance team!

Have you talked to your dad recently? Pause to feel awkward because what she really wants to know is whether he's been on a date lately. Dance team!

"It's okay. It makes me happy to see you so happy." She gets up because we both need napkins.

"Thanks. I am. Happy, I mean. With dance team. And . . . and because of other stuff."

She says the part I didn't. "Since you and Karl broke up. I've noticed." She smiles. "You've started singing in the shower again."

"I sing in the shower?" How. Embarrassing.

"You do. Loudly. And off-key." She kisses the top of my head. "And I love it."

Friday, August 14
ANA

had hoped a summer would help people forget. It didn't. The first week of school is no different from any of the weeks last year. When I'm at my locker switching books, a football player leans in and whispers, "Slut," before continuing down the hallway. *Idiota*, I whisper back. I only whisper it in my head, but it still helps. A couple of cheerleader girls who are friends with Melanie Jane give me dirty looks as I pass them. *Malevolent hags*. It's been almost a year since the Party-That-Must-Not-Be-Named, and my subsequent departure from the cheerleading squad, but it may as well have been last month. At least I still have my guys— the merry band of nerds I've belonged to since diapers. I can get through anything with them.

I get a text from Melanie Jane (only it shows up in my phone as THE DEVIL) while I'm weaving through school to get to the parking lot. It's to all three of us.

Recon this weekend! Don't forget!

Seeing her picture pop up on my screen after all this time is like an electric shock. I think about what she did to me, and my teeth clench, and I want to throw my phone against the wall. As much as I want to get revenge on the football team, I don't know if it's worth teaming up with my former BFF–current nemesis.

Getting texts from her. Planning check-in meetings. Having to listen to her yammer on about stupid pageant crap. I am very tempted to text back something along the lines of "Screw this. I'm out" when I run into a burly shoulder.

"Excuse you," says the voice I hear in my nightmares.

Chad MacAllistair stands in front of me, and life stops for one terrifying second, and I think I might vomit and cry and claw his eyes out all at the same time. A glimmer of recognition flickers in his eyes. "Oh, hey, Ana."

He takes a step closer. The apparent safety of the open hallway is an illusion. I hate hearing him say my name. Seeing him smile that half smile like he didn't tear my entire world apart. Like I don't know what kind of person he really is. Part of me wants to run away and never look back. The other part wants to strap him to a medieval torture device until he tells me every last thing that happened that night.

"Okay, well, I'll see you," he says. And just like that he's gone. Not another look. Not another thought. Because even though he did what he did, everything is always totally freaking peachy in Chad MacAllistair land.

Joining forces with Melanie Jane is worth getting even with him. *Anything* would be worth getting even with him. I text back:

I'm on it.

I know it's kind of dumb. An inflated piece of pigskin isn't going to counterbalance what happened to me—I don't care if it is the Football of '76. The scars I'm hiding are bigger than the ones you get from being called a slut or getting dumped by your loser boyfriend. A silly little revenge plot isn't going to erase them. But the idea of being united instead of facing the great heaving darkness alone? That feels like it could change everything.

I drive shakily to Jake's to put in a couple of hours and pick up my pay stub before heading home—being the first sophomore with a license is one of the few perks of getting held back because of my English when we moved here in second grade. Shouts are coming from my backyard when I pull into the driveway, so I follow the noises through the grass along the side of the house. The kitchen window is open, and the smell of *feijoada* tumbles out—I can practically taste the black beans and pork trimmings. My embarrassingly PDA parents are drinking red wine and looking like they might eat each other instead of the food.

I round the corner of the house and burst out laughing at the scene that is currently taking place in my backyard. Grayson is trying on an embroidered jacket, Toby is making dragon eggs, Isaiah is slashing at the air with a fake sword, and Matthew is filming it all with a digital video camera.

"Ana!" they yell when they see me.

I hop over and give each one a squeeze. These are my boys. My best and truest friends. They were there for me when I made the cheerleading squad in seventh grade—thus unexpectedly catapulting myself into the popular-kid stratosphere—and they are still here for me now, after my fall from grace.

"How are we doing?" I ask, digging around in my bag for my new lip balm.

"Pretty good," says Grayson. "The first couple of episodes are going to be brutal, but after that we won't have as many new props and costumes to make, so it'll get a lot easier."

We have this year-long assignment for our broadcasting class: start a vlog and post a one- to five-minute video each week. Naturally, we decided to reenact *Game of Thrones*, Season 1, in one-minute episodes. We're also posting clips of how we're making some of the props and stuff.

"Cool. Well, I can help out for most of tonight." I grab a box of thumbtacks and carry it over to Toby. "What's up, Tobes? Need some help?"

"Sure."

He passes me a Styrofoam egg, and I get to work pushing in thumbtacks so they look like tiny scales. It's monotonous work but not in a bad way.

"Are we painting them today too?" I ask Toby after a few minutes.

He doesn't answer, so I push his shoulder. "Toby?"

"Huh? Oh, sorry." He rubs at his eyes. "Man, I'm tired."

"Why are you so tired? School just started. Are you addicted to video games again?" I tease.

He fumbles with his handful of thumbtacks and almost drops

them. "No, but I had to, like, assist a friend with something late last night."

"That's the sketchiest thing I've ever heard."

His face is turning redder by the second. "Oh, no. It's nothing bad. It's nothing bad."

I laugh. "What, are you a drug dealer now?"

"It's nothing bad. I just don't want to tell you." He goes back to his dragon egg.

"Yeah, I'm just gonna assume you're a drug dealer until you tell me otherwise," I say. "You can't bring something like this up and not tell me."

Toby sighs. "Well, it's just that I have a new girlfriend, so I need to spend a lot of time with her. Cool?"

Like with a question mark. Like he's asking me if it's cool.

This time I force myself to keep the laughter on the inside. "Yeah. Yeah, that is very cool."

He gets this smug grin that is both goofy and adorable. "Thanks. For some reason, I just didn't want to tell you."

This does not surprise me. I'm always having to convince one or another of them that they are not in love with me. I don't mean for it to sound like I'm some great beauty. It's just that I'm the only girl most of them have regular contact with, so it's not all that surprising that at some point they have all confessed their undying devotion. Except Grayson. Based on the number of times he's fought me over who gets to be Princess Daenerys, I suspect there is something he hasn't told us yet.

"You know, I guess it *was* a pretty jerk move to keep it a secret, so here's how you're going to make it up to me," I say. "I have questions. About the football team."

Toby is one of their trainers (which is a fancy way to say "water boy"), plus he's the kind of guy you just want to tell secrets to, so I have a feeling he hears *everything.*

He snort-laughs. "You do?"

I shrug and go back to thumbtacking my egg so as not to seem too interested. "Yeah, I mean, that stupid football, for instance. Do they really only take it out for games? I bet they take turns bringing it home at night and snuggling with it."

Toby rolls his eyes. "They don't do that. But, well, there are certain *special occasions* they take it out for."

"Really? Like what?"

"Well, you know they take it out for the scavenger hunt."

"Oh, yeah, everybody knows about that."

I am not exaggerating. For all their secret brotherhood BS, the football team can't keep their collective mouth shut when it comes to bragging about the scavenger hunt. It happens every year the weekend before Homecoming, and the new guys have to get through an entire list of crazy dares, and at the very end they get the football. Oh, and if they fail, they have to walk onto the field naked at Homecoming. That's weeks away though.

"They're taking it out next Saturday too," says Toby.

"Really? What for?" I manage to keep my tone disinterested (I hope).

"This induction thing for the new Varsity guys. They're doing it at midnight in this abandoned barn at Big Tom's, and it's supposed to be the 'most badass thing ever.' I'm not allowed to go." He jabs a pin into his egg with an unnecessary amount of force. Then his eyes get big. "Hey, please don't tell anyone what I told you, okay? The guys would kill me."

"Of course not," I say, but the lie makes me feel like the worst friend ever. I have to make a getaway before the guilt becomes intolerable. "I think it's almost time for dinner, so I better go. I'll come back after though."

I wave bye to the rest of the guys and open the door to the kitchen—loudly so my parents know to stop making out. I'm greeted by a frenzy of licks.

"Falkor!"

When I was nine years old, I watched *The NeverEnding Story* for the first time and realized that my life would not be complete until I owned a luckdragon. You should have seen me at the pet store when the owner told me they didn't sell those—I bawled the entire way home, against my dad's entreaties that we buy a dog or maybe a guinea pig. I insisted nothing but a luckdragon would do and locked myself in my room with my book copy of *The Neverending Story.*

Two weeks later, I got Falkor for Christmas. He was sixteen

pounds of wiggly Great Pyrenees goodness, and he looked pretty dang close to a luckdragon. But my dad wasn't finished there. We bought out the nearby Michael's of all their faux pearls and rhinestones, and my dad helped me build a custom-made harness that was a precise replica of Falkor's back. You should have seen him holding the tiny pearls in his huge fingers, painstakingly applying each one as I directed. The harness was, and still is, a thing of beauty. For a six-foot-three, two-hundred-and-thirty-pound Brazilian man, my father is quite the BeDazzler.

I spent the rest of Christmas break dressed up like Atreyu, taking Falkor on walks around the neighborhood, pumping my little fist in the air.

I scratch Falkor behind his ears the way he likes and drift over to the pan of *pão de queijo* (the Brazilian version of cheese bread) my mom just popped out of the oven.

"Not yet, *princesinha*, they're hot," she says, squeezing me into a hug and kissing both cheeks.

I pause, my fingers centimeters away from the one with the most cheese sprinkled on top. My dad winks at me as he snatches one up and bites into it.

"Ah!" He drops it back on the tray.

"Told you," says my mom without turning around.

I snicker and hand him a glass of water.

"Thanks, *princesinha*. Hey, what do you have there?"

I flip over the piece of paper I'm holding. "Pay stub."

"It's a lot to keep your grades up and have a job." He wraps his arm around me tight because I've been in the house for a whole thirty seconds and haven't received one of his bear hugs yet. "I'm really proud of you, you know?"

"Thanks," I say without looking at him.

If he knew what happened at that party last year, I wonder if he'd still be saying that.

RANBURNE PANTHER SCAVENGER HUNT

In Ranburne:

1. Fill a condom up with water. Draw a face on it. Put it on Principal Corso's doormat, and ding-dong ditch. (One person)

2. The egg-on-a-string trick. Hang an egg from a power line by a string and watch a car run into it. (Everyone)

3. Paint the David Bowie statue at Old Lady Howard's corn maze. (Everyone)

4. ~~Chair race through Walmart. (Everyone)~~

5. Get a picture of the team with the Ranburne Panther. (Everyone)

6. ~~Go to the Dawsonville football field. Find that stupid rock they touch before their games. Pee on it. (Everyone)~~

In Nashville:

7. Visit the illustrious Delta Tau Beta fraternity at Vanderbilt. Have a beer with Panther alum TJ McNeil and take a picture of the legendary scar he got during a game-winning play against Dawsonville. (One person)

8. Go to LP Field and reenact the "Music City Miracle." (Everyone)

9. Go to Centennial Park and jump into the pond behind the Parthenon. (Everyone)

10. Go to The Jackrabbit Saloon. Walk to the very middle of the dance floor and attempt to do the worm. (One person)

11. Go up to a girl who is totally out of your league, get down on your knees, and ask her to marry you. (One person)

12. Go up to a fat girl and tell her "You're so beautiful . . . for a fat chick." Bonus points if she throws her drink on you. (One person)

13. Hug a biker. Bonus points if he has a mullet. (One person)

14. Get a girl to give you her thong. (One person)

DARES REMAINING: 12

7:10 P.M.

ANA

The boys could be anywhere. Leaving a prophylactic at
Principal Corso's house. Hanging an egg over any of Ranburne's
dusty streets. Driving up to the front of the school *right now*
where they'll catch us, and figure out exactly what we're
doing, and maybe—probably—murder us. The girls laugh as
they cluster around the panther statue, Liv jumping onto his
back while Peyton and Melanie Jane plant a kiss on each of his
granite cheeks. I want to join in, but I can't shake the dread I'm
feeling.

I attach the camera to a tripod and aim it at the panther.
What happens if Chad figures out there are girls doing the hunt?
And that I'm one of them? I sweep my bangs out of my eyes
and force all thoughts of Chad from my mind. He's probably at
The Jackrabbit Saloon already working on getting drunk off his
ass. I don't have to worry about running into him. Yet.

I set the timer and run at the panther, climbing on his back
behind Liv. By the time the camera flashes, I'm smiling, but I
know it's not a very good one.

"We need to get out of here," I say, rushing back to the
camera.

My friends are still laughing, and I look up from where I'm
dismantling the stand. "C'mon. I have a bad feeling."

That's a good enough reason for Peyton. Melanie Jane and Liv shrug and hurry along behind us. They offer to help me carry the camera equipment, but I'm all right. Scooping ice cream all day gives me mad biceps. The girls decide the egg-on-a-string prank is next. I need to get us a safe distance from the school. To a road where we're not likely to run into the boys. I turn out of the school parking lot. My head darts left. Then right. Is anyone around? Did anybody see us?

Melanie Jane touches my arm. "Ana, calm down, no one is going to—"

Peyton screams, and my heart almost explodes. Somehow, I manage to slam on the brakes in the middle of the intersection. A truck skids around us, and there's the sound of a horn blaring, and I don't know if it's theirs or mine or both. The truck fishtails to a stop in front of a ditch on the other side of the road.

"It was green! I swear the light was green!" I tear up almost instantly now that I know we're okay.

"It was. I saw it." Melanie Jane's voice is steady, calming my raw nerves. "The other car ran a red light."

The other car. I wipe my eyes and really focus on the shiny red truck, the back of which I suddenly notice is crammed with swearing boys. The taillights cast enough of a glow that I can make out cans of something (beer?) in their hands.

"Go! It's the boys! Go!" yells Liv.

I floor it even though my hands are shaking so bad it feels like they might slip right off the steering wheel. The truck shrinks in my rearview mirror.

Melanie Jane recovers first. "That was way, *way* too close."

"We almost got caught," says Peyton.

"We almost DIED," says Liv.

"I told you I had a bad feeling!"

"Next time you have a bad feeling, I'm listening." Melanie Jane shudders, and then wrinkles her nose. "Ughhh. I'm totally sweating now."

I smirk at her. "What's the matter? Running out of baby wipes?"

She narrows her eyes in a fake-mad kind of way. "You be nice or I'll hide your lip balm."

She snatches it from the center console and waves it back and forth in front of her like a magician does before they make something vanish.

"Go for it. I have at least three others in this car right now."

"You are one sick individual."

I laugh, remembering what it was like to be like this with her. My fingers finally relax on the steering wheel—my brain already figured out we're safe, but sometimes it takes a while for the message to trickle down.

Liv points out a good spot for the egg prank, and I park my car on the next street over because I sure as hell don't want anyone taking down my license plate number. We traipse through the woods with our supplies (egg carton, string, video camera), and stare up at the power line that Liv has deemed ideal pranking material. The girls get started while I videotape.

I thought it would be easy. *Thought* being the operative word. We break four eggs and almost get hit by a car trying to get the damn thing into position. Melanie Jane eventually throws a rock tied with string and makes it over the power line. She ever so carefully ties the string around egg number five, and we duck behind some bushes and wait.

And wait.

And wait. This. Blows. The moon is already out, and despite their drunken handicap, the boys are beating us, and I can't do anything but sit here and hope a car comes along. I'm about to suggest moving to a busier street when Melanie Jane points into the darkness.

"Look," she says. "Lights."

The lights get closer. And bigger. Holy crap, that is one big-ass truck. It tears past us, the egg exploding against its windshield. It slams on the breaks. Tires squeal against the road.

Melanie Jane claps her hands together. "It worked. It really worked!"

I squint at the truck through my viewfinder. "Is that like one of those monster-truck-show trucks?"

Liv giggles. "Oh my gosh, it is. It's like: come see Gigantor take on the egg. THIS. SATURDAY. ONLY."

She makes her voice deep and twangy, and we all crack up laughing. I watch the truck, waiting for it to drive away, possibly to the nearest gas station where the driver can clean off its windshield. Instead, I hear a door slam. Oh, shit.

"You guys," I hiss. "Someone's getting out of the truck."

There's a flurry of whispers and swearing around me, and then silence, thick and scared.

"Y'all think that was funny?" a voice yells.

I am 97 percent sure the voice belongs to a big, scary redneck, and 98 percent sure he intends to kill us all. I hear the scrape of work boots against the gritty street, and then he steps in front of the headlights, and my blood freezes in my veins.

He's got a gun.

"I said." *Ah sayud.* He cocks the gun with a terrible *click-click.* "Did y'all think that was funny?"

No, please, no. It wasn't funny at all. Please don't kill us. And then he starts yelling about what he's going to do to us, a symphony of threats and obscenities. The girls don't move. They must be paralyzed with fear like I am. I stare at the gun while panic churns my insides. He's waving it around when it happens. A flash of light. And then a blast, so loud I'm sure I've been shot. But no, he's got the gun pointed in the air.

The shot is what finally gets us moving. I tear my eyes away from him. I hear the gun cock again, empty shells clattering against the road, and I race through the trees with my friends, praying we all make it back to my car with our young lives intact.

It's only after we're safely inside that I calm down enough to think about how dangerous that really was. And not just because of the gun. There could have been an accident. But they do this, year after year, hunt after hunt. Drinking and driving and hazing and racing and fighting. It's a wonder the football team hasn't killed anyone yet.

3

'll have to see Trevor. Tonight. I don't want to, but I know he's going to be there, and I know with the same certainty that I won't be able to avoid him this time. I've been taking circuitous routes to all my classes, ignoring his calls and texts. It was harder to avoid him at dance team practice, but after Coach Tanner used her megaphone to call him out for lurking, he couldn't very well let the football team see him hovering around our practices anymore.

So I'm dreading tonight, but sometimes the dread feels kind of like excitement. I try to distract myself with some of my favorite things:

1. Makeovers. Is it just me, or are they way more fun when you're doing them on people like Peyton who are shy and don't wear very much makeup? Marley obviously feels the same way because she practically attacked Peyton with styling products.

2. Getting ready. Because don't be fooled—the best part of any party is not the time spent at the actual party. It's the time spent gossiping with your girls while you do your hair and then gossiping again in the morning over bagels. Nothing brings out the flavor in good gossip like hazelnut cream cheese.

3. Dancing. Which I haven't actually done yet but will do the millisecond we arrive.

Marley parks at the back of a line of cars trailing from Casey Martin's house, and we all pile out (as dance team members, we are physically incapable of arriving at parties in groups smaller than three). Climbing Casey's driveway in high heels feels like an extreme sporting event, but we all make it in one piece. A few hours from now, when Casey's front door vomits out drunk people, I doubt everyone will be so lucky.

The last time he had a party here was just a couple of months ago. Trevor and I were standing in the front yard, surveying the Driveway of Death. I pulled off my heels because I felt like it would be safer, but then my toes curled into the softest, most luscious grass you can imagine. Seriously, Casey's mom must have an in with the guys who landscape golf courses or something because the stuff was unbelievable.

"You have to feel this!" I said, sinking onto my butt and pulling Trevor with me.

His mouth turned upward in an amused smile. But not amused like I-think-you-do-weird-dumb-stuff amused. More like you-are-the-kind-of-puzzle-that-makes-me-happy amused. "What am I feeling?" he asked.

I grabbed his hand and raked our fingers through the grass together. "This! Isn't it spectacular?"

"Mmm," he replied, really taking it in. "Oh, yes. This is a whole new level of grass."

"Right?! So I think we know how we're getting back to the car." I pointed to where his dad's rusty Ford sat waiting at the bottom of the hill.

Trevor's smile came back. "We're rolling down the hill?"

"Hell, yes, we are. Because, one, there is no way I'm making it down that driveway without a flesh wound. And, two, THE GRASS." I leaned back and made a grass angel for emphasis and also for fun.

And he could have looked at me, with my grass angels and my childish suggestions, and laughed. Or pulled me up by the hand saying, "How about I just help you down the driveway?" He could have said any number of things. What he did say was, "Race you to the bottom!" before diving into the grass and rolling down the hill. And as I came tumbling after, all I could think was: *I. Am. So. Hopelessly. In. Love. With. You.* And, okay, maybe a small part of me was thinking: *I hope I don't die.*

Trevor rolled to a stop at the bottom of the hill, but I must have picked up more speed because I barreled into him, limbs crashing into limbs, bodies rolling over bodies. And suddenly, Trevor was kissing me like we were in one of those black-and-white movies where the couple tumbles around in the sand while the ocean licks at their feet (which is wildly romantic until you figure, with all that thrashing, there is *definitely* sand in uncomfortable places). We stuttered to a stop with Trevor's body over mine. He stopped kissing me and pulled a blonde curl away from my eyes.

"I love you," he said.

It wasn't the first time he said it. Or the last. But it's the time I can't stop thinking about.

"Hey, look out." Peyton pulls me sideways by the elbow so I just miss walking into an impromptu wrestling match. A couple of guys are trying to pin each other on the lawn while people cheer from the front porch. I shake my head. One of the football team's hobbies is getting drunk at parties and beating the crap out of people. Often each other. The guys are getting dangerously close to rolling down the hill, and somehow I don't think they'll find it as magical as Trevor and I did.

Trevor. I have got to stop thinking about him. I spent two hours yesterday playing sappy breakup songs on my guitar. It's really getting sad.

We file inside and head to the kitchen because Marley says she is going to spontaneously combust if she doesn't get vodka-cranberried, stat. Casey pours one for her, and then the rest of us too because we're with her. The vodka he's using comes from a plastic bottle and looks incredibly high class.

Peyton stirs her vodka-cranberry with her straw, but doesn't drink any.

I walk over and bump her with my hip. "You don't have to drink that, you know."

"I know."

"If you don't want it, give it to me!" says Marley. "Never throw away alcohol. There are starving people in Alabama."

Marley keeps cracking inappropriate jokes because it's so easy to shock Peyton into giggles. I can almost see the moment when a friendship forms between my old friend and my new one—it's like the room gets a little brighter.

We decide the kitchen is boring and take a lap around the party.

"People are looking at me," whispers Peyton.

I grin. "That's a good thing. Now let's get going. We have a job to do." A job that will be much easier while Trevor isn't here.

I find the nearest Varsity football player and introduce myself. Then old-school Ludacris starts blaring from the living room that has been declared a dance floor by this guy Purdeep from my AP US history class, who happens to be the reigning deejay of every party ever.

I grab the guy's hand. "We have to go dance! Now! Ludacris is my favorite!" And I'm not just saying that to get this guy to dance with me. Ludacris is like the bacon of music. He can make any song better.

He follows me without question. Of course he does. They all think I'm a mega-slut—he's probably expecting this to end with sex in the laundry room or something. I decide this could work in my favor and attempt to hypnotize him with my Shakira-like hip action.

"What year are you?"

"I'm a senior."

"Wow, so you must be a pretty big deal on the team then?"

He watches my hips swirl around. And around. "Um, yes?"

"That's so cool. Do you get to know all kinds of insider stuff, like where they keep the keys to the trophy case with that special football?"

"The Football of '76?" He frowns, possibly because I just gave their most prized possession all the respect of a blankie. Or maybe I went too far too fast. "Only Coach Fuller and the team captain have keys to the trophy case. Why do you care anyway?"

And that's pretty much how my conversations go with every football player for the next hour. The guys are all into me, and then I bring up the football, and then they turn into these weird, macho, football-protecting robots. About the only useful thing I figure out is that there are two sets of keys, and Coach Fuller and Chad MacAllistair have them. I wonder if Peyton's doing any better. I catch a glimpse of her silver halter whipping around the corner so I rush after her. And come face-to-face with Trevor.

"Hi," says Trevor.

"Hi," I say back.

We stare at each other for several painful seconds, during which entire civilizations in parallel universes spawn, rise, and self-destruct. Trevor's friend and Peyton glance back and forth between us and each other until they are unable to stand the awkwardness anymore.

"I'm Rey," says the friend, who is built like a California redwood.

"I'm Peyton."

He looks at us again and clears his throat. "Do you want to go with me to get something to drink?"

Peyton's eyebrows raise just enough to let me know she's silently asking my permission to go, so I give her the tiniest of nods to tell her I'll be okay. She still watches me until the last possible second when she steps into the kitchen.

"Can we go somewhere and talk?" Trevor asks once they're gone. "Please?"

He reaches for my hand, and I pull it away. The words *leave me alone* are on my lips, but then there's this small pathetic part of me that wants him to tell me every detail of every conversation he ever had with them about breaking up with me.

"Okay," I say.

We manage to find one of the only quiet places in the whole

house, the laundry room. (If any of his "friends" spot us, they'll assume he's just getting me out of his system.) I hop on top of the dryer and sit cross-legged, elbows on knees, chin in hands.

Trevor closes the door behind us. "I'm really sorry."

I keep my eyes focused on the floor.

"This wasn't what was supposed to happen," he says.

"No shit."

He winces and scuffs one shoe against the other, and when he looks up again, his face is pleading. "Those things you heard them say, you know I don't think that, right?"

And my plan to keep silent and make him suffer goes up in flames because there are things I have to know. "But why do they think it? You're the only guy I've ever had sex with, not that it's any of their business. I don't understand why I'm getting dumped for things that aren't even real. Why didn't you stick up for me?"

"I *did* stick up for you. This is why I wanted to talk to you first." His voice is heavy with the kind of hurt I've been carrying around all week. "They can force me to break up with you, but they can't make me stop loving you."

He squeezes my hands in his, and his eyes are full of questions and apologies, and a part of me believes him. Loves him. And another part of me hates myself for it.

"So, you really were going to break up with me." It's more a statement of fact than a question.

"I didn't have a choice," he says. Which is kind of like saying he loves me, *but*.

"What does that even mean? They're a football team, not the mafia. They can't force you to do things."

"They don't need to hold a gun to my head to ruin my life." He paces around the laundry room like it's a cage. "Football is everything for me. It's my one chance to get out of here and do something better because you know my parents can't afford college."

It's true. My mom may work two jobs, but Trevor is the kind of poor where you get free lunch at school.

"If I don't do what they say, they'll beat the shit out of me at practice, they'll make sure I never get the ball in games. I've been fighting to get on Varsity since freshman year, and now that Chris graduated, I finally get my shot. But I've only got two years to prove to the college scouts that I'm worth anything." His voice cracks. "They'll ruin me. And everything I've been working for will disappear."

"I can't believe they can really do that," I whisper. They're horrible, the things he's saying. That these guys are willing to completely torpedo someone's life because he's dating an alleged slut. But even though my heart is breaking for him, it doesn't excuse what he did to me.

He sighs. "So, yeah. I can't be seen dating you. But that doesn't mean they can keep us apart."

Now I see where this conversation is going. I understand what he wants from me. And I'm not okay with it.

Nothing good is going to come out of me staying and talking

to Trevor. Because life isn't fair. If it was, my dad wouldn't have been able to break all the rules and have a perfect life while my mom who did everything right can barely keep it together. And still, she's the one facing all this judgment, like if she'd only had sex with her husband more or been sweeter or cooked better, it all would have been okay. I remember Mama getting advice from one of the ladies from church when I was supposed to be cramming for a test but had instead crammed my ear against the space between my bedroom door and the carpet. The woman was telling her to spice things up, as if buying lingerie or making French cuisine can patch a sinking submarine, as if "spice" or relationship-fixing when your husband is straying is entirely the responsibility of the woman. I remember watching Mama tear her hair out over the stove trying to figure out how to make a béarnaise sauce, and then going to my room and stuffing my fist in my mouth and crying because I knew it wouldn't make a damn bit of difference.

So if Trevor doesn't love me enough, I've already learned there's nothing I can do. My only fault is being stupid enough to believe he loved me enough in the first place. No one ever loves anyone enough. Not forever anyway.

He stands in front of me again, his hands resting on my kneecaps. "Liv, you know how much I love you."

And I know what he's asking, but I just can't say yes.

"Then, tell them," I say. "Stand on the coffee table, and tell the whole party how much you love me. Tell them you are so sorry being on the football team made you forget that."

He hangs his head. "I can't."

"That's what I thought."

"But we could—"

"We could what? Have a relationship on the DL? Keep me as your dirty little secret? Your friends may think that's all I'm good for, but I know I'm better than that."

He opens his mouth and closes it. Opens it again. "I'm sorry," he says.

I remember when I was little and pretty much anything could be fixed by those two magic words. It's too bad we're not little anymore. "I'm sorry too."

"So, this is it for us then?"

"Yes." I didn't realize one little word could hurt so much. "Maybe you could call me when you graduate, though."

"Yeah. Yeah, okay."

He walks out of the laundry room utterly defeated. I put my head in my hands and cry. I made the right decision, didn't I? I don't deserve to be called a slut. Or to be someone's secret, on-the-side girl. So, why do I feel so horrible right now?

"Hey," says a deep voice.

I jump. I didn't realize I wasn't alone. It's that guy Rey from earlier.

"Oh, um, hi." Crying in front of a total stranger. Exactly how I want to spend my Friday night. Rey must have noticed too because he winds his big fingers together in supreme discomfort.

"He's really torn up about having to break up with you," he finally says.

"Yeah? Well then, maybe he shouldn't have done it," I snap. And then I feel guilty because this guy doesn't seem like the ones that were talking about me. "Sorry."

He shrugs. "It's okay. From what your friend was saying, it sounds like you're pretty torn up too."

Remind me to have a chat with Peyton about sharing my feelings with football players.

"You need to know, he didn't want to do it," Rey says. "He felt like he didn't have a choice."

I frown. "But he did have a choice. He could have picked me. He could have told them no."

"If you saw the email, it might not seem like such an easy decision to you either."

"What email?" *There's an email? Hopefully, one that will explain why my life sucks so much right now.*

"I shouldn't be talking about this." He pauses, shifting his weight from one foot to the other. "Let's just say you weren't the only girl this happened to. There may have been . . . a list."

"Are you *kidding* me?" A spark of anger sizzles through me, effectively cauterizing my tears.

His face is kind, but serious too. "I shouldn't have said anything, but Trevor's my friend. You can't tell anyone."

"You have to forward it to me."

"I can't do that."

"Do the other girls even know the football team made their boyfriends dump them, or do they think their broken hearts are just a coincidence?"

"I don't know," he says in a way that makes me think the other girls have no idea.

"This is ridiculous."

I jump off the dryer. Worry flashes in his warm brown eyes.

"Where are you going?"

I put a hand on his shoulder, stretching to reach it because he towers over me. "Don't worry. I'm not going to tell anyone you told me."

But that doesn't mean I'm not going to tell anyone.

Saturday, August 15
MELANIE JANE

"Are you serious right now?!" I don't mean to yell, but that's kind of how it comes out. I am so angry I'm pretty sure there is steam coming out of my ears. "I can't believe those jerks have a list! Am I on it?" I don't give Liv a chance to answer. "Of course I'm on it. I just got dumped. I can't believe they put *me* on a list."

"I don't actually know who's on it," says Liv. "I didn't get to see it."

"Well, I know how to find out. Where's Weston?" I think I saw him watching a fight in the front yard.

Liv catches me by the wrist. "We aren't supposed to know. You can't say anything to him."

"I can't know something like this and not do something about it!" It comes out louder than I mean it to again, and this time people hear. And not just any people. Cheerleader people. Crap.

A few of the girls flit over, all raised eyebrows and sideways glances at each other. Aubrey leads the charge, putting a hand on my arm and cocking her blonde head to the side in concern.

"Are you okay, sweetie? Is it about Weston?"

"He totally sucks," says Chloe.

Beth nods fervently. "The whole squad hates him for what he did to you."

"I'm fine, y'all, really. I am so over him," I say with a winning smile.

Liv stands at my side, but they aren't really acknowledging that she's there. High school caste system in action. Chloe and Beth are giving me sad, hopeful looks. Sad because that's what they're pretending to be. Hopeful because they're failing. They are actually prissy debutante hags who would like nothing more than to see me go "crazy train" over Weston in public.

"Do you want to go somewhere and talk about it?" asks Beth.

I think I've had about all the heart-to-hearts I can take for the night.

"Nah. I'm off to find my next victim."

"Text me if you need anything," says Aubrey, who is actually pretty great to talk to even if she can't keep a secret to save her life.

"I will. Wish me luck." I grin at them before I walk away.

I kind of said that stuff to get away from them, but boy-finding really was part of my plan for tonight. Plus, Weston totally deserves it since he broke up with me over a freaking list.

The kitchen is the heart of any party, so that's where I head first. There are not one but two kegs—the guys have really gone all out this time, and the winding beer line is where I begin my search for my next boyfriend. I have to work fast. Whoever moves on first wins.

Being on a guy search makes me feel like I'm some kind of robot girl. I can practically see the info on each boy pop up in my view screen as I assess the candidates. There's a guy from my health class pumping the keg.

Terry Hanes. Blond hair. Track team. Kind of goofy. Expiration date: five months from now. Meh. I think he has horrible breath.

The guy standing next to him with an empty cup, I've known since second grade. When he used to sneak behind the cubbies and eat glue. He hasn't changed a whole lot since then. I'm kind of surprised he got an invite. And is that a faint white residue I detect on his lips? Hell. No.

In the dining room, Big Tom tortures some rookies with forties duct-taped around their wrists.

"This is the sorriest game of Edward Fortyhands I've ever seen. Mason, I had no idea you were such a little bitch."

He pushes one guy, Mason, I guess, in the shoulder. The bottle slips out of Mason's mouth and beer spills down his shirt.

"I gotta pee," whines Mason in a voice that makes me fear for Casey's mom's dining room chairs.

"Well, then I guess you better drink faster."

Some guy vomits in the corner, and Mason gets a reprieve.

"Vomiting is an immediate disqualification," yells Big Tom.

I stifle my own gag reflex and move to the living room. Music blasts over the speakers, a few girls dancing while Purdeep Patel and Judd Baker play deejay.

Purdeep Patel. Gorgeous smile. Eyelashes I would kill for. In all the smart-people classes but still cool. Expiration date: ten to twelve months. Huh. I never realized Purdeep and I were so compatible. Bonus: he's completely unlike Weston, which would totally piss Weston off. Not-so-bonus: my parents, well, my mother at least, would hate the idea of me dating him because I don't know a lot about the Hindu religion, but I'm pretty sure it does not include Jesus.

Judd Baker, on the other hand . . . reasonably attractive, but smokes way too much pot and has no discernible life goals. Expiration date: two months. Tops.

I'm thinking about going over to flirt with Purdeep when this other guy, Michael, joins them. There he goes in his Boston College shirt, slapping Purdeep and Judd a high five and looking deceptively safe. I've been actively avoiding Michael ever since I met him in physical science last year and thought I might be in love with him.

We were working on this lab together, and I felt the prickly feeling I get when I catch someone noticing my finger. I made sure to keep it tucked in even farther as I wrote.

"Why do you do that?" he asked.

"Do what?" I shook my hair over my shoulder as if to say, *I am certain I don't know what you're talking about.*

"Hide it." He stopped my hand and unbent my knuckle so my pinky was showing, all the way out to its nail-less tip. "You're beautiful. People aren't going to stop seeing that if you let them see all of you."

And then he *touched my finger.* And when he did it, when

he ran his thumb over those thousands of nerve endings, I could have sworn he was touching my soul. Unlike some people, I find the sensation of having someone plunge their hand into my chest and grab my still-beating heart to be extremely unpleasant. Feelings that strong are scary. Feelings that strong for someone you just met are even scarier. There's a term for them in Japanese—*koi no yokan*—the sense you get when you've just met someone but feel certain you're going to fall in love with them. *Koi no yokan* is part of why I started dating Weston in the first place. I needed an emergency exit.

I realize I need to stop with the staring before he notices, but it's too late. When he tilts his head up and our eyes meet from across the room, I get the same feeling I got last year.

He's dangerous.

He gives me a smile and my insides feel all toasty, like I've just gulped down a mug of hot chocolate. I retreat to the kitchen. I eat some chips and salsa, which normally I wouldn't do because eating at a party shortly after a breakup makes you look mopey and desperate, but I estimate I need to stay here at least another few minutes before it's safe to walk back through the living room. Before my heart rate returns to normal.

"Hi."

"Holy jeez!" I almost flip the entire contents of the salsa bowl onto my dress because I was so not expecting for someone to—to—

Michael stands in front of me, his eyebrows raised at my

obvious weirdness. Perfectly groomed eyebrows, I might add. Guys actually taking the time to do personal upkeep is kind of a turn-on of mine, and most guys in this town just . . . don't. Memo to high school boys everywhere: Axe body spray cannot be used in place of actual hygiene.

"I'm Michael. I think we had class together last semester," he says. He's so much taller up close. Mmmm. Tall guys are my Kryptonite.

"I'm—I'm Melanie Jane." Seriously? Stuttering? Pageant queens do not stutter. I am nothing if not well spoken—with all my training it's like I can't even help it. I take a breath. Maybe this is a good thing, him finding me. Maybe I was wrong before, and I can find out all kinds of annoying things about him, and he'll turn out to have an expiration date measured in weeks. Maybe.

"Why'd you run away back there?"

"I didn't." I flip my hair over my shoulder in an attempt to center myself and get some of my swagger back. "I just really wanted some chips."

"Oh. Well, in that case." His hand brushes against my forearm in the very best way as he snakes around me to snag a chip. He dips it in salsa and pops it into his mouth with a James Bond grin. "I'll have chips with you."

"Accidentally" brushing my arm. Trying to be all suave. Things like that don't work on me. Maybe he's just nervous or maybe he really *is* that cheesy and my guy-finder needs recalibrating. Whew. Now that I know he's not a threat, I can relax. I hop on a bar stool, and he takes the one next to me, and we just talk. Not about anything vitally important. He asks me questions about my friends and my family. And he listens, really listens, and it's not the I-want-to-get-into-your-pants kind of listening I'm so used to with guys. I find out he's from Boston, and he misses his friends like crazy. His stories about his family's attempts to acclimate to Tennessee have me laughing so hard I almost spit chip pieces everywhere. I wipe my mouth, embarrassed, and reach for another chip. He reaches for one too, both of us still laughing. Until it happens.

Until our fingers touch in the half-empty bowl, and a jolt ricochets down my arm, and suddenly we're staring at each other all serious. And it's not like salty fingers + one lingering glance = me seeing visions of us getting married and having perfectly eyebrowed children, but wow, holy wow. I was right to call him dangerous. If my *Terminator* vision popped up right now it would say something like:

Michael I-don't-even-know-his-last-name. Gorgeous. Charming. Deliciously tall. Makes me laugh in unladylike ways at parties. Expiration date: indefinite.

And I don't mean "indefinite" as in "Oh, I just haven't figured it out yet because I don't know him well enough." I mean "indefinite" as in he's the kind of guy who might not have an expiration date. Who I could fall for so completely that I might as well put my heart in a blender right now because it would hurt less. Who I could want with the kind of passion that makes you forget important things like the promises you make to yourself. I am terrified. Because the last time I let myself fall this hard, I learned that a lack of control sets you up for heartache and that maybe I shouldn't trust my heart anyway if it picks guys like Chad MacAllistair. Now I know the only safe boys are the ones who fit neatly into expiration date–stamped packages. I know exactly what to do in this situation.

I run.

I make an excuse first about how I desperately need to use the powder room and the downstairs one always has a crazy-long wait, but running is what I am doing. I need to purge Michael and his taller-than-six-foot self from my brain. Stat.

And I know I hardly know the guy, and really I'm not dumb enough to believe in love at first sight, but you hear people like my dad say he knew he was going to marry my mom from that first day when he saw her carrying an entire crate of books up the stairs of their freshman dorm by herself and in heels. He nearly took out two other guys and an RA so he could be the one to open the door for her. And I guess what I think is, sometimes when you meet someone Big, you know. You can't love them. You just met them. But you have this irrepressible feeling that they could change your life forever. It's kind of like how I felt when I met Ana. We were drawn together at that first practice because we were the only two brunettes on the seventh-grade cheerleading squad, but it was about so much more than hair color. I met her, and I knew I wanted her to be my best friend.

And that turned out so well.

By the time I finish reapplying my lip gloss, I am no longer thinking about Michael. I'm thinking about Ana. All the memories of what happened last year—being at the first football party of the year, walking uncertainly down this very hallway, and seeing *them*. I shiver, feeling as though I've been transported back in time. The door at the end of the hallway is cracked open, and I hold my breath as I walk toward it. I push it open wider, my fingers quivering just a bit, my stomach knotting up.

It's empty.

Of course it is. She's not even here. It's not like I'm going to see some replay of last year.

But it does replay, in my head.

I was wearing a new pink dress and a ton of body glitter, and I totally looked like I was trying too hard because I wanted like anything for Chad MacAllistair to notice me that night the way I'd noticed him every day for the past two weeks. I had this idea that he was going to be Big, and if I could just get myself looking hot and into his line of sight, something Big would happen to me. I had talked Ana's ear off about him, and she had dutifully listened and squealed, only making me stop when I started comparing him to all the colors of the rainbow. She's a really good friend.

The first football party was supposed to be the big night, but I panicked every time I got near him, so Ana said she would talk to him for me. But then half an hour went by.

I checked the basement one more time and then the back-yard again. It was like they'd disappeared! I went back inside through the kitchen door and accidentally kind of slammed it behind me.

"Something wrong, princess?" asked a football player I didn't know.

"No." I glared at him. I liked when my dad called me prin-cess, but something about the way this guy said it bothered me.

The cluster of guys surrounding the keg laughed.

I decided maybe I could use his help after all. I hopped up on the counter beside him so my hip touched his bicep. "Actually, I'm looking for my friend Ana. Long, black hair? Freshman cheerleader like me? I just wanted to make sure she didn't leave without me."

"Is that the girl who was talking to Chad?" asked another guy.

"Maybe," I replied, even though I knew good and well the answer was yes.

"Oh, her," said the guy beside me. "Don't worry. They just went upstairs. I'm sure they'll be back in a little bit."

A couple of guys snickered, and I died a little on the inside, but I tried not to show it.

I gave him a smirk as I squeezed his shoulder. "Thanks. *Princess.*"

Then I hopped off the counter and headed to the staircase.

"Wait!" he called. "You can't just go up there."

I pretended not to hear.

When I reached the upstairs hallway, I didn't feel so brave. Could my best friend really do this to me? She knew he was supposed to be Big—I told her about things like that, my crazy theories on the Bigness of people. The first room was empty and the second one was occupied by Big Tom and two girls from band doing things I hoped didn't scar me for life. And then I heard what I thought was the sound of salvation or, more accurately, the sound of vomiting. Lots of it, happening in the bathroom right next to me. I foolishly hoped Ana was in there puking her guts out while Chad innocently held her hair, not even once glancing in the direction of her butt.

It wasn't them. It was a couple of sophomore girls. Which left only one door, the one at the end of the hallway. My stomach knotted up as I gently turned the handle. My fingers shook as I eased the door open.

And there they were.

My best friend, flopped spread eagle on the bed, purple panties crumpled in a ball on the floor. And the guy who was supposed to be Big, his hand moving around under her skirt.

"What are you doing?!" I practically shrieked it.

In less than a second, Chad was three feet away, his body pressed against a dresser instead of Ana. My yelling has that effect on people. "I wasn't! I mean, she—I mean, what?"

"You knew I liked him!" I started crying then, in public,

which completely went against all of my Southern belle training.

Chad's eyes bugged a little, and his face started to get its color back. "I'll just let you girls work this out, then," he said before making a quick exit.

I moved beside the bed, hands on hips, waiting for the apology I wasn't going to accept.

Ana just looked confused. "Mel-Jay?"

She tried to sit up, but didn't quite make it. And when I moved to help her, she vomited all down the side of the bedspread . . . and my new dress.

Fantastic. On top of everything else, she was wasted, and there was no one to take care of her but me. I could have just left her there, but I knew how strict her parents were, and I didn't want her getting in trouble, even if she was a heartless, guy-stealing lush. So because I am *such* a good friend, I carried her home and snuck her into her bed without her parents noticing.

And then I cut her out of my life.

Sunday, August 16
ANA

wake up to my phone vibrating its way off my nightstand. My hand fumbles around on the floor for it. If I can just reach it, I won't have to get out from under the covers yet. I snag the corner of it with my index finger (success!) and slide it until it's close enough to pick up.

> The Devil: I got nothing out of that party.
> Peyton: Me neither.

I text the girls back:

I have something :)

A few seconds later, my phone buzzes again.

The Devil: What? You weren't even at the party.

I smirk as I text back:

I have my ways.

Liv chimes in later.

Liv: I have something too! We should meet up!

The Devil: Yeah, but we need to keep this on the DL.

People will get suspicious if they see us together.

I roll my eyes. Translation: I'm Melanie Jane Montgomery, and I'm too cool to be seen with you people.

Liv: SECRET RENDEZVOUS!!!

Me: I have to open at Jake's this morning. Want to meet me there at 11? No one comes in before noon.

Peyton: Works for me.

The Devil: Me too.

Liv: SECRET RENDEZVOUS + ICE CREAM!!!

I get to Jake's early and clock in. My manager's getting the register ready, but she retreats to her office when she's done. She knows I've got this. I turn on all the lights, prep everything that needs prepping, make some coffee (the inferior, stateside kind), and check all the rooms and bathrooms just in case, even though they should still be clean from closing last night. Just as I'm finishing up, there's a knock at the door. I unlock it and let in Peyton and Liv even though we don't open for another ten minutes.

"Hey, you guys want anything?" I ask.

"Oh! I'll have Strawberry Fields in a waffle cone," says Liv.

I make one for her, and then a Key Lime Piescream for Peyton, and a Chocolate Slap Yo Mama for myself. Liv takes the opportunity to prowl around the store like a secret agent even though I already told her we're the only people here. When the bell jingles at the front door, she pops out of one of the side rooms, looking a little disappointed when she sees it's Melanie Jane and not an enemy spy.

"We can meet over there." I point to a tiny room with squishy mismatched chairs and an antique bookcase painted the precise shade of a baked sweet potato. "That way I can hear the bell if anyone comes in."

I scoop up a cup of Brown Sugah Vanilla for Melanie Jane and hand it to her without making eye contact. Sometimes it's hard to be around her without launching into a rant about how she's a stupid *vaca*, and she should have been there for me, but wasn't. Not that I care. I shake my head. I used to tell her *everything*. Even the weird, embarrassing stuff like how I believe dragons are real and the only reason we don't see them nowadays is because they propagate backward through time. But when I needed to tell her something really important, she wouldn't listen.

We all get comfortable, Peyton tucked into a high-backed chair that almost swallows her whole, Liv sitting on the floor in a butterfly stretch that would make me whimper in pain, and Melanie Jane perched on the edge of her cushion with her legs crossed at the ankles. (She never crosses at the knee because she says the pressure can cause varicose veins. Because, you know, that's something normal for a fifteen-year-old girl to worry about.) I take the seat closest to the door in case I need to jump up and help a customer.

"So, how did it go last night?" I ask.

Peyton and Melanie Jane mostly eat their ice cream and shrug. They weren't kidding when they said they had nothing. Liv did a little better.

"I know who has the keys to the trophy case!" she says.

The floor-to-ceiling case takes up almost an entire wall at the front of the school, and it's filled with trophies and other random football crap, and of course, at its center, is the Football of '76, letting off an otherworldly glow under its custom track lighting. I heard the glass protecting it is bulletproof, but I think that might be BS.

"Nice," I tell Liv. "Who's got them?"

"Coach Fuller and the team captain," she says. "So, Chad MacAllistair."

I focus on keeping my expression neutral. Is it weird that hearing a name can make you feel like your eyelids are stapled open and you're being forced to watch the worst night of your life on replay? I feel Melanie Jane's eyes on me.

"Well, I have Coach Fuller for health, and he pretty much loves me," she says. "I'll think of an excuse to borrow his keys. I'm sure he'll give them to me."

"Oh! And if that doesn't work, I'll try to steal Chad's," says Liv. "He was one of the guys I heard telling Trevor to break up with me, so I wouldn't mind getting back at him." She's smiling, but there's sharpness behind it. "I can plan a fake seduction for the next football party! He'd totally fall for it."

I narrow my eyes. "That's not a good idea."

I didn't mean for it to come out that way. Almost like I was snapping at her. Melanie Jane is definitely staring at me this time, and so are Peyton and Liv.

"He's—well, he's just not a nice guy, you know?" Understatement of the year. Just thinking about him makes my pulse feel like it's exploding in my ears. I try to channel some Liv-like excitement. "Plus, I haven't even told you guys what I found out yet!"

"Oh, yeah, I almost forgot about that," says Peyton just as Liv says, "Spill!"

Melanie Jane isn't so easily distracted. She keeps watching me, a tiny wrinkle between her eyebrows.

"Right, so the football team is having this initiation thing a week from today, and that means they're going to have the football out of the case. It's supposed to happen in this abandoned barn at Big Tom's around midnight, so I figure we sneak in early and wait for our chance to steal it."

"We're going to watch their secret boy ceremony? That's awesome!" says Liv.

"How did you find out about all this anyway?" asks Melanie Jane. *Ha! She's impressed.*

"My friend Toby is a water boy. You guys really can't tell anyone about this. Toby's supernice, and I don't want anything to happen to him."

"We would never do that. We promise," says Peyton, and she

looks so serious I half expect her to make the Girl Scout sign.

Liv and Melanie Jane nod.

We make plans for this Saturday, excitement sizzling in the air around us. We laugh like supervillains and feel like badasses and use our empty ice-cream cups to act out our plans even though it is completely unnecessary. It's times like this that I get so caught up in what we're doing that I almost forget why I wanted to be part of this in the first place. Almost.

Melanie Jane elbows Liv. "Hey, aren't you forgetting something?"

"A pen that doubles as a hidden camera?"

"The List?"

"Oh, right! The List." Liv slams her hands down on the table in front of her, making us all jump. "Those assholes made a list."

"What kind of a list?" I ask. Girls we've banged. Girls we hate more than anyone else in school. I could be on any number of lists.

"A list of girls the guys had to dump," says Melanie Jane, venom in her voice. "And we are *not* telling anyone."

I stifle a snort. That kind of list would completely submarine the perfect reputation she's worked so hard to build.

"Who else is on it?" I ask.

"We don't know," says Liv. "Really, I'm the only one we know for sure was on it, and that's only because Rey told me."

"Rey?"

"That crazy-big freshman from Samoa who just made Varsity."

I still have no idea who she's talking about but I nod like I do.

"Rey stays in the cone of silence too," says Liv. "He may be one of them, but he seems like a really nice guy."

"Well, clearly, I'm on The List too because they made Weston dump me," says Melanie Jane because the attention being on someone else for a minute during her time of crisis is just too much for her to handle.

"The other girls probably don't even know. They just think their boyfriends decided to break up with them." Liv shakes her head.

"That's horrible," says Peyton. "We need to find out who they are so we can help them."

"How do we do that?" asks Liv.

"Check online?"

"Yeah, that could work." I whip out my phone and so do the other girls. "We can just see if any other football team girlfriends got dumped last week."

"Month," says Liv. "I got the feeling they'd been wearing Trevor down for a few weeks at least, so we need to check the past month."

It takes some searching, but we eventually find two other girls who got dumped a couple weeks before Liv and Melanie Jane. Natalie von Oterendorp, this girl in the band who is a total sweetheart but definitely not the coolest girl in school. And Abby Clayton, who I don't think I've talked to but who is, erm, full figured. It takes about a second to look at their pictures and know why they made The List. And then another second to feel sick to your stomach that you just snap judged them the way the football team did.

Liv rests her head against the chair beside her—for once she has nothing to say. Melanie Jane seems even more pissed off than before, but it's probably only because she was lumped in with these girls.

"They're such jerks!" Peyton shoves her phone away, and we all turn toward her. I don't think I've ever seen her angry. I don't think I believed she was capable of getting angry. "Natalie is one of the sweetest girls I know. She *doesn't* deserve this. No one deserves this. We need to tell her. And Abby too. Can you imagine how they're feeling right now?!"

"Yes," say Liv and Melanie Jane simultaneously.

"Oh, yeah." Her cheeks turn a little pink. "But we should tell them, right?"

Melanie Jane runs a hand through her dark, glossy hair. "I don't think we should."

I give her a look that says, *Seriously?* even though I should know better than to expect her to help someone if it means going against the other popular kids.

"No, I mean it," she says. "Finding out you're on that list hurts. Bad." She glances at Liv, who nods in corroboration. "I don't think we should go telling anyone they're on it unless we know for sure."

"But we do know," I say. "It's obvious because of when they got dumped."

"We know they're *probably* on The List," says Liv. She shakes her blond head. "I agree with Melanie Jane. I'm not about to gut someone over 'probably.'" She squeezes Peyton's knee. "But, hey, I promise, as soon as we know something for sure, we'll tell."

Peyton sighs. "So then what are we going to do? We can't just wait around doing nothing."

Melanie Jane smiles like a Disney villain. "We get our hands on that list."

RANBURNE PANTHER SCAVENGER HUNT

In Ranburne:

1. Fill a condom up with water. Draw a face on it. Put it on Principal Corso's doormat, and ding-dong ditch. (One person)

2. ~~The egg-on-a-string trick. Hang an egg from a power line by a string and watch a car run into it. (Everyone)~~

3. Paint the David Bowie statue at Old Lady Howard's corn maze. (Everyone)

4. ~~Chair race through Walmart. (Everyone)~~

5. ~~Get a picture of the team with the Ranburne Panther. (Everyone)~~

6. ~~Go to the Dawsonville football field. Find that stupid rock they touch before their games. Pee on it. (Everyone)~~

In Nashville:

7. Visit the illustrious Delta Tau Beta fraternity at Vanderbilt. Have a beer with Panther alum TJ McNeil and take a picture of the legendary scar he got during a game-winning play against Dawsonville. (One person)

8. Go to LP Field and reenact the "Music City Miracle." (Everyone)

9. Go to Centennial Park and jump into the pond behind the Parthenon. (Everyone)

10. Go to The Jackrabbit Saloon. Walk to the very middle of the dance floor and attempt to do the worm. (One person)

11. Go up to a girl who is totally out of your league, get down on your knees, and ask her to marry you. (One person)

12. Go up to a fat girl and tell her "You're so beautiful . . . for a fat chick." Bonus points if she throws her drink on you. (One person)

13. Hug a biker. Bonus points if he has a mullet. (One person)

14. Get a girl to give you her thong. (One person)

DARES REMAINING: 10

8:20 P.M.

PEYTON

When Liv removes the box of condoms from their brown paper bag, it is all I can do not to snatch the bag and start hyperventilating into it. Liv must be able to tell because she grabs me by the shoulders.

"You don't have to do this, you know. One of the other girls can videotape me. It's totally fine."

"I want to. Really." My jittery hands are clearly saying the opposite, and Ana half grimaces as she passes me her camera.

She shows me what all the buttons do, and I hold it steady. Well, as steady as I can. I really do want to do this. Partly because I want to be an active part of this team and partly because of what this particular prank symbolizes for me. I am taking a stand against our school's special treatment of football players. Against the teachers who give them endless extensions and undeserved passing grades, and the administration's complete inability to care. Against a school system that thinks making sure Casey Martin plays football is more important than making sure I get the education I need. I'd never have the guts to walk into Principal Corso's office and tell him these things, but leaving an anonymous smiling condom on his doorstep is just as good, right?

My grip has tightened on the camera. I make sure I still

have it trained on Liv, who is currently using her water bottle to turn a condom into a water balloon. She draws a face in black Sharpie, really taking her time with the bushy eyebrows. Bushy eyebrows that look strangely familiar.

I cock my head to the side. "Is that . . . ?"

"Supposed to be Principal Corso? Yes."

The four of us burst into giggles, but mine don't last because now it's time to walk up to the front door of my principal's house, and ding-dong ditch.

I feel so vulnerable. Principal Corso's street has an unseemly number of streetlights, and everything is lit up like daytime. Liv skips down the sidewalk like we're delivering a welcome basket, and I trail along beside her. We thought it would be a good idea to park around the corner and walk.

She skids to a stop in front of a blue house with hydrangea bushes the size of boulders obscuring the front porch. "It's this one with the flower boxes on the windows."

"Are you sure?" Because we could totally turn back.

She nods. "Marley lives two houses over. Apparently, he likes to mow the lawn shirtless, and his chest hair looks like a sweater-vest."

We stare up the incline of his driveway with wrinkled noses.

"There's no car. Do you think that means he's not home?" I ask hopefully.

Liv squints at the blackened windows of the garage. "There might still be a car in there. Can't tell."

"Yeah."

There are luna moths flapping around in my belly. We could still turn and run. Liv starts walking, but my feet are rooted to the cement next to the mailbox.

"We better get going," she says. "Who knows what dare the boys are on right now."

She means we need to hurry because we have no idea how far ahead they might be, but the thought of them showing up here and catching us finally gets me moving. I force one foot in front of the other in slow, terrified steps that lead me to the porch.

"Hey, look," says Liv.

Sitting on the doormat in the glow of the porch light is a condom with a sloppy smile and uneven eyes.

She smirks. "My smiley face is *so* much better than theirs."

"He must not be home." I feel a flood of relief.

"Yeah, or the boys were too scared to ring his doorbell."

And the relief disappears.

A car zooms by on the street behind us, and I clutch Liv's arm.

She laughs. "It's okay. Just a passing car. Nothing to have a heart attack over."

"Right," I say, feeling a little embarrassed.

Liv starts up the stairs, and I follow. My heart races, knowing what happens next, but I try to keep calm and not act like such a dork. I keep my mind occupied with technical stuff. Checking that the tiny red light by the record button is still blinking. Making sure I'm not cutting off Liv's head. She sets her condom next to the one the boys left. It really is superior in every way, especially the eyebrows. I wish I could add a thought bubble that says *Stop the favoritism*. Or leave a sternly worded letter. Of course, then they'd know exactly who did it.

Liv looks at me, eyebrows raised, silently asking if I'm ready. Before I can nod, I hear another car. I turn, determined not to freak out this time, but the car is slowing down.

"Liv."

It's turning into the driveway.

"Liv!"

She flies into action, ringing the doorbell with one hand and grabbing my arm with the other. "This way!"

She practically drags me down the porch. I bang my knee on a wooden rocking chair, and reach down to rub it, but she's already vaulting over the porch railing. I follow without thinking, landing with a soft thump on the pine straw below. Snowballs of white flowers surround us on all sides.

Liv's eyes are frantic. "Do you think he saw us? Ohmygosh, he saw us! I am never getting into college!"

I squeeze her hands. "It's going to be okay. I think the bushes hid us."

Liv continues to jabber about college in a much-too-loud voice, and a car door slams, and I clap my hand over her mouth.

"We have to go. Now. It's our only shot," I whisper.

Her mouth closes, and she shakes her head up and down in a manic nod. We squeeze between two of the mammoth hydrangeas, their branches digging into our clothes and hair like they want to keep us. The last thing I hear before we tear off through the neighbor's yard is Principal Corso's voice saying, "What in the hell?"

4

Monday, August 17

P E Y T O N

We've been in school for less than a week, and already geometry is kicking my butt. It doesn't help that my teacher is Coach Mayes and he thinks sports tangents make great teaching tools. Or that I suck at math. Or that there are four football players in this class, and they've made a game of seeing what they can get away with behind Coach's back. Pelting each other with Skittles. Texting each other pictures of porn stars. Having lewd hand gesture showdowns.

Things I have learned in this class:
- Skittles hurt more than you'd expect.
- Gianna Michaels does not have fake boobs.
- Flipping someone the bird < the BJ motion < flicking your hands against your pelvic bones in the way that means "suck it" < full-on dry humping your textbook.

Things I have not learned in this class:
- Geometry.

It also doesn't help that I have ADHD so even if they weren't doing all that ridiculous crap, I'd still have trouble paying attention. And the thing is, I actually do okay in school—in non-math things. I like reading, and as long as I'm interested in something, I can be a pretty fast learner. But the math. Ugh. It's like one minute Coach Mayes is up there blathering on about angles and the next minute I'm thinking about how chipped my nail polish is and then I notice that Jessica Swanson's toenail polish is a shade of green that makes me imagine a flesh-eating bacteria is feasting on her toes and now I'm wondering whether a flesh-eating bacteria really could eat up all your skin. And before I know what's happened, we're on an entirely different problem, and I have no idea how much I missed.

Today, we're doing these problems where there are all these lines intersecting to make angles, and even though they only give you like two of the angle measurements, you're supposed to be able to guess all the others. I'm trying like anything to focus. Unfortunately for me, the football team is playing the penis game.

"Lines that look parallel are parallel," says Coach Mayes.

"Penis," whispers Brian.

"If we know this angle is one hundred fifteen degrees, what do we know about the angle on the other side?"

"Penis," whispers Casey, just a smidge louder than Brian.

"Penis," whispers Weston, but at least he has the decency to blush.

"Anybody? Come on, if this angle is one hundred fifteen degrees, the other angle has to be . . . ?" His question hangs in the air. No one makes eye contact.

"Penis," says Nate in a voice just louder than a whisper.

Coach cocks his head up. "What was that, Nate?"

Nate grins. "Sixty-five, Coach."

The other guys snicker.

"Sixty-five. Nice work."

Sixty-five. Oh, yeah. I guess that makes sense. I add the number sixty-five to the diagram I copied from the board and try extra hard to block out the crescendoing cries of "Penis!" for the rest of class. *Finally*, Coach Mayes notices what the rest of the class picked up on over half an hour ago, but all he does is laugh and say, "All right, guys. Knock it off." Not that that actually stops them. Nate, determined to end class with a bang, jumps into the air as he leaves the room, slapping both hands against the door frame and yelling "Penis!" at the top of his lungs.

I hang back.

"Um, Coach Mayes?"

He turns from where he's erasing the board. "What's up?"

I pull at the bottom of my shirt, my fingers fidgeting with the hem. "Well, I was wondering, I mean, I know the homework was due today, but I'm meeting with my math tutor this afternoon, so I was hoping I could get an extension?" Whew. I hate asking people for things. It makes me feel all sweaty and vomit-y.

"Mmmm." Coach Mayes is making the "no" face. I must be an easy person to say no to because people make that face at me a lot. "I'll have to take ten points off for being late. It's in the syllabus."

"Yeah, I know, it's just . . ." I bite my lip and check to see if there's anyone within hearing range. Casey and Brian are still sitting on desks at the back of the room. I lower my voice even more. "I have an IEP. So I'm supposed to get a little more time."

Coach frowns. "I don't have an IEP on file for you."

"You don't?"

He shakes his head.

"Oh." And then Casey and Brian are standing behind me, so I just say, "Okay, thanks, Coach," and make a quick exit.

I lean against the wall outside the classroom. How could I not have an Individualized Education Plan? I've had one ever since second grade when they tested me for ADHD. Did my parents forget to do something this year? I wouldn't be surprised with the way they've been acting lately.

Loud voices, boy voices, drift out of the classroom.

"Hey, Coach, I was in the gym all weekend getting ready for the Canyon Springs game this Friday, so I didn't have time to do the homework," says Brian.

"Yeah, me neither," says Casey, who I think is taking geometry for the second time. "It was a serious workout weekend."

Uh-huh. With the amount of beer I saw them both drinking on Friday, I have a feeling they spent the better part of Saturday working beastly hangovers out of their systems.

"Okay, but make sure you get it in tomorrow." I can hear the smile in his voice. "And make sure you bring the pain when we play Canyon Springs. I want to literally beat the piss out of those guys."

My mouth hangs open. I can't believe he just gave them the extension he wouldn't give me. An extension I actually deserve! Casey cocks his chin at me as he passes. You. Have. Got. To. Be. Kidding. This is eighty different kinds of unfair.

I am in a spiral of suck. When I got home from school, Karl called, and like an idiot, I answered. I don't know why I keep doing this to myself. I tell myself we're over. That I have to stop letting him and his poison back into my life. But then he calls, and I have to pick up. Or I'll see him coming toward me in the hallway, and my feet will forget how to move. I wish he'd up and transfer to another school, because I can't seem to tell that boy no. I never have been able to.

Mom brushes my hair out of my face. "You okay, there?"

"What? Oh, yeah, I'm fine."

"You don't have to tell me what's wrong. But do you maybe want to call Candace?"

Candace and Karl? Not buds. He practically did a happy dance when she moved, and she was so proud when I finally dumped him. But since I don't feel like admitting to her that I let him get to me again, I just say, "I'm fine. I promise."

"You sure? You're usually digging into Thai food before I can get the bags open."

I join her at the counter, unpacking the Penang curry and pot stickers. The tamarind shrimp smells so good I want to eat it straight from the box. Mom slides a plate in front of me just in time as if she can tell what I'm thinking.

"That's better," she says.

Ever since she and Dad got divorced, we're like bachelor girls. We eat take-out food all the time (girly, healthy takeout—the kind we could never get Dad to agree to). We do yoga before church on Sunday mornings. Sometimes we feel more like roommates than mother-daughter. Sometimes I like it. I don't like when she goes out with her single friends and I stay up worrying about her. And I definitely don't like hearing about the guys they meet. Mostly, I hate how everything's a competition between my parents now. Mom gets a cat, Dad gets a puppy. Dad buys a motorcycle, Mom buys a convertible. Who can act the most young and fun? Who's recovering from the divorce the fastest?

I want my parents to act like parents. I want a fridge filled with more than just diet shakes and to not run out of toilet paper all the time because they're too busy going on dates and saying "YOLO" as a justification for doing all manner of stupid, embarrassing crap. Instead, I have a dad who highlights his hair, and a mom who steals my clothes. Which reminds me.

"Hey, Mom?"

She sets down her fork. "What's up?"

"I had a problem in geometry today. I asked for extra time on the homework, but my teacher didn't have an IEP for me. Did we forget to do something this year?" I say "we" because as annoyed as I get with her, at least she's here. With me.

She shakes her head. "You don't have to file a new one every year. They should have everything from last year, and it should get sent to all your teachers. There haven't been any major changes."

"Oh." I'm really glad I said "we" now because it seems like it wasn't her fault.

"It's probably just a mix-up or something. I'll call your case manager tomorrow and get it straightened out."

And because I'm still feeling guilty for thinking it's her fault, I tell my cynical side to shove it when it wonders how many days it will actually take her to call and if it would be easier to go see my case manager myself.

Thursday, August 20

MELANIE JANE

N ormally, I hate gym days. Gym days mean Coach Fuller has us file into the gym (or worse, outside to the track) for the physical education portion of our health/PE class. They mean he makes us do something god-awful like play dodgeball or see how many sit-ups we can do before our ab muscles give out. Worst of all, they mean I get sweaty. And as dainty and belle-like as I pretend to be, I sweat like a pig. Or a whore in church. Or a turkey on Thanksgiving. Or a fat man eating hot wings. Take your pick. Mama always has a variety of metaphors on hand to describe the fact that what I do not sweat like is a girl. I don't glow. I don't glisten. I sweat bullets and buckets and great big drops of grossness.

And it's not so bad if I get sweaty at cheerleading practice because then I can go home and shower, but I have two more classes, plus lunch, that I have to get through after PE, and I'd rather not do it coated in a sheen of my own electrolytes.

What this all means is Coach Fuller is no stranger to me coming up to him and asking if I can do some different (and by different, I mean "sweat free," but he doesn't have to know that) activity. Which, for today, is perfect. I put on my best pageant smile and skip on over to where Coach Fuller is instructing people on how to properly serve a volleyball.

"Hey there, Coach. Do you mind if I get a yoga ball from the closet? Miss Nashville's right around the corner, and I really need to work on my core."

I smile bigger. I can feel my dimples popping on my cheeks. No one says no to my dimples.

He scratches his head and leaves the volleyball players alone for a minute. "Work on your core, huh?"

"Well, yeah." I giggle. "The swimsuit competition knows no mercy." I playfully poke at his tummy, which is actually impressive for a guy his age. "You probably know all about core exercises."

He grins and holds himself a little taller. "I may still do sit-ups every day."

"I thought so. Can I have the key, then? To the closet?"

His head is still cloudy with the compliment I just gave him. "Oh, sure. Sure." He pulls a key ring out of his pocket. Jackpot. The key to the trophy case has to be on there. And . . . I won't be finding out because he slips a single gleaming key off the ring before pocketing the rest. "Here you go," he says. "Bring it back when you're done. And good luck with, you know, your core."

So what can I do but go to the sports closet and grab a big pink yoga ball? I had visions of this working perfectly and me presenting the girls with the football later tonight. It's okay, though. We'll get another chance at that football initiation thing. And at least I don't have to go through the rest of the school day with sweaty hair plastered to the sides of my face. A fact I am extremely thankful for when I turn the corner onto the A hallway after PE and run smack into Michael.

"Hey!" He grins at me as he dislodges his arm from my backpack. If he had a tail, it would totally be wagging right now.

"Hey." I smile too because seeing him again sends a rush of tingles up my back, but underneath, I am freaking out.

"I was worried I'd never see you again." He blushes a little when he says it. "You always end up running away. Actually, you kind of look like you might run right now."

"What? No way." I wasn't just planning the best exit route in my mind. Nope. Not me.

He grins again. Man, is he happy. "Well, good. Because there's something I wanted to ask you."

"Oh, yeah?" My eyes dart from side to side, and then I forget all about Michael for a second because a hulking figure in a letter jacket I used to wear is lurking just a few lockers away. Weston.

". . . this Saturday," finishes Michael.

"What?" I cock my head to the side, trying to get my brain to replay the rest of what he just asked.

"This Saturday? Are you free?" For the first time, his smile falters. "But, hey, if you're not, it's cool." He must think I'm stalling so I can think of a way to say no.

Weston is eyeing us like he owns me, tight jaw and a vein pulsing in his forehead. I half expect him to start cracking his knuckles. Hot rage slices through me. *Who does he think he is?* He broke up with me based on a list. A list I can't even talk to him about. But you know what I *can* do? I can stop being afraid of this other guy who is probably better than Weston in every way. I can stop beating myself up because the last time I liked a guy this much it cost me a broken heart and a best friend. I can say yes.

"Yes." I grab Michael's arm to stop him from walking away.

His eyes light up. "Really?"

"Well, no. I mean, I can't this Saturday because I already have plans, but how about next Saturday?"

"Next Saturday is great!" He can't keep the exclamation point out of his voice, and it is kind of adorable.

We trade phone numbers and he walks, no, bounces, down the hallway, and I would bet you anything that when he rounds that corner he punches his fist into the air.

My heart is in so much trouble.

I lift my chin high as I pass by Weston, determined not to talk to him. My plan doesn't really work because he throws an arm out and practically clotheslines me.

"Excuse you." I push him away and shoot laser beams through him with my eyes.

"Hey, who was that?" He's wearing that pouty look that used to be cute but is now irritating as all hell.

"He's none of your business. You broke up with me, remember?"

"Sometimes it feels like the other way around."

I flash him a pageant smile minus the smiling with the eyes part. "Not my fault."

He's still stuttering behind me as I stride away. Life is as it should be. Except that I'm going out with a guy who might not have an expiration date.

I slide into my desk in Spanish II, still wondering whether saying yes to Michael was a good idea. Or rather, wondering just how bad of an idea it was. Señor Barbas hands back our homework. He passes the paper to my right side, but I take it with my left hand because it's way too hard to grab a paper and keep my finger hidden at the same time, especially with Chloe Baskins sitting right next to me. I check the grade at the top: 100 percent correct, with smiley face. Not that I'm surprised. I love foreign languages. I'm probably the only person in this school taking both French and Spanish. I can't wait till college when I can take something really cool like Arabic or Mandarin.

When I was little, Mama told me that if I could read, no one would be able to write down secrets and keep them from me—it's the whole reason I learned. She was wrong though. Grandma helped me figure that out.

My grandma used to tell me all kinds of wonderful stories about when she was a kid. She had the best and bravest adventures, a new one every time I came to visit. Stories about saving a band of children from a cave inhabited by a yellow jacket big as a house, and a journey to the North Pole to meet an Ice Man, and a daring escape from an old woman named Spearfinger who liked to catch children and eat their livers. Later, when I was older, my mom told me the stories weren't real. Or, well, they were, just not how I thought. My grandmother had taken all these Cherokee legends and inserted herself as the star. It didn't really change the important thing though—that my grandma was the best story-teller in the whole world and could weave words into otters and eagles and intrigue.

One day I let Grandma in on my plan—the one where I learned to read so that no one would ever be able to keep a secret from me again. She kind of ruined it for me. It wasn't her fault—the plan had a gaping flaw. If I learned to read, no one would ever be able to keep a secret from me again. *In English.* She opened my mind to the idea that people could talk and write in all kinds of other languages and those are secrets too. They could even write in code. That idea stuck in my brain like a weed, and I decided I wanted to learn as many languages as possible.

But then it got better. My grandma knew a language that almost no one else could speak: Cherokee. And if she taught it to me, even Mama wouldn't be able to tell what we were saying, and would I like to learn it? Um, obviously. The idea of having a secret language from my mom was reason enough. Unfortunately, I only learned six words from Grandma on that visit, and we never got to have another one because of the heart attack. I still remember those six words though:

Wahya (wolf)

Saloli (squirrel)

Ugidali (feather)

Ama (water)

Nvda (sun)

Ditlihi (warrior)

"Mel-Jay? Are you even listening to me?" I realize Chloe is staring at me and looking kind of annoyed.

"Sorry. What?"

"I said I just ran into that bitch Ana Cardoso in the hallway, and she actually had the nerve to act like it was my fault." She flips her white-blonde hair over her shoulder. "I can't even believe she still goes to school here. Wouldn't you, like, move to another state or something?"

My mind runs over every mean thing I've seen someone do to Ana in the past year. "Yeah, I probably would," I say. But I don't mean it in the vengeful way, not like I would have before.

Chloe giggles. "Why were you ever friends with that slut anyway?"

"She—"

But I'm saved from having to answer because Señor Barbas starts class.

Sometimes I think back on the day of the party, when I caught Chad and Ana. Betrayal and humiliation and this feeling of being less than, a feeling I've struggled to hide my entire life, compressed inside that one moment. In Czech, they call it *litost*, that acute sense of clarity and agony that drives you to lash out in revenge. But if I hold up the memory and peel all that away?

I don't know. I wonder if I really saw what I thought I saw. I was only fourteen when it happened, and I'd only ever kissed a boy. I was certainly no expert on the things men and women do in dark rooms alone. I'm still no expert.

I think about our meeting at Jake's. About the look on Ana's face when Liv brought up Chad MacAllistair. And for some reason, I feel inexplicably sick to my stomach.

RANBURNE PANTHER SCAVENGER HUNT

In Ranburne:

1. ~~Fill a condom up with water. Draw a face on it. Put it on Principal Corso's doormat, and ding-dong ditch. (One person)~~

2. ~~The egg-on-a-string trick. Hang an egg from a power line by a string and watch a car run into it. (Everyone)~~

3. Paint the David Bowie statue at Old Lady Howard's corn maze. (Everyone)

4. ~~Chair race through Walmart. (Everyone)~~

5. ~~Get a picture of the team with the Ranburne Panther. (Everyone)~~

6. ~~Go to the Dawsonville football field. Find that stupid rock they touch before their games. Pee on it. (Everyone)~~

In Nashville:

7. Visit the illustrious Delta Tau Beta fraternity at Vanderbilt. Have a beer with Panther alum TJ McNeil and take a picture of the legendary scar he got during a game-winning play against Dawsonville. (One person)

8. Go to LP Field and reenact the "Music City Miracle." (Everyone)

9. Go to Centennial Park and jump into the pond behind the Parthenon. (Everyone)

10. Go to The Jackrabbit Saloon. Walk to the very middle of the dance floor and attempt to do the worm. (One person)

11. Go up to a girl who is totally out of your league, get down on your knees, and ask her to marry you. (One person)

12. Go up to a fat girl and tell her "You're so beautiful . . . for a fat chick." Bonus points if she throws her drink on you. (One person)

13. Hug a biker. Bonus points if he has a mullet. (One person)

14. Get a girl to give you her thong. (One person)

DARES REMAINING: 9

8:45 P.M.

LIV

The football team is still ahead of us. At least, I think they are. But we're catching up, we just have to be. And that means we need to be extra careful. The boys could be at Old Lady Howard's this very minute, and I definitely don't want to run into them again. I wonder what Trevor's doing right now. Is he studying the scavenger hunt dares and planning their next move? Aiming a can of spray paint at the goblin king's fabulous hair? Laughing in the background and snapping photos? Is he thinking of me too? Scratch that last one. I'm not pathetic enough to want the answer to that.

There are no other cars in the dirt lot next to the corn maze. Either the boys are gone or they parked on the street. We creep toward the cornfield with our flashlights off, tripping over rocks and each other. A few flickering mosquito lanterns sway in the breeze on Old Lady Howard's back porch. In the feeble halo of light, I can see we're alone. And based on the empty cans of paint and beer that litter the grass surrounding the statue, the football team has already been here.

Melanie Jane approaches the goblin king and touches a tentative finger to his thigh. "It's still wet," she whispers. "We can't be far behind now."

"Damn straight." I clap my hands together. "They better watch their backs!"

"Shhh," hisses Ana. She cocks her head toward the house. "She's probably still awake."

We circle around the statue, surveying their paint job in crisscrossing flashlight beams. It's terrible. And I don't just mean their technique—clumsy streaks of spray paint in black and silver with a little purple thrown in too—Panther colors. They've sprayed the words *Panther Football Rocks* across his chest, a purple penis directed at his mouth, a silver one at his butt, and does that say what I think it does? I shine my light at his crotch where someone has painstakingly painted the word *Fag* in skinny purple letters.

Ana looks like she's grinding her teeth into dust. "What do you want to bet Big Tom was behind this?"

"How do you know?" I shine my flashlight at her, and she squints. Oops.

"Because a few weeks ago he—" She catches herself. "It's not my secret to tell, but let's just say intolerance is one of his hobbies." Her eyes are so angry, I swear they could split that statue right down the middle. "We need to fix this before I punch something."

Peyton rustles through her Walmart bags. "Here." She holds out two cans to Ana. "Do you want black or silver? I also have—"

"Those'll work." Ana takes them both, and eyes the statue in disgust. "I'll be on hate-crime duty."

"Do you have any hot pink?" I ask Peyton.

She grins. "Yes."

"Excellent. I know the goblin king didn't have hot-pink boots, but I totally feel like he should have." I bounce over and get to work on the wardrobe change.

Melanie Jane drags a tree stump over so she can reach his face. Peyton alternates between photo documentation, shining her flashlight so we can see better, and throwing the trash the boys left into an empty Walmart bag. Oh, and turning her head to glance at Old Lady Howard's house at five-second intervals because she is still peeing her pants over the thought of getting caught.

I finish the front half of the boots, stretch, and check out Melanie Jane's handiwork. She has somehow managed to cover different parts of his face with a bag while spraying so the paint looks almost like makeup. I move around to the back. Ana has painted over his entire cloak in black so you can't see the penis anymore, and is just finishing up a huge silver equality sign on his back.

"Nice," I say.

"You too." She smiles at my pink boots, which I have to say do look pretty amazing.

Ana paces around to the front and is about to black out *Panther Football Rocks* when I say, "WAIT!"

She holds up her hands in confusion. "What? I didn't realize

'Panther Football Rocks' was a critical message to share with the rest of the world."

I giggle. "Just black out the 'Rocks' part, okay? I'll take care of the rest."

We exchange evil-genius eye glints. "Cool," she says.

I'm putting the final touches on David Bowie's go-go boots, when I hear it.

Music.

Softly at first, and then it's blaring through the yard over the outdoor speakers. Floodlights tear apart the night sky, and we blink like frightened mice. Old Lady Howard stands silhouetted in the doorway, nightgown billowing around her, silver hair reaching in every direction like it could snatch moths from the air and gobble them up.

I think I hear Peyton whisper, "We're all going to die."

"What are you doing?" she asks with a voice like rusty nails.

Me? Is she asking me? I always thought her lazy eye made her look kind of sweet and discombobulated, but now I can't tell if she's looking at me, and it is absolutely nerve-wracking!

Melanie Jane recovers before the rest of us and bravely approaches the wooden porch with the warped slats. "We can leave right now," she says, her voice impressively calm. "We're very sorry to have disturbed you. There's no need to call the police or anything. We're leaving right now."

When she stops talking, I catch a few words of the song. ". . . power of voodoo . . ." Wait. Is she playing "Magic Dance"?

She *is*. I feel an odd sense of relief. Anyone blaring music from *Labyrinth* probably isn't going to maim us or send us to jail. Right?

We back away with slow, careful steps, edging ourselves away from her and in the direction of the car.

"Just where do you think you're going?" she shouts.

I cringe and stop moving. "We were just going to leave, ma'am. If that's okay."

She nods at the Bowie statue. "Did you finish the job yet?"

I blink. Does she mean what I think she means? We compare notes with our eyes, all wondering the same thing.

"You didn't disturb me," she says, leaning against the railing for support. "Them boys did. Hootin' and hollerin' like a bunch of banshees. And I ain't gonna call the police neither." She points a gnarled finger at Peyton, who nearly faints on the spot. "I seen this one picking up trash."

I close my eyes and thank the Lord that Peyton loves the environment.

"You better make sure you're finished, though. I don't like people leaving a job half done." Old Lady Howard creaks down the steps and out into the yard, where she circles the statue with eagle eyes. "Not bad. Not bad at all. Are you sure you're done?"

Ana and Melanie Jane nod furiously. When I say "Almost," I think they are going to skin me alive.

I pick up my can of paint and spray the word *Sucks*

underneath *Panther Football* in bubbly pink letters. "There." I smile and tuck the can of paint into our makeshift trash bag.

"Anyone else?" asks Old Lady Howard.

Peyton, who up until now hasn't even touched the statue, takes a step forward. "Well, actually, um . . ."

She removes a round container from one of the bags and approaches the goblin king with delicate steps. A lid pops off. Her dainty fingers reach inside. And she sprinkles the crystal ball on the end of his cane with glitter. GLITTER. Can you believe it?

"That looks real nice," says Old Lady Howard before she hobbles back into the house on arthritic knees.

I throw my arms around Peyton's neck. "Have I told you that I am in love with you?"

5

Thursday, August 20

A N A

I catch Grayson by the sleeve on the way to my last class of the day.

"Hey, I don't have work today. You want a ride?"

He holds out his hands like Lady Justice. "Hmm. Riding the bus with the unwashed masses or getting chauffeured by one of my best friends? I'll meet you in the parking lot."

"Cool." I squeeze him on the shoulder and head to class.

It's usually just the two of us on the days when I don't work. The other guys have clubs or sports or whatever, but Grayson and I aren't really joiners. Well, I'm not anymore anyway.

I don't see him in the hallway after the last bell. He isn't in the parking lot yet either, so I sit in my car and wait. It's safer that way. Standing around while the other kids pass me by is asking for trouble because you never know who's coming out of those double doors next. I check my phone, but there's nothing. He would have texted me if he'd changed his mind—and then I'd have to wonder if his body had been taken over by aliens. I guess I can give him a few more minutes. I flip on the radio and am hit with an insatiable need for lip balm. I dig through my purse because there's always at least one tube in there, and I swear I can feel the skin around my lips cracking. My fingers close around some Burt's Bees Pomegranate. Whew. I run the lip balm over my lips, my eyes closing, a satisfied sigh escaping me. My obsession with non-dry lips used to crack Melanie Jane up. She called them my "Lip Balm Panic Attacks," and the guys picked it up too.

When my eyelids flutter open I finally see Grayson. And I know something is wrong.

His shoulders are hunched, his backpack hanging from his hand and bumping against his leg as he walks down the stairs. Grayson is usually one of those ray-of-sunshine people. It's the kind of personality I find annoying on most people but endearing on him. The closer he gets, the more I worry. His hair is messed up, and not in the artful, Grayson way, and there are splotches all over his shirt. They're white and they look kind of like . . .

I roll down the window. "Is that—?" I can't even bring myself to say it.

"It's mayonnaise," he says.

I fall back against my seat in relief, but only for a second. "What happened to you?"

"Big Tom and a couple of other guys jumped me in the bathroom." He opens the door and sets his backpack on the floorboard. "They roughed me up a little and squeezed mayonnaise packets all over me. I'll be fine." He looks down at his shirt. "I guess I shouldn't wear this in your car though."

He pulls his polo over his head, but his white undershirt sticks to it in the places where the mayonnaise seeped through, and I catch a glimpse of the angry red welts on his stomach before he can tug it back down.

"Oh my gosh! Grayson!" I caught at least five places where they pinched and twisted his skin, and I didn't even see that much of him.

"I'm fine." He sits down and smooths his hair back, and when he takes off his sunglasses, his eyes are red.

I think I can actually feel my heart breaking. "You're not fine," I say softly.

"Can you just take me home?"

His voice has pent-up tears in it, and I know how horrible it is to cry where someone might see you, so I don't say anything else. I drive to our neighborhood in silence.

When I get to his driveway, though, I have a hard time staying quiet.

"This is really screwed up. Has it happened before?"

His lack of an answer means it has.

"But they can't keep getting away with this. You have to tell someone."

"You mean the way you told someone?"

There isn't enough air in the car. "I don't—"

"Oh, come on, Ana. We know you don't want to talk about it and we're all okay with that, but you can't pretend like nothing happened."

Grayson would understand. I know he would. But I've gotten so good at hiding the old wounds that the thought of opening them again, everything fresh and raw, is overwhelming.

"I can't," I whisper.

He pulls my hand into his lap and squeezes it. "I can't either," he says sadly.

I can't cry in Grayson's driveway when he's the one who got beat up at school. I'm pretty sure that would make me a bigger drama queen than Melanie Jane. I can't cry in my own driveway either because one of my parents might see me, and they'd be all, "Are you okay, *princesinha*?" and then I might tell them what happened, and then they might disown me.

I drive a couple of blocks until I'm halfway between my house and Grayson's and halfway blinded by tears. Not telling is definitely the best policy. I learned that pretty quickly after. I only told two people. The first was one of the school counselors.

It was the Monday after the party. They're always saying how "the door is always open." And "you can talk about anything." The first part was true.

I had knocked on the door even though it was, in fact, open. A small knock. Quick and light. An I-don't-want-to-be-here, please-don't-hear-this-so-I-can-turn-and-go knock. The counselor saw me before I could take more than a step away from the door.

"Ana?" Damn.

"Oh, yeah, hi." I shuffled into the office and closed the door behind me. There was no way in hell I wanted anyone overhearing this.

"What can I help you with?" Her smile was so big it hurt to look at it. I was a freshman cheerleader. School had just started. She probably thought I was there for a schedule change. What kind of problems could a girl like me possibly have? She'd know in a minute.

"I needed to talk to someone," I said to the coffee mug on her desk. "About something."

She frowned, but it still wasn't nearly serious enough. "Well, sure. What do you need to talk about?"

"I was at a party this weekend. And someone did things to me." I somehow got the words out. My hands clenched into fists on top of my jeans. "I didn't want him to." I cracked open, and the pain spilled onto the floor.

"It's going to be okay." She finally looked properly horrified. "Have you told the police or your parents? Have you been to a doctor?"

I shook my head.

"Do you want to talk about what happened?"

This was the hardest thing. "I don't really know. I mean, I know something happened. But it's hazy. I remember . . ." That awful shot. Dancing. Euphoria. Lines between objects melting together like watercolors. His breath in my ear. Stumbling. A bed. Hands where I didn't want them. Heavy eyelids. Dead limbs. "Things. Chad gave me a shot and after—things happened." I sank my teeth into the inside of my lip, a distraction from the other kind of hurt.

"Chad? Chad MacAllistair?" And it was like her whole face changed.

I nodded. "I think he put something in my drink."

"Why do you think that?"

"Well, I felt so out of it so fast. And I only had one drink." One horrible-tasting shot that clung to the inside of my mouth.

"Are you sure?"

The question caught me by surprise. "Yes."

Wait. Did she not believe me? Was that what this was about?

Her eyes were sharp. "But you said your memory is hazy. It's possible you had more drinks after the first one?"

It wasn't, and I knew it. But did I? Really? There were bigger things about that night that I didn't know.

"I guess so," I finally said.

She nodded. "And maybe the first one was very strong."

I shrugged. "Maybe."

She nodded again like now we were getting somewhere. "So, you were with Chad and you were drinking. What happened next?"

"Well, we were dancing. I started feeling really dizzy, so he said we'd go upstairs and get me some water. And then we ended up in this bedroom, and—" My voice cut off, and the sick feeling in my stomach became almost unbearable. I never realized memories could feel like physical things that tore at your insides. I took a deep breath and tried again. "He was kissing me, and I know he did other things too."

"And during this time, did you tell him no? Did you try to stop him?" Her voice was kind, but I had an uneasy feeling, like I was on a witness stand and she was the lawyer for the other team.

The powerless feelings flooded me again. I wrapped my arms around myself. "I said no. I couldn't move very well, I think because of the drink."

"And then you and Chad had sex?"

That was the question that broke me. I started crying then, great big angry sobs that shook my whole chest. She handed me some tissues. It was a long time before I could talk again. "I don't know exactly because everything went dark."

The ugly, broken thing was out there in the open. The part that made me want to never get out of bed again and turned my insides cold. Because how was I supposed to explain to my dad, the man who had taken me to mass every week since before I could remember that I didn't know if I was a virgin anymore?

The counselor held my hands and let me cry for a while. Then she was back to business. "I want you to think very carefully about what to do next," she said. "What you're telling me is you and Chad were drinking and dancing and then you went upstairs with him. You said no, but you didn't do a whole lot to try to stop him, and you don't actually know that anything happened."

Her words cut like a knife. When you put it that way, I sounded like a lying, conniving slut. She was twisting everything. "But—"

She held up her hands to stop me. "I'm just saying to be careful. Chad's one of the best receivers in the state. He's probably going to get a football scholarship to a good college. Do you really want to ruin all of that for him over something you're not sure even happened? Do you really want that kind of spotlight on you? It might be better for everyone if you could forgive him."

She had this look on her face like the right answer was clear, and I just needed to see it. And she was right about the spotlight part. I hadn't thought about that. I couldn't imagine everyone knowing. Facing that kind of judgment. But she was wrong about everything else and I knew it.

It was all too much, and I felt like I was on my own. I found myself saying, "I'll think about it."

Friday, August 21
PEYTON

I might as well be naked. The three-inch strip of skin between the top of my tight, black pants and the bottom of my cropped zip-up hoodie feels like it's on fire. The sparkly dance top underneath pushes my girls up in a way that violates laws of physics and the school dress code all at once. That dream you have where you show up to school without any clothes and everyone stares at you? I'm living it. The girls at Friday Morning Fellowship are tearing me up one side and down the other with their eyes, and it's all I can do not to run away and hide in the bathroom. They're dressed as scandalously as they can be (some of them are probably hoping to catch a Christian boyfriend here, after all), but they have to adhere to the school guidelines or face the wrath of Vice Principal Crutcher, and I get to sidestep those same guidelines because this is the official dance team uniform.

I see a girl glance at me and whisper something to her friend, and I can't handle it anymore. I zip my hoodie all the way up even though that's not technically how we're supposed to wear it. I want to clamp my arms around my waist too, but I figure that would only draw more attention, so I hurry to find a seat and hope this will all be over soon.

Pastor Dave steps up to the microphone—he's a youth pastor at a church nearby, and he always leads Friday Morning Fellowship. "Hey, guys. Before we get started today, Rey Lemalu has an announcement to make."

Rey steps up to take the microphone from Pastor Dave, practically casting a shadow on him he's so big. The entire auditorium goes quiet. Everyone knows who Rey is, even though he's only a freshman. Most freshmen aren't six two and 210 pounds, and they aren't starting at defensive end for the Varsity football team. And in case you're wondering why I know his exact height and weight, no, I'm not a creepy stalker. It's just that the coaches here at Ranburne were salivating over Rey the whole time he was in middle school, so people are always talking about him. How big he is. The number of sacks he got last year (thirteen). Whether he really got tattoos over the summer when he went back to Samoa to see his family.

Rey clears his throat. "Yeah, hi." His voice is softer than you would expect. He's the kind of person who doesn't say a whole lot, but when he does talk, it's important. "So, I have this idea I'm hoping you guys can help me with. I've been volunteering with a group of elementary school kids over the summer—it's been really great. They don't have a lot, and their neighborhood isn't really safe for trick-or-treating. One of the teachers was telling me a lot of them don't get to do it. So I thought it would be cool if we set up the gym here with booths and candy. Maybe a haunted house and some games and activities and stuff. I know it's only September, but we'd have to start planning now. The kids are so great, you guys. They treat me like I'm a hero just because I taught some of them how to catch a football. They get so excited over having someone care about them. Anyway, I think it would be a really cool way to make a difference."

I see nods around the auditorium. I'm definitely in. We'd be helping so many kids. That's my favorite part of religion, connecting to other people in a bigger way, feeling like what you're doing means something. Plus, the way Rey talks about things, he's just so inspiring. I know other people are feeling the same way. This is the Rey Lemalu I met at the party on Friday, the one who seemed so concerned about Trevor and Liv. The real thing is so much more interesting than the football myth.

While everyone else is singing and listening to Pastor Dave, all I can think about is Rey's Halloween idea and how I can help. I walk to class without even noticing whether people are staring at my clothes, though at least one person must have been because one of the senior dance team girls swoops in to return my zipper to its proper boob-baring height.

When I get to geometry, the high I'm riding on dissolves. Casey whistles as soon as I enter the classroom.

"Woo, did you know Church Girl was hidin' a body like that?"

Snickers erupt all around him, but I try to ignore them because I have more important things to worry about. I pull my IEP out of my backpack. You get one if you have any kind of special needs, and mine has pretty standard modifications for ADHD:

I have to sit at the front of the room.

I need both visual and verbal instructions (because if it doesn't get written on the board, there's a 200 percent chance I'll forget it).

I get more time on assignments and stuff.

I need "cuing." This one totally sucks because every time a teacher catches me spacing out and redirects my attention, I'm positive everyone in class knows what's going on and thinks I'm stupid.

I have to have a learning environment with minimal distractions (so, pretty much the opposite of geometry class).

I stand by Coach Mayes's desk for a very long two seconds before he notices me.

"Hi." I hand him my folder. "Dr. Barnes gave me a copy of my IEP to give you."

He flips open the folder and glances over the front page before shoving the whole thing into a desk drawer. "Yeah, Dr. Barnes told me you talked to him." Something flickers in his eyes. Anger maybe. Or annoyance. Did Dr. Barnes tell him I mentioned how distracting the learning environment was? Is that what this is about?

I feel super awkward, so I just say, "Um, okay, sounds good," and make a quick retreat.

Casey whistles again as I take my seat two desks ahead of him. He nudges Nate.

"'Scuse me, gentlemen."

He moves to the desk behind me and taps my shoulder. "Hey, you sure are lookin' good."

"Um, thanks?" I say, but what I'm really thinking is: you sure do sound like that guy from *Deliverance*.

"Hey. Church Girl." He taps me again.

I turn around. "It's Peyton."

"Peyton." He thinks it over for a minute. "I like it."

Before he can say anything else, Coach Mayes starts going over the homework from last night. I face the board, never happier to learn about the wonders of geometry. My relief is short lived. A few problems in, I feel another tap.

"Hey, Peyton," Casey whispers.

I don't respond.

He leans over his desk so his mouth is right next to my ear. "Hey, Peyton," he whispers again. "You wanna come out with me tonight after the game?"

Again, he doesn't seem deterred by my lack of response.

"We could drive around in my truck, and you could show me what else you're hidin' under that uniform."

He traces a finger down my neck, and this time he does get a response. I jerk away and twist around in my seat so I can glare daggers at him. "No. I don't want to," I hiss.

He grins. "What? You think Jesus would mind?"

"No, but I—"

"Miss Reed?"

I turn to face Coach Mayes, my cheeks burning. "Yes?"

"The answer to question number seven," he says. "It's your turn. Please pay attention."

"Sorry. Casey was distracting me," I mumble.

Casey snorts. "Are you kidding? She's the one bein' distracting. Look at what she's wearing."

Coach frowns. "Miss Reed, why don't you move to another seat so you can concentrate. There's an open one over there."

He gets that flicker in his eyes again, and I'm more sure than ever that it has to do with what I told Dr. Barnes. I don't bother arguing with him about why *I'm* the one that has to move. I just want the humiliation to end, so I grab my stuff and take it to the empty desk, which, of course, happens to be right beside the two girls who ignored me at dance team tryouts. I sit down with a tense smile that says, *Don't worry, I'm not going to try to talk to you again.*

"Hey, Peyton," says the girl directly beside me.

"Hey," echoes her friend.

I'm shocked they're speaking to me—extra shocked they know my name. I forget to say anything back, I'm so flustered between that and what just happened with Casey. I try to stay focused for the rest of class, but let's be honest, that's difficult for me on a good day, and today, well, today is not shaping up to be so great. It only gets worse at the end of class when Coach Mayes gives back our quizzes. At the top of mine, circled in red pen, is a giant D+. The bell rings, and I hurry out to the hallway before Casey can think of any other clever remarks. I lean against the wall with my quiz and try not to cry. I'm so confused, I can't even figure out why most of my wrong answers are wrong.

"Hey, are you okay?"

I look up to see Rey standing beside me. It makes me a little nervous, being around someone who could snap me like a twig, but I know he's not like Big Tom. He has sweet eyes and a voice like caramel.

"I'm fine," I say. "I'm just having a rough day. And I suck at geometry."

I flash my quiz so he can see the grade even though I'm usually really embarrassed about stuff like that.

His eyes light up. "I can help you with that. I'm pretty good at math. Here." He writes his phone number next to the D+. "If you ever want to get together and study, just let me know."

"Cool." He starts to leave but I say, "Rey?"

He pauses at the door to the classroom. "Yeah?"

"I really liked your idea today. At FMF?"

He grins. "Thanks."

As I stuff my quiz into my book bag, I realize Karl is watching from across the hallway, but before he can come over, Liv bounces up to me. I say a silent prayer of thanks.

"Hey! How's it going? You look hot!"

"Thanks," I say, but it's hard to feel enthusiastic after the morning I've had.

"What's wrong?"

"It's just— I guess I feel kind of uncomfortable." I tug at the bottom of my jacket. "People have been staring at me all morning, and I know the girls at FMF were talking about me."

She puts her arm around me, and we walk to my next class. "Ignore them. They're just jealous. If you see people staring, it's because you look amazing. And hot. Have I told you how hot you look, yet?"

I giggle. "You might have mentioned that."

People stare at the pair of us in our twin uniforms that are almost identical in their scandalousness. (Mine is tighter across the boobs; hers is tighter across the butt.) When people stare at Liv, I don't assume it's because they think she's skanky or half naked. It's because she looks amazing. It occurs to me that maybe, just maybe, people are staring at me for the same reason. I've been hiding up until now. But I stop. Because for the first time today, I feel good about what I'm wearing. And I realize, as I weave through the crowd with a slightly straighter spine, that it has nothing to do with what the other people in the hallway are thinking.

Everything is electric. The music. The stadium lights. The screaming fans. When I ran onto the field for the halftime show, I felt dozens of butterflies—the tiny lavender ones that come out in early spring. But now, with the bass pumping through me, and the night air warm against my skin, I feel powerful. I kick and shimmy and leap and pirouette. I shake my nonexistent butt. I don't think about my uniform. Or about what people are saying.

I live this moment just for me.

And when it's over, when the music fades and I'm left panting in my final pose, I know that I was phenomenal. That not dancing like this meant keeping the best part of myself hidden. And that coming back to dance was the best decision I ever made.

I search for my parents again as we jog back to the sidelines amidst cheering and wolf whistles. I know neither of them is here, but I can't help but look anyway. I'm filled with this fragile hope that I'll see their faces in the crowd and they'll have flowers and be like, "Surprise! How could you ever think I'd miss your first halftime show?" It's the only thing missing to keep tonight from being perfect.

I made plans to have Liv's mom drop me off at my house, so I find them as soon as the game is over. While her mom chauffeurs us around, we chatter and giggle and go over and over the awesomeness that was tonight's performance. When we get to my house, though, we fall silent. It's dark except for one sad porch light.

Mrs. Lambros gives me the concerned-mom frown. "Is anybody home?"

I shake my head. "My mom's at a concert in Nashville. A girl's night. They've had the tickets for a really long time, though," I rush to say. "And my dad, well, he couldn't make it either." I stare at the floorboard. "They said they'd catch the next one."

I focus on counting the Cheerios scattered around my feet because the urge to cry has hit me so hard and so suddenly, and I won't do that in front of Liv. I won't.

"Nope," says Liv, an authoritative answer to a question nobody asked. "Nope, we're definitely not dropping you off. You're coming home with me, and we're having a sleepover."

"You don't have to."

"Are you kidding? I'm embarrassed I didn't think of it earlier. Sleepovers are my favorite."

I can't remember the last time I had a sleepover. Actually, I can. It was the night before Candace moved away, and we stayed up all night eating cupcake batter and ugly-crying. It's not that I didn't want to make new friends, but I can only talk to people after a prolonged process of getting past the initial awkward barrier. Luckily, Liv doesn't seem to have an awkward barrier.

Half an hour later, we're wearing our pj's and those weird toe-divider thingies, sprawled on the carpet with our backs against Liv's bed. She paints her toes the brightest shade of pink I've ever seen. I choose lavender.

"My dad wasn't at the game either. He only came to one of them last year," she says, her usual exuberance gone. "How long have your parents been divorced?"

I almost botch the polish on my pinky toe. "I didn't think I told you."

"You didn't. But I have divorce-dar."

"Oh. Well, they just got divorced last year."

"Ouch."

"Yeah. I guess it's better than the fighting. I don't know. I had kind of gotten used to falling asleep to it." I shut my mouth fast. I almost never talk about my family stuff. Maybe the nail polish fumes are burning away my inhibitions.

Liv nods like someone who has been through it already. It's a gesture that could feel dismissive coming from the wrong person. From her, it feels like comfort. "The first year is pretty bad. And when one of them meets somebody else. That's bad too. You lose them a little." She breathes a slow breath out through her lips like she's doing yoga. Or trying to forget.

"I feel like I've already lost mine."

Having that kind of gaping loss is dangerous. It turns you desperate. There were times when Karl felt like the only bright point in my life. Him and the promise of college. I always envied caterpillars. So many times before I met him, I wished I could crawl into a cocoon and come out when high school was over. Sometimes I still wish it.

I realize Liv is watching me with sad eyes, and I have the sudden feeling of exposing too much.

"I'm sorry if I made you sad," she says. "I don't have anyone to talk to about this stuff."

"You don't?" She's always surrounded by people.

"Nah. Marley's amazing, but her parents are still hopelessly in love, so she doesn't get it. Sometimes I used to talk about it with Trevor. But not anymore."

I nod. "I used to talk to my friend Candace about stuff like that, but she lives in Vermont now. And I can't really talk to Karl anymore either. Um, my ex-boyfriend."

"Why'd you guys break up?"

"Because he's an asshole." And then I clap my hand over my mouth because I can't believe I just said that.

Liv snickers. I try to keep calm, but it's contagious. And then I'm giggling through my fingers, and she's laughing, and we're both rolling around on the floor.

"Say it again. You have to say it again." There are tears streaming down her cheeks.

"I can't." I can't even get words out right now.

"Pleeease."

"Okay, okay. Okay." I try to stop laughing, but I can't. We are the kind of delirious that can only be achieved by staying up late and ingesting large quantities of high fructose corn syrup.

Liv pushes herself up on her elbows, determined not to miss it. I take a deep breath and steady myself by grabbing the nightstand. My lips twitch.

"Asshole."

"AHHHHH! You said it. You said it. Ohmygosh, it burns." Liv clutches her side and doubles over, her cheeks turning red.

I tilt my head to the ceiling, my arms wide open. "My ex-boyfriend is an asshole!" I was doing it just to be silly, but the sense of triumph flowing through me is undeniable. "Oh, wow, you have got to try that."

She tilts her face up to match mine. "MY EX-BOYFRIEND IS AN ASSHOLE!"

"Girls!" Mrs. Lambros raps on the door, and we freeze. Did I really just do that? Did I really just swear loud enough to wake my friend's mother? "Go to sleep," she says.

Her footsteps move back to her bedroom. We are properly shamed into silence. Until our eyes meet. Then we collapse into giggles all over again, our hands pressed against our faces to muffle the sound.

"My ex-boyfriend. Is an asshole," whispers Liv in between staccato laughter.

I'm wheezing like I've got the black lung, but when I turn her words over in my mind, I stop. "Do you think he is, really?"

Now she stops laughing too. "Of course he is. You know what he did to me."

"I know, but, well, I've dated a bad guy. A really bad guy. And Trevor seems more like a good guy who made a mistake."

My whole body feels tight with waiting for her to respond. I didn't mean to push, but she's my friend. And I want to be a good friend.

"Maybe he isn't," she finally says. And then a few seconds later, "Hey, if your ex-boyfriend is such a jerk, why do I always see you talking to him in the hallway?"

I feel myself flush because that is a very good question and sometimes I forget I have a choice. "Maybe I shouldn't."

RANBURNE PANTHER SCAVENGER HUNT

In Ranburne:

1. ~~Fill a condom up with water. Draw a face on it. Put it on Principal Corso's doormat, and ding-dong ditch. (One person)~~

2. ~~The egg-on-a-string trick. Hang an egg from a power line by a string and watch a car run into it. (Everyone)~~

3. ~~Paint the David Bowie statue at Old Lady Howard's corn maze. (Everyone)~~

4. ~~Chair race through Walmart. (Everyone)~~

5. ~~Get a picture of the team with the Ranburne Panther. (Everyone)~~

6. ~~Go to the Dawsonville football field. Find that stupid rock they touch before their games. Pee on it. (Everyone)~~

In Nashville:

7. Visit the illustrious Delta Tau Beta fraternity at Vanderbilt. Have a beer with Panther alum TJ McNeil and take a picture of the legendary scar he got during a game-winning play against Dawsonville. (One person)

8. Go to LP Field and reenact the "Music City Miracle." (Everyone)

9. Go to Centennial Park and jump into the pond behind the Parthenon. (Everyone)

10. Go to The Jackrabbit Saloon. Walk to the very middle of the dance floor and attempt to do the worm. (One person)

11. Go up to a girl who is totally out of your league, get down on your knees, and ask her to marry you. (One person)

12. Go up to a fat girl and tell her "You're so beautiful . . . for a fat chick." Bonus points if she throws her drink on you. (One person)

13. Hug a biker. Bonus points if he has a mullet. (One person)

14. Get a girl to give you her thong. (One person)

DARES REMAINING: 8

10:35 P.M.

LIV

The night is perfect and full of possibilities. We walk past house after house of catcalling college boys, and I bask in the attention. I am so full of energy I can feel my blonde Disney princess curls bouncing with each step.

"There it is. Delta Tau Beta." I lead the girls up the walkway to a three-story brick structure ornamented with columns and filled with boys.

Two burly security guards preside over a table in front of the house.

"Ladies, can we have you sign in?" the burlier one says to the girls in front of us.

"What for?" I hear one of them ask.

"This is an official party, so we have to keep tabs on everyone who enters and give wristbands to those who are twenty-one and over."

The girl seems annoyed, but she and her friends bend over the list and write their names anyway. I peek over their shoulders. Trevor's name is there. So are Weston's and Rey's. *They signed their real names? Amateurs.*

I sign my name next: Ashley Benson. After I finish, I look over my shoulder at Peyton and wink. She's blushing like crazy when she catches up with me on the stairs.

"Your face is bright red," I whisper. "Did you sign a fake name too?"

She nods sheepishly, and I let out a belly laugh. "This is going to be the best night ever."

Melanie Jane and Ana are right behind us. "What are we going to do if the guys are here?" asks Ana.

I shake my head. "They're not. I texted Trevor on the way over to ask if I'd see him at The Jackrabbit soon, and he said they were just leaving a Vanderbilt party."

Melanie Jane bumps me with her hip. "Nice work, ninja."

A blond guy lounging on the front porch leaps up from his rocking chair when he spots us. "Girls!" he yells.

"Boy!" I yell back.

He picks me up over his shoulder and spins me around.

"Do you know him?" asks Melanie Jane when he sets me down.

I shrug. "No."

"I'm Jack," he says.

"I'm Olivia." Using my full name is enough of a cover. No one ever calls me that.

"You girls wanna come up to my room and have a drink with us?" Jack asks, gesturing to himself and a couple of pledges.

"Sure. I'm actually looking for someone, though. A guy named TJ?"

Jack rolls his eyes. "Every girl is looking for TJ." He sighs.

"Come on. He's my roommate."

Peyton and I follow Jack and the pledges upstairs. A thin coating of grime covers each step, and I have to hop over a large, sleeping Labrador named Bob Marley while navigating the landing.

Jack stops in front of a room with a ripped futon, two wooden lofts overhead, and a blond guy pulling a beer from the fridge. "Here he is. The football star."

TJ, aka the Football Star, throws beers around the room while we introduce ourselves. He sure has skinny arms for a quarterback. I pop my beer open and "cheers" him (I'm the one doing this dare), all the while scrutinizing his legs. Luckily, he's wearing shorts today. I spot the gnarliest scar on the back of his calf. It almost looks like a kraken or something. One of the boys starts talking to me, but I get distracted by the beautiful Hamer Sunburst tucked behind the futon. I picked up my first guitar when I was eleven, and since then, I've been obsessed.

"Jack, is that guitar yours?" I ask.

"It's TJ's, but mine's in the closet."

"We were having a jam session before you girls came over," says TJ.

TJ is now the most interesting person in the room as far as I'm concerned. QB1 status aside, I am picking up a rock-star vibe, and it is hot. Without thinking, I grab TJ's arm.

"TJ, will you play a song for me?"

"Sure," he replies. "What do you want to hear?"

"I'm feeling old school today. How about 'Over the Hills and Far Away'?"

TJ starts playing, and he is good. Even better than me. I find this immensely attractive. We talk between songs and find out we like all the same music.

"Can I play one?" I ask after a few songs.

"You play too?" His eyes spark with interest.

I nod, and he passes me the guitar. I strum the strings lightly a couple of times like I don't really know what I'm doing. Then, I play Aerosmith's "Walk This Way." His eyes goggle when I get to the first solo. I grin. Surprising boys with my guitar-playing skills never gets old. I hand his guitar back to him.

"You're awesome. Let's play together sometime."

My eyes light up. "Oh my gosh, we should totally start a band."

"What should we call it?"

"I don't know, but we need a fantastic name. And a drummer and singer."

TJ nods seriously. "And someone to play the tambourine."

Just then, my phone vibrates in the back pocket of my skirt.

"Ah! My butt is vibrating!"

TJ laughs, and I whip out my phone.

"My other friends just texted me. They're leaving." I let out an exasperated sigh. The text is actually from Peyton who is still in the room. She needs his legs to turn to the side so she can get a good picture of the scar. I give her a nod. The sigh was real though. We *are* going to have to leave soon, and I am really starting to enjoy this TJ character.

"I'd better go."

"If you have to," says TJ, pushing out his bottom lip.

When he pouts, I can't help but notice that his lips look irresistibly kissable. On impulse, I lean over and press my mouth to his, pinning him to the couch so his legs twist to the side. Then I grab Peyton and dart out of the room.

"See you later, TJ," I call over my shoulder.

For the second time that night, TJ looks pleasantly stunned by the force of nature that is me.

"Did you get the picture?" I ask Peyton. "Because I could totally go back and do that again."

She laughs. "I got it."

Melanie Jane and Ana pounce on us as soon as we enter the stairwell. There's a small platform at the top of the stairs with the fraternity's seal painted on the wall behind it. I guess they've been waiting here.

"What are you guys doing?" I ask, just as Melanie Jane grabs my wrists.

"Did anyone see y'all?"

"Um, no." I pry back her fingers. Ohmygosh, she's so strong. "I told you, Trevor texted me. The guys already left."

She shakes her head. "Trevor left. But there's a guy shotgunning beers in the room right across the hall, and I swear he's on the football team."

Before I can tell her I'm pretty sure we're safe, a yell travels up the stairwell.

"Greg! Where'd you go, you drunk son of a bitch?"

Melanie Jane's eyes go wide. She mouths a name at us—Weston.

Heavy footsteps echo on the stairs below. We back away from the railing as one, pressing as close as we can get to the wall with the seal.

"Greg, the other car already left for LP Field! If I have to walk out at Homecoming naked because of your drunk ass, I *will* kill you."

The footsteps are getting closer. We won't be able to make it through the door in time. He'll see us. But if we wait here, he'll definitely see us. I'm just considering whether knocking him unconscious and hiding him in a closet somewhere would be too extreme, when Ana hisses, "In here."

What the crap? The wall with the seal is actually a door, and my friends are all rushing through. Melanie Jane grabs me by the arm and pulls me along with her because I'm having trouble doing anything besides staring. Ana closes the door with seconds to spare. I can hear Weston on the platform now, still hollering an assortment of threats and insults. We wait in the dark until the door slams behind him. Then, light floods the room, and I see Ana standing by a switch.

"What is this place?" Her nose wrinkles. It smells like grain alcohol and armpits in here.

I take in the room—it's the weirdest combination of a man cave and the place where we had model UN semifinals. Couches of questionable cleanliness are raised up at different levels so they form a lazy-man's stadium surrounding the tables at the front. I watch Melanie Jane pick up a book and turn it over slowly. And then all the color drains from her face.

"I know where we are."

She sounds so serious, I pull my hands away from the podium even though I desperately want to bang the gavel.

"This is a chapter room. Both of my brothers are in fraternities at Tennessee. This room, it's like where they have all their secret stuff. No one's allowed in here except members. Definitely not girls. We need to get out of here before someone finds us."

We don't have to discuss it. We are all in agreement. Even though there's a chance that Weston or someone else might see us, we will open the door and race down the stairs. Because men can get a little crazy about their secrets. And there is nothing more dangerous than getting caught trying to uncover them.

6

PEYTON

We giggle like kids with a secret as we dress all in black, and Liv paints dark stripes under our eyes. As we pile into Ana's car, all of us talking over each other about how awesome tonight is going to be. Ana turns onto a dirt road, and Liv bounces in her seat, and we all crane our necks for that first glimpse of the barn.

"There!" says Melanie Jane.

She points out the window, and I lean across the backseat. Liv can't see from up front, and it is just killing her, so she rolls down her window and sticks half her body out, so she can look over the top of the car.

"The car is still in motion!" Ana attempts to tug her back inside by her belt loop, but Liv wriggles farther out the window, so Ana settles for stopping the car instead.

"I guess we can get out here since some of us can't wait."

I eye the barn again, high up on a hill over the fields, a good half-mile hike away. The place is dilapidated, at best. The wooden walls are a sun-faded gray—only a few boards show reminders of the original red paint. The tin roof is dark with rust. An army of kudzu crawls up the back of the barn, its tendrils curling over the roof, like it's about to drag the barn into the forest. My eyes dart around the property, scanning for any signs of life, and I have a realization.

"If we can see the barn, doesn't that mean anyone who comes there later will be able to see the car?"

"Shit, you're right," says Ana.

She drives farther down the road, snailing along because Liv is still hanging out the window, and stops once we're out of sight of the barn. The boys will be coming to the barn straight from Big Tom's house, so it should be safe here.

As we climb over the rough wooden fence and wade through clumps of scratchy grass, I feel anything but safe. First of all, I didn't wear my hiking boots, and there could be snakes. And second of all, we are breaking and entering. Well, entering any-way. I don't think any of us are planning to break anything. But, still, that's got to be a felony or something. Although, if I'm really being honest with myself, getting caught by the police scares me much less than getting caught by the football team. My thoughts run to Charlotte Fisher, and I shiver even though I'm sweating.

"It is hot as *blazes* out here, and this grass is scratching my legs, and I'm pretty sure one of my shoes is *ruined*." Melanie Jane flails around dramatically behind us.

"Maybe you shouldn't have worn designer shoes to a barn break-in," Ana calls over her shoulder.

I glance at Melanie Jane's Marc Jacobs ballet flats that are as adorable as they are impractical.

Melanie Jane glares at Ana, but before she can open her mouth, I say, "Here. Walk behind me. It'll be easier on you if you follow my steps."

"Thanks," she grumbles.

I hate it when they get like that. I know I'm overly sensitive to tension or conflict or whatever, but I think even Big Tom would pick up on whatever it is that's going on between them.

We get to the top of the hill and tiptoe inside the barn. It's empty. Of people, I mean. As soon as the other girls realize this, they run around the barn giggling and speculating. There are all kinds of things to be investigated: crates, candles, a two-handled metal vase, piles of black sheets. We are definitely in the right place.

"So, I guess we should set up in the hayloft?" says Ana, and everyone comes to a halt.

They tore around the barn like crazy people, but when it comes to climbing into that loft, they're all so hesitant. I take in

Melanie Jane's ballet flats, and Liv curling her hair around her fingers protectively, and even Ana—even she wore lace shorts and a fedora. That's when I realize—I'm the tomboy. I mean, I don't wear trucker hats or punctuate my sentences by spitting or anything, but out of these girls, I have to be the first to climb the ladder into the dirty, scary hayloft. I have to be the brave one.

"I'll go," I say.

Liv takes a half step like she wants to stop me. "No, Peyton, you don't have to."

"It's fine." I step onto the first rung of the ladder. "I don't mind."

It makes me feel good, like I can do something useful, like I'm not just some pathetic girl tagging along behind these shining goddesses. Once I've climbed to the top, the other girls follow, but not without reservations.

Melanie Jane seems hesitant to touch the rungs. "Ew! I am going to get ringworm!"

"Do you think there are rodents in here?" asks Liv. "Because I'm *terrified* of rodents."

It takes a while for them to get comfortable (and by comfortable, I mean non-terrified) and for Ana to set up her video camera so it'll record even in next-to-no lighting. She wants every second of the football-stealing recorded for posterity. There's a blanket behind some hay bales, and it's nice enough to sit on as long as you don't stop to think about why Big Tom would have a blanket in his hayloft.

We get to talking and kind of forget why we're here. I wonder if my parents suspected anything when I said I was going to a sleepover. I thought about telling someone—not them, but *someone*—what we're up to in case we get caught and are never heard from again, but it didn't seem right. None of the other girls told anyone, and I keep my promises.

"Mel-Jay, aren't you supposed to be watching the window?" asks Liv.

"Oh, right." She skips over to the window and peeks out. "Someone's coming."

Ana crosses her arms. "Ha-ha."

"No, really. I see flashlights."

Liv stands on her toes so she can see over Melanie Jane. "Someone *is* coming. A lot of someones."

We rush to our positions on the blanket behind the hay bales, and just in time, because the barn door creaks open with a noise straight out of a horror movie. Liv squeezes my hand in excitement. We can't see anything without getting up on our knees, so for now we just listen. It's not enough for Ana, though. She tries to push herself up into a crouch so she can see what's going on, but she can't keep her balance. At the last second, she saves herself from falling out from behind the hay bale (aka certain death), but she can't hold it in. She squeaks. Loudly. Melanie Jane claps her hand over Ana's mouth, and we all duck. *Please don't let them notice. Please don't.*

"Hey, did you hear something?"

Crap.

"Yeah, I think it was coming from the loft."

Flashlights cut back and forth over our heads. I close my eyes tight like that'll help hide me.

"Should we go check it out?"

No. No, you shouldn't. You should go back to setting up for your stupid thirteen-year-old sleepover séance.

"Naw, it's all right," says Big Tom, and I'm finally able to breathe again. "There's a pack of rats living up there. That's probably all it was."

My eyes snap open in time to see Liv mouth, *"Rats!"* with a panicked look. I grab her hand and force her to lock eyes with me. *It's going to be okay. Calm down. I've got you.* I try to beam these thoughts directly into her brain, but I don't think our mind meld is working because her breathing keeps getting faster and louder. If I can't think of some way to calm her down soon, they're going to hear her, and who knows what they'll do to us.

Whenever my mom's stressed out (which is often), I give her a hand massage, so I try it now with Liv because I don't have any better ideas. All I do is take her hand between my thumb and fingers and massage out the tension, working my way around so I get her fingers and knuckles and especially that loose skin beside her thumb. By the time I switch to her other hand, her breathing has reached subaudible levels. She smiles sheepishly and mouths, *"Thanks."*

Saturday, August 22
ANA

That was close. Waaay too close. I stay put for a while even though I desperately need to record what's happening. Dozens of feet shuffle against the barn floor below, but other than that, the boys are silent. At first. Someone must be setting things up, and the tribe is getting restless because I hear rustling and a few clanks and then a thunk followed by the f-bomb and several "shhhhs." Ha. When it comes to their man ceremonies, these guys can shush like old ladies.

As quietly as we can, we slip onto our knees and peer over the hay bales. This time I don't fall over. The barn looks pretty much the same, except now all the candles are lit, and there are a bunch of dudes standing around in black robes. I make sure to get it all on camera.

"Are we ready for them?" The voice comes from the biggest robe—it has to be Big Tom.

Another robe nods, and Big Tom leaves the barn. He is clearly not pleased with what he finds outside.

"What the fuck is this?" I hear him yell like he's right beside me. "Did I or did I not tell you to do push-ups until I came back for you?"

Someone must have answered, but I can't make it out.

"Well, then why the fuck would you stop?"

There is a great deal of shouting and assigning of calisthenics before Big Tom feels satisfied that the "pack of vaginas" outside deserve to be allowed to follow him into the barn. He appears in the doorway, accompanied by a bunch of guys in boxers who look like they want to pee themselves. They're covered in . . . something. I think the first round of aerobics might have taken place in a field with a lot of cow pies. I also think I can smell them. Ewww.

Melanie Jane silently gags beside me, her hand cupped over her mouth. I roll my eyes because even in a barn, in the dark, mid–dry heave, she has taken care to position The Finger so it doesn't show. But that's the running philosophy at our high school. Hide anything about yourself that isn't pretty and perfect because if the rest of them find out, they'll shun you. I can't believe I was ever dumb enough to think our friendship might be worth her going against them.

I turn back to the barn floor where the herd of guys stands, awaiting the inevitable. A couple of them seem to be shaking, whether from fear or exhaustion, I couldn't say. After what seems like an eternity, someone finally speaks.

"Gentlemen," booms the voice. I know it's Chad by the way my fingernails involuntarily dig into my palms. "We are gathered here tonight to honor an ancient tradition."

Well, I don't exactly know that the '70s qualifies as ancient.

"Only the best men have worn the Panthers uniform and played for glory on our field. Only the most determined, the strongest, the fastest, can claim a spot on our team. We are men of honor. Our values and ideals are second to none."

Men of honor, my ass. Men of honor wouldn't have beat up Grayson. And they don't drug girls at parties. Watching all of those new guys stare up at Chad like he's God's gift to mankind and he's spewing pure gold instead of bullshit—I can't take it. I'm going to explode.

"Tonight, you will become part of an elite brotherhood. If you're scared, if you're not willing to give everything to this team, you can leave. Now."

He waits all dramatic-like, but nobody moves. Too bad. That would have been fun.

"Joining this brotherhood is a commitment. It should not be taken lightly. You're going to have to put a lot of work into proving yourself. That's why we have this ceremony. So you understand what it means to be a part of this team and join it with the proper amount of respect. And serious . . . ness."

I can't help it. I snort. Not loudly or anything. Nobody hears me. But they're so ridiculous and pompous, and for what? High school football? It is really very sad. The football players at this school think they're gods or something. Probably because everyone in this town treats them like gods. There's got to be some way to break the horrible cycle. To shake everyone up and make them see reality.

Liv flicks my arm and points down at the boys. I frown. I

don't know what's so serious that— Oh. The football. Chad holds it high overhead like that old baboon did with baby Simba in *The Lion King*, and with much the same results.

It's right there, taunting me. Just a few yards away. Now all we have to do is figure out how to get it.

Saturday, August 22
LIV

f I were to jump out of the loft and tackle Chad, I could probably grab it. Not that I'm thinking about doing that. Okay, maybe I am, but even I have a little self-control.

Chad clears his throat. "All right, men. Weston Albright, you're first."

If Weston hadn't just dumped Melanie Jane, I might feel bad for the guy. I note how his head ducks as all the hooded figures turn to watch him walk to the front of the barn in his underwear. How his chest rises and falls so rapidly as he stands in front of Chad. I think I even see his Adam's apple bob up and down like a cartoon character's.

"Weston Albright." Chad's voice booms louder than before. "Place your right hand on the game ball of '76." Weston does it. "Do you swear to uphold the values of the Ranburne High School football team, to put the needs of the brotherhood before those of yourself, to trust and respect your family and obey their guidance, to put everything you have into being a better player and to winning State this year?"

Weston hesitates, clearly unsure of what to do next. "I do," he finally says in a squeaky voice.

Chad snorts. "We're not getting married." The guys snicker in their hoods. "Say, 'I swear.'"

"I swear," says Weston, his face turning red.

I glance to my left and notice that Melanie Jane is smiling at his misfortune.

Chad says, "Welcome, brother," and does the manly hand-shake-pat-on-the-back hug. "You're part of this team. You may now drink the sacramental wine and claim your spot."

Big Tom hands Weston a gigantic urn—the poor guy can barely lift it, and it sloshes down his chest when he takes a sip. Someone else places a black robe over his shoulders. You can see the pride shining on his face, which is pretty funny considering he's half naked and covered in poop.

Some other guys go, and before I realize what's happened, it's Trevor's turn. He steps up to Chad in his SpongeBob boxers. His straight back says he's not afraid, but his finger scratching against his thigh says the bravery is just a show. Chad feeds him the same oath the other guys got. For just a moment, Trevor hesitates, and I get the idea that maybe he'll turn the whole thing down. I lean forward, wishing so hard I forget to breathe, but then he says, "I swear," just like everyone else, and I feel stupid for thinking anything different might happen.

As they place the cloak upon his head, I whisper into the straw in front of me, "I hope it's worth it."

Rey is next, but he doesn't seem scared at all. I notice Peyton sits a little straighter to watch him, but that's the only tell that he's any different from the other guys in boxers. Then there's a light scratching noise behind me, and all I can think is *THERE ARE RATS UP HERE!* Peyton's voodoo calming powers may have worked before, but if I see an actual rat in this barn, I'm screaming, and nothing and no one will be able to stop me.

We have to suffer through a billion more of these ridiculous ceremonies before they're finally finished. The novelty of seeing what the football team gets up to in secret wore off a long time ago, and all four of us are yawning.

Peyton nudges me. They seem to be wrapping up.

"Welcome to the team, gentlemen," says Chad. "Now, let's go get drunk!"

Hooting and hollering fills the barn. The newly minted members of the football-cult-of-everything-that-is-wrong-with-this-town file out first and the other guys follow. Including Chad. Who is taking the football with him. *Crap.*

Crap. Crap. Crap.

Well, what did I think was going to happen? That he'd leave it there on a platter with a note that said, "Just in case anyone wants to steal me, go ahead"?

"I can't believe we went through all this for nothing," mutters Ana.

"Right?" says Melanie Jane. "I spent all night in a stinky old barn—I ruined a shoe! And we're still not any closer to getting that stupid football."

Peyton blows listlessly at her bangs. "They probably never let it out of their sight. I don't see how we're ever going to pull this off."

And even though they're saying all the things I'm thinking,

I don't want anyone else feeling like the night was a total loss.

"You guys, don't talk like that. We'll find a way. There are keys to the football when it's locked up—we can still try that. I know tonight was disappointing, but think of it." I jump to my feet. "We got to see something tonight that no girl has ever seen. We penetrated the football team's inner sanctum."

Ana snorts. "You said *penetrated*."

I roll my eyes. "This is huge! We have them on tape. We know their secrets. And we didn't get caught." I'm buzzing with energy now. I can feel every nerve ending, each individual hair standing at attention. I've managed to hype myself up—that's what pretending to be positive can do. "We are amazing. We are badasses. And now we're going to do something we'll never forget."

They look confused. "We are?"

"Yes! Follow me!" I climb down the ladder and grab the lighter from the table. Light up the candles the boys left snuffed out all around the barn. I pick up the urn of "sacramental wine" and sniff. Smells like Boone's Farm to me. I dump out what's left, splash around some wine from the bottle to disinfect because, you know, football-player germs. Then I refill it and set it on the table.

Melanie Jane is regarding me with extreme curiosity. Or dread. Sometimes it's hard to say which with her. "What are you doing?"

I grin. "*We* are going to say our own vows."

I have to do something to turn this night around, and I think this is my best chance.

"Um, that sounds cool," says Peyton.

I throw one of the robes over my clothes and lean over a crate so the candles cast eerie shadows on my face.

"Tonight we honor an ancient tradition," I say in my best spooky voice. Peyton moves to stand beside me. Ana starts to hang back, but Melanie Jane prods her along.

"You are about to become part of an elite sisterhood. We are brave. We are strong. We have honor . . . and some other lame shit."

Ana smirks and steps forward. I've got her now.

I turn serious. "Tonight we did something no one else has ever done. We started something. And we're going to finish it. We will steal that football. We will have our revenge. And we will change this town."

I pause. No one is smirking now. There is only hunger on their faces.

"It won't be easy. But it will be worth it. And the only way we can make it happen is if all of us are in this together. If you're in this, say 'I swear.'"

I barely get the words out of my mouth before Peyton says, "I swear." Her voice is soft, but her face isn't. I offer her the wine, and she drinks.

Melanie Jane is next. "I swear."

She sips the wine and wrinkles her nose and scoots the urn

in Ana's direction. We all wait for Ana, standing there with her arms crossed over her chest—she's the only one I'm not sure about. She stares us down for a few uneasy seconds before letting out a prolonged sigh and gripping the urn with both hands.

"I swear," she says, and something like surprise flutters behind her eyes.

She passes the urn of wine back to me, and I lift it to my lips. "I swear."

As the words roll off my tongue, the most unearthly tingle crawls up my spine. Like the vow we've made tonight is bigger than all of us.

RANBURNE PANTHER SCAVENGER HUNT

In Ranburne:

1. ~~Fill a condom up with water. Draw a face on it. Put it on Principal Corso's doormat, and ding-dong ditch. (One person)~~

2. ~~The egg-on-a-string trick. Hang an egg from a power line by a string and watch a car run into it. (Everyone)~~

3. ~~Paint the David Bowie statue at Old Lady Howard's corn maze. (Everyone)~~

4. ~~Chair race through Walmart. (Everyone)~~

5. ~~Get a picture of the team with the Ranburne Panther. (Everyone)~~

6. ~~Go to the Dawsonville football field. Find that stupid rock they touch before their games. Pee on it. (Everyone)~~

In Nashville:

7. ~~Visit the illustrious Delta Tau Beta fraternity at Vanderbilt. Have a beer with Panther alum TJ McNeil and take a picture of the legendary scar he got during a game-winning play against Dawsonville. (One person)~~

8. Go to LP Field and reenact the "Music City Miracle." (Everyone)

9. Go to Centennial Park and jump into the pond behind the Parthenon. (Everyone)

10. Go to The Jackrabbit Saloon. Walk to the very middle of the dance floor and attempt to do the worm. (One person)

11. Go up to a girl who is totally out of your league, get down on your knees, and ask her to marry you. (One person)

12. Go up to a fat girl and tell her "You're so beautiful . . . for a fat chick." Bonus points if she throws her drink on you. (One person)

13. Hug a biker. Bonus points if he has a mullet. (One person)

14. Get a girl to give you her thong. (One person)

DARES REMAINING: 7

11:20 P.M.

PEYTON

"What's next? What's next?" Liv is still on a high from her stolen kiss. She keeps asking to see the scar picture every five minutes. "Doesn't it look like a kraken to you? I think it looks kind of like a kraken!"

I check the list. "LP Field is next if we go in order. And then jumping in that pond at Centennial Park. Maybe we should save that for last since we're going to get all wet."

Melanie Jane walks shoulder to shoulder with me so she can read the list at the same time. "I think we should go straight to the bar. If we beat them there, we could get some of this stuff done without them seeing."

"Yeah. That's a good idea," says Ana.

She unlocks her car, and we pile in. Melanie Jane mans the GPS and gets us there in record time, while Liv and I discuss exactly what it was like kissing the legendary TJ McNeil.

We walk through the swinging doors of The Jackrabbit Saloon, which is everything you expect when you hear the words "honky-tonk bar." A stage stretches almost the whole length of the main room with a band playing country music, complete with fiddles and harmonicas. There are tons of people dancing. Tons. And even more at the various bars and the bull-riding arena and smaller rooms I can't see the inside of. The decor is kind of hokey—rough wooden walls, barrels for tables, riding gear and wagon wheels and so many animal heads I'm tempted to have a moment of silence. It's definitely over-the-top country. So are most of the people here.

Liv races off as soon as we get inside and returns with the biggest grin on her face. "They're not here!" she squeals. "The old Varsity guys are playing pool in one of the other rooms though, so if we want to do dares, we need to do them in here."

"Perfect." Melanie Jane points to the dance floor where the line dancing is going full force. "You ready to do the worm?"

Liv's grin disappears. "I can't do the worm."

"What?!" Melanie Jane and Ana both look like they're going to have coronaries.

"How can you not do the worm? You dance better than anyone in school," says Ana.

Liv lets out a serious sigh. "And it is one of my great downfalls as a dancer that I am unable to do the worm."

Melanie Jane paces in her heels. "Well, what are we going to do? I can't do the worm."

"I can do the worm," I mumble.

Ana takes a quick peek at the list before shoving it back in her purse. "It says attempt. We just have to attempt it."

"I can do the worm," I say a little louder.

Ana grabs my arm. "Wait. What?"

I sigh. "I said I can do it. The worm, I mean." I can completely humiliate myself in public and have everyone stare at me and probably contract a disease from lying on the floor of a bar.

"Peyton!" Liv spins me around. "This is amazing!"

My eyes don't leave the dance floor. So many people. "I guess so." I gulp.

I walk the path to the dance floor like it's my very own green mile. I can do this. People will watch. People will laugh. But it will be over soon, and it has to happen. We need this in order to beat them. I weave to the very center of the wooden floor, taking care not to bump any of the dancers. *I hope no one steps on me,* I think as I lay down and try to ignore the sticky spot under my right arm. I take a deep breath. And then, in a feat of nearly impossible muscle coordination, I send a ripple down my body. Once. Twice. Three times. I alternately contract and relax my muscles in isolated segments, creating, what I have to say, is a very impressive wormlike effect.

I stand up to cheers all around me. To huge hugs from Ana and Melanie Jane and a tackle hug from Liv that nearly lands me on the floor again. I'm sweating, that's how nervous I was, and I know my cheeks are redder than red. It feels amazing.

The country band fires up a fast one, so we celebrate with some victory dancing. The girls agree I've done enough daring for now and could use a break. Liv, inspired by my worminess, demands to go next.

"Find someone out of my league!" she tells us. "I'll do the asking."

She grabs my hands, and we dance around while Ana and Melanie Jane have a debate that goes something like this:

Melanie Jane: OMG. That guy is so cute.

Ana: Yeah . . . no.

Melanie Jane: Are you kidding?

Ana: He isn't.

Melanie Jane: Is.

Ana: Not. You'll have to excuse Melanie Jane. She has tall goggles. It's why she always dates athletes.

Melanie Jane: Not always.

Ana: Okay, who?

Melanie Jane: Someone. Michael. His name is Michael, and oh, by the way, he's meeting us later.

And then she's all tongue-tied and blushing and totally un–Melanie Jane–like. Ana doesn't push her on it because at that moment a seriously gorgeous man walks past us. Not even his Lee jeans and plate-sized belt buckle can eclipse that kind of breathtaking splendor.

"Him!" we all shout simultaneously, and then burst out laughing.

Liv salutes us all and follows him to the bar, where she gets down on one knee and proposes as I take a picture. He's laughing as he helps her up. He's got to be at least ten years older than us. Then he kisses her hand and tips his hat and goes back to ordering his drink.

Liv skips all the way back to us.

"And that, ladies, is how it's done. Next."

"I'll go next," says Melanie Jane. "Some bikers just sat down over there. We weren't lucky enough to get a mullet sighting, but one of them kind of has a rat tail."

Ana nods with mock seriousness. "I feel a rat tail is a perfectly acceptable mullet substitute."

Melanie Jane links her arm through mine. "Come with me. I need you to take the picture."

I'm glad she picked me because there's something I've been meaning to talk to her about. "Hey, um, how's it going with Ana?" I ask as soon as we're far enough away.

"I tried to talk to her, but it didn't really work." She's staring at Ana with longing and regret stamped all over her face, but luckily Ana is preoccupied with making sure Liv doesn't climb on top of a table.

"I think it helped. She's been . . . different. Maybe you should try again."

Liv is gesturing wildly, and it's clear she thinks both she and Ana should be dancing on the table. Ana stands with her arms crossed.

"I don't know," says Melanie Jane.

"You should. I feel like, I don't know, like tonight is this magical night, and there's this window of opportunity where anything could happen." Melanie Jane is staring at me now instead of Ana. "It's dumb."

"No. I kind of feel it too." We watch them for another

minute, and then she bumps her shoulder against mine. "C'mon. Let's go hug some bikers."

For the first time, I take a good look at said bikers. I am marginally concerned. These guys are huge. And old. And they have tons of tattoos and scary leather jackets with skulls and did I mention they are *huge*?

Melanie Jane struts right into the circle of intimidating bikers and squeezes Rat Tail's arm. "Ohmygosh, are you Chance Foster?"

Wow, she's always had an accent, but she just kicked it up, like, eight notches. He peers up at her from whatever he's drinking. Whiskey? Moonshine? The blood of his enemies?

"No."

She giggles like this is hilarious. "Oh, I'm so sorry. It's just he's this local country singer. And my dad is such a big fan. And, well, you look just like him."

He grins at this, and his teeth are straighter and whiter than you would expect. "Nah. I'm no singer." Except he says it "sanger" not "singer."

Melanie Jane looks at him through her eyelashes like she's this shy Southern belle. Ha. "Okay, so, this is going to sound weird, but would you mind if I took a picture with you? Just to show my dad and all. He'll never believe me. You really do look *just* like him."

His friends chuckle, but Rat Tail seems to be enjoying the limelight.

"Sure. Why not?"

"Awesome! Thank you so much." Before he can blink, she puts one arm around his back and another across his chest and squeezes him into a hug as I snap the picture.

"Thank you again!" she drawls. "You totally made my day!"

"That's what I'm here for. Making dreams come true."

His friends all belly laugh and go back to their drinks while we run over to show Liv and Ana the picture. We celebrate with more dancing, and I try to teach Melanie Jane how to roll her hips, but it isn't going so well. She's just starting to learn how to relax her body when we see them. The football team. And clustered around them, the cheerleaders, because didn't you know they're incapable of not being in the same place at the same time? It's like magic or physics or something. They can't have been here long. The space by the bull-riding arena was empty the last time I checked. I scan their faces. I see Trevor. And there's Weston. I wonder where Rey is.

There's a tap on my shoulder. I turn around to see Rey bending down in front of me. His hands reach for mine and swallow them up.

"Hi there." He grins. "Will you marry me?"

A light flashes. Someone taking a picture. People are clapping and staring all around us. Is this really happening? Wait. Does this mean Rey thinks I'm out of his league? I feel my cheeks go pink. Oh, no. Am I supposed to answer? What do I say?

"Thanks for the help," he says, preventing me the embarrassment of having to stumble through a response. "It was for that scavenger hunt thing we're doing."

"Right." I nod awkwardly. I'm not supposed to know that already.

We both stand there, not dancing, not talking, just staring at each other, and not in the comfortable way. Just when I think this moment can't get any more agonizing, Casey appears. I guess the older guys are finished playing pool.

He slings an arm around my shoulders. "Hey, Church Girl, I didn't know you were coming out."

"Her name is Peyton." Rey says it before I can.

Casey narrows his eyes, first at Rey rising from the kneeling position, then at me, the pieces clicking into place in his brain. He squeezes his arm tighter around me. "What are you doing talking to my girl?"

In his intoxicated state, Casey seems to have forgotten a number of things: my name, our relationship status, societal norms about personal bubbles. And most important, the fact that Rey is twice his size.

"I think you're making her uncomfortable," says Rey.

"Like hell I am."

He lunges at Rey, who holds out an arm in self-defense. Casey runs into it, effectively clotheslining himself.

And then Chad's in the middle of them, trying to keep Casey from hurting himself any further. All Rey is doing is standing there—he isn't even speaking, but Casey tackles Chad to the floor trying to get at Rey. Something falls out of Chad's pocket in the scuffle. Keys. On the floor. Right in front of me. The girls are at my side, asking if I'm okay, but when they see the keys, they stop mid-sentence. I know what they're thinking. What we wouldn't have given to get our hands on those keys a few weeks ago.

Big Tom pins Casey's arms behind his back and jerks him away. Chad pockets the keys and puts a hand to Rey's chest.

"All right, Casanova. Let's get going."

The boys are pulling at him and the girls are tugging at me, but our eyes refuse to let go of each other.

They keep pushing, but he manages to get out some last words: "I'm sorry."

"Me too," I say, but they've already dragged him away.

I'm sorry for what I'm about to do to you.

7

MELANIE JANE

ey Thievery—Take Two. If I ever want to have a future in the CIA, I should at least be able to steal a key from a bumbling high school football coach. I knock on the door to his office. Classes just ended, but maybe I can catch him before he leaves for any all-important game night preparations.

"Come in," he bellows. And then when he sees I'm not a teenage boy, "Oh, hi. What can I do for you?"

I recite my carefully prepared speech. "The cheerleading squad wanted to make a special banner for tonight's game. We were going to use some of the old plaques and trophies and make rubbings of them. Kind of like a victory-through-the-ages-type thing?"

"Well, that sounds real nice. You know, I'm in one of the pictures where we won State way back when." He goes back to his playbook like the conversation's over. Then he realizes I haven't moved. "Was there something else?"

"Yes. We need the key. So we can get the plaques and stuff out of the case? I promise we'll be super careful with everything, and I'll bring the key back to you when we're done."

I look around his office, taking in the motivational sports posters on one wall, pretending I couldn't care less about whether or not he decides to give me that key.

"Well, sure," he says. Perfect! "I'll walk down with you and unlock it myself. I need to get something before the game anyway."

Oh.

"Sounds great. Thanks, Coach!" I say brightly.

When we get to the trophy case, I try very hard not to stare longingly at the football. Instead, I pretend I actually care about the history of the Ranburne empire, and stand at one end of the case staring at awards given to boys who thought they were gods only to be disappointed when they tried to assimilate into the real world. The key clicks in the lock, turns with a scrape, and still I don't allow myself to look away from the glass. I wonder if it really is bulletproof like people say. I tap at it with a fingernail and nearly jump out of my skin when Coach Fuller jingles the key ring in my ear.

"Here you go." He hands over the keys. "Make sure to lock up and give them back to me as soon as you're done."

"No problem."

I make a note of which key goes to the trophy case, so I don't have to try every single one when I close it. I try to decide the best course of action—making a copy of the key, maybe? I can't very well steal the football right now. It'd be obvious I did it. I wonder if they have any kind of surveillance going. As I'm scoping out the walls and ceiling for hidden cameras, it hits me.

The football. It isn't there.

Did Coach Fuller take it with him? I wasn't paying attention. He must have—it was there when he opened the case. He probably took it for tonight's pregame football-rubbing ritual. The track lighting seems extra bright as it highlights the empty space. I tell myself this is fine. The key is what I need right now, not the football. I can go make a copy and be back before—

"Mel-Jay!"

I turn to see Chloe and Beth balancing a huge roll of banner paper between them, and Aubrey carrying art supplies. Oh, right. The banner. I had kind of forgotten we're actually making that.

Twenty minutes pass, and I am still in banner-making hell. Liv, Peyton, and Ana haven't returned my calls, and I can't find any excuse good enough for the rest of the cheerleaders to let me slip away. In fact, they seem kind of offended when I try, especially Aubrey. I feel guilty because I know I haven't been around so much lately, and she deserves a better friend. I just, I don't know, ever since Ana, I've been scared to put myself out there. I don't think I'm ready for the BFF-necklace-level of friendship. Now or maybe ever. I'm struck with a terrible sense of wanting. For Ana? For that kind of closeness in general? I couldn't say. There's a Portuguese word for the longing that comes with losing something you love: *saudade*. The word even sounds like how I feel.

I put the old trophies and plaques and stuff back in the case since we're finished with that part of the banner. Just as I'm locking it closed, my phone rings. It's Ana, and it's perfect timing.

"Perfect timing," says a voice behind me.

Wait. What?

I answer my phone and turn around, and there is Coach Fuller taking the keys from my hand. I want to grip them tight in my fist and run out the door.

"Hello? Hello?"

"Hi, Ana. Sorry. Thanks, Coach."

"What's up? Did you need something?" asks Ana.

I sigh. "Not anymore."

I wonder if I had worked it out with Ana ahead of time if she could have made a copy fast enough that Coach Fuller wouldn't have noticed. It was stupid of me not to tell the girls, but I really wanted to be the hero, okay? I trudge back over to where the rest of the squad is giggling and painting like "OMG, making a banner is the funnest thing ever." This sucks.

Saturday, August 29

The day after I gave Michael my number (not three days later), he called (not texted, not emailed) on a real, live phone, and we talked until we couldn't keep our eyes open. Then, yesterday he called again to ask if he could pick me up at four p.m. to go on a good old-fashioned date. My mama would approve. If she knew about it. I frown. I haven't told either of my parents about him. I keep telling myself, "Well, it's not like it's serious or anything. This is our very first date." But I'm lying.

In eighth grade, she saw me holding hands with Charlie Swanson after school one day. She forced me to bring him round for dinner, then interrogated him about his family and their connections, his extracurriculars and life goals. She did all this while comparing him alongside another boy she felt would be a more appropriate choice ("You know, Matthew Lawrence already has plans to intern at his father's company."), ignoring my father when he coughed the words *eighth grade* into his napkin.

I've brought home other boys since then because I didn't care. Taking them home to Mama is a safe thing to do because it gets rid of them faster. The fact that I don't want to tell her this time shows just how serious it really is.

"Who's the lucky boy?" I hear my mother's voice before I see her. It nearly sends me into a panic spiral.

"What?" How did she find out?! I've been so careful!

She runs her fingers over the pile of discarded clothes on my pink comforter. "This amount of reject outfits says first date. So, are you going to tell me about him or not?"

I try not to visibly breathe a sigh of relief. She doesn't know. Yet.

I plaster on a smile. "Mama, I have to look extra good after breakups too. You never know, I could run into Weston, so even though I'm just going out with the girls, I have to dress for revenge." I say this with a tinkling, Southern belle laugh, like revenge is something only delicate women can pull off properly.

Mama analyzes my sundress. "Well, in that case, you need to change. Peach isn't your color." She flicks through my closet. "Here." She hands me another dress like I don't get a say in the matter. It's a shade of green that would look hideous on most people.

I slip out of the peach dress and into the green one, hurrying before she can notice something about my body to complain about. I kind of want to cover up the mirror when I see my reflection. The dress fits me perfectly, and the color—like grass dialed up to an intensity that should never appear in human clothing—makes my green eyes pop and my tan skin glow. I want to take it off in protest. But I also want Michael to see me wearing it in half an hour. Which flavor of pride will win out today?

"Well?" She is smiling the most satisfied smile. I really, really want to take off the dress.

I shrug. "It looks okay. I'll think about it."

"Whatever you want to do is fine." She stands beside me in the mirror and kisses me on the temple. "You look really beautiful."

And as much as she frustrates me, I love that I never have to doubt her compliments. I want to store them in glass jars like fireflies, wrap them around my wrists like bracelets.

She floats away before I can say thank you.

I peek out my window for Michael for about the fifth time. I know it's too early, but I can't squish down my excitement. Believe it or not, there is actually an Inuit word for this specific subtype of anticipation: *iktsuarpok*. I close the blinds. Since Michael clearly isn't going to materialize outside my window, I text him to ask what we're doing today, because as cute as this dress is, I have no idea whether it's practical. Then I carry a couple of dirty dishes down to the kitchen. Daddy is there making a peanut butter and Nutella sandwich. (Seriously, where is he keeping all these contraband items?)

"Want a bite?" he asks when he sees me.

"Um, obviously." I lean over to take the offered bite of sandwich and promptly ascend to a higher plane of Nutella-enhanced being. "Mmm. How did you get Nutella past Mama?"

"I have my ways." He winks. "You look beautiful, princess."

I love that he would say it even if I was wearing a burlap sack and sporting leprosy-like acne, but I simultaneously know it doesn't mean as much as when Mama said it. Daddy's compliments make me feel comfortable and happy. Mama's make me soar.

"Thanks."

"What are you up to today?"

"Oh, um." I am incapable of lying to my daddy outright. Which means I am screwed. Luckily, my phone rings. I glance at the screen and see that it's Michael. "Oops, sorry, Daddy, gotta get this."

I kiss him on the cheek and hurry out of the room, so I can answer the phone.

"Hey! Where are we going today?" I ask once I've reached the safety of the hallway.

"To a maize maze."

"A what?"

"You know, one of those mazes made out of corn. A maize maze."

"Oh, perfect! I love going to Old Lady Howard's. She makes the best apple cider." Plus, a sundress is totally corn maize–appropriate attire. If you're me, I mean. I'll have to ditch the heels for some flats though.

"Awesome. I'll pick you up in fifteen?"

"Sounds good."

I hang up, and my blood pressure returns to normal. Talking on the phone with Michael. Hiding talking on the phone with Michael from Daddy. It's a bit much.

Even though I know I didn't lie to my dad, I get the grimiest feeling from being evasive with him. The situation can't be helped though. Telling my father would be tantamount to telling my mother, and there is no way I'm telling the woman who has crushed many a fledgling relationship. My brothers are scared to bring their girlfriends home for Thanksgiving for the very same reason. This is just how things are in our family, I tell myself. I still feel gross when I sneak to the bottom of my driveway.

Michael opens the car door for me. This is the sort of thing my brain normally files away in a mental spreadsheet of pros and cons, possibly with a comment like, "A Yankee who opens car doors! Will wonders never cease!" Michael is more than checks and balances. He is skipped heartbeats and a tingle on the back of my neck and sweaty palms and a thousand daydreams about what his lips would feel like against mine. He turns me into one of those dumb girls who believes in white horses and all kinds of other sentimental crap. I wonder if he knows how terrifying he is.

I realize his hand is resting on the console between us. Is that his way of inviting me to hold it? He seems so relaxed though. Maybe he's just one of those people who likes driving one-handed. And his hand is facedown. If he wanted me to hold it, he would have put it faceup. Right??? Why am I such a mess?! Normally, I'd alternately encourage and repel him, a carefully choreographed dance where I am in control. Instead, I have all these *feelings* in my stomach. Bubbly ones, like at any minute I'll spew out champagne. Or vomit. I don't like them one bit. He smiles at me from the driver's seat. I hope they never stop.

A squirrel darts in front of the car. He has to slam on the breaks and grab the steering wheel with both hands, and I'm saved from having to make any life-altering decisions of the hand-holding variety.

When we arrive at the maze, the sun is hanging high overhead, a fat tangerine. The cornfield spans out in front of us like an ocean, stalks whispering secrets when the breeze makes them rub together. I try to inhale the scent of fall: the earthy smell of dead leaves, the sweet smell of corn, but it's too early for that. Summer is five months long in Tennessee. Michael buys two tickets from the guy behind the wooden stand, and we read over the "few simple rules," an exhaustive list printed on a sign bigger than Michael's SUV.

"'What to do if you become lost in the maze.'" Michael laughs. "These rules are neither few nor simple."

"Well, at least now you know we aren't allowed to use profanity in the maze or drink alcohol and throw dried corncobs at each other."

"Good to know. Because I was planning on throwing some corn at you."

"I wuttin' recommend it," speaks up a surly old woman guarding the entrance to the maze with her lazy eye. Old Lady Howard. I hadn't realized she was sitting there. "Them corncobs hurt."

Michael blushes. "Oh, I wasn't really going to."

I giggle. "Good. Because it says right here on the sign they have undercover 'corn cops' on the lookout for rule breaking."

I tap my fingers to the sign and head toward the maze, but the entrance makes me hesitate. I flash back to being nine years old and sneaking downstairs to watch *Children of the Corn* from behind the sofa. I half expect to see red-eyed demon children jump out at me from the thick rows of corn. We don't see any of those, but we do see David Bowie. Or, well, a statue of David Bowie in full *Labyrinth* glory with '80s hair and ruffled collar and pants so expertly rendered, they make stone look like spandex. Michael studies the statue with a mixture of amusement and fear.

"Um?" He snickers at the goblin king's substantial package, which, to be fair, the artist has taken creative liberty with in regard to size.

"Old Lady Howard's a huge Bowie fan. And by 'fan,' I mean she's obsessed, and small children are afraid of her. She had them put *Labyrinth* characters all through the cornfield, and they carve the maze around them each year. There's another David Bowie just outside the exit near the house that people sneak in and paint all the time, like with sports team rivalries and stuff. The cheerleaders painted it as a bonding thing after we got back from summer camp this year."

"Huh," he says. "That's . . . well, okay, it's kind of weird."

I laugh. "It is, right?"

For the first leg of the maze, we amble along on paths carved like bizarre alien crop circles into the cornfield. We talk easily, and when he takes my hand (so he did want to hold it!), I let him, even though my cheeks turn red and my PDA meter quivers near overload, especially when he slides a finger across my pinky.

It isn't long before we reach a fork.

"Do you want to split up?" he asks. "We could see who makes it out of the maze fastest?"

My eyes spark at the idea of a challenge. "Loser buys snacks?"

"Done."

I take off at a sprint, completely ignoring what that means in terms of my sweat glands. I vaguely remember my mother saying something about how you're supposed to let boys win because losing makes them feel inadequate as providers. I consider this idea for all of two seconds before rejecting it. Michael directly challenged me to a competitive event. Date etiquette be damned. I race through the maze like there's a legion of evil children chasing me.

Minutes later, I burst past the corn at the front of the maze. I bend over panting and pull pieces of husk from my hair. Then I scan the benches and the concession stand. No sign of Michael. I hurry over to the concession stand and buy two apple ciders and an enormous sheaf of cotton candy. Then I grab napkins by the handful and wipe any part of my body I can reach. I check my reflection in my compact. I don't look great exactly, but it could be a whole lot worse. When Michael emerges from the maze a minute later, I'm perched on a bench with the snacks looking (mostly) like I haven't spent the last several minutes battling through corn.

"Michael," I call with a wave.

"Hey." He's panting too. Good. A guy who would let me win

would be almost as bad as a sore loser. "How long have you been here?"

"Just long enough to get some cider and cotton candy." I smile and search his face for any sign of irritation at being beaten by a girl. "I love cotton candy to a ridiculous degree."

He eyes the cotton-candy mountain. "I can see that. It was really sweet of you to get the snacks."

He smiles down at me. A genuine one—not a trace of "I'm actually pissed about losing to a girl," which means he passes my sore-loser test—and on the first date too. It's better he finds out sooner rather than later that losing is a hazard of dating Melanie Jane Montgomery.

Saturday, September 5
LIV

Someday, it's going to stop hurting. Seeing Trevor in the hallway. Going over to my dad's house and having his sparkly new life thrown in my face. Someday, those things won't seem so overwhelming. But someday is not today.

I pull my duffel bag out of the trunk and try to mentally prepare myself for twenty-four hours in an alternate universe. It's just me this time. My brother and sister can't come over right now because being in the third trimester makes my stepmom so tired. I'm sure if she could think of a reason not to have me here too, she would. Their life is perfect, organized shapes pressed into dough, and we are the sad, broken pieces you tear away from the cookie cutters to make the pretty stars and gingerbread men. A man next door waves vigorously while he mows his lawn. Dad's neighborhood creeps me out a little. The houses are all the same: clean gutters and freshly pruned hedges. The paint on the wrap-around porch is so shiny it hurts. Sandra, my stepmom, is waiting to pounce when he opens the door for me.

"Hi, Liv!" She gives me this huge smile with way too many of her teeth showing.

"Hi."

"Want to see the baby's room? We're finally finished!"

"Um, sure," I say, even though I really don't.

I drop my duffel bag in the foyer and follow her upstairs.

Sandra's life's work is decorating and redecorating this house. She doesn't have a job. Even before she was seven months pregnant, she didn't. I hate seeing her projects. Not because they're ugly or anything, but whenever I see their new silk rug (A bargain! Only $4,000!) or a rocking chair imported from Germany, all I can think of is Mom begging for extra shifts at the restaurant and our recliner that is held together by duct tape.

Mom and I are fighters. We're the kind of people who don't ever get anything the easy way. Who, after anything good happens, have to look around in fear wondering when the inevitable "tornado of suck" is going to hit. We have to work ten times harder to get things that seem to be handed to other people. But that's okay because I think it gives us a secret strength that the people who coast through life will never know. People like my dad. People like Sandra.

When you've earned something, I mean really earned it, no one can make you doubt that you deserve it. They can't say it isn't yours. There's something about getting a thing that you've bled and fought for that makes the getting that much sweeter.

Sometimes I wonder if I'd fight as hard if my dad were still here. If I wasn't trying so desperately to get him to notice me.

"Well, what do you think?"

Sandra sweeps her arm across the room like a game-show model. I try to manufacture a smile.

"It's . . . great." I get the feeling I've stepped into a catalogue. I take in the crib that probably cost more than our mortgage, the wooden rocking horse, the fresh coat of paint with its stenciled animals. "It's really pretty." I reach out to touch a turtle.

"Don't you love those?" she gushes. "Your dad painted every last one of them. It took days. Can you believe it?"

I can't. My dad was never the type to do crafty things. Or really any things at all.

I force another smile. This one almost breaks my face. "Not really."

"I know, right?" She laughs like it's hysterical. "But he's been *so* involved. He's been researching the safest car seat and planning a college fund and making sure I take my prenatal vitamins every day. Pregnancy brain. I can't remember anything!"

I busy myself with inspecting the mobile—sun, moon, and stars revolving over the crib—because I know I won't be able to conjure a fake smile this time. It would be wrong of me to hate this kid. I've made a promise to myself that I'll never let that happen. But it's hard not to be jealous. He or she is going to get a life I never had—a life I wish for, for my brother and sister. Birthday candle wishes, all smoke and no substance.

Dad doesn't feel like my dad anymore. He feels like this other kid's dad. Which makes him my what? Uncle? "Uncle" feels about right. I really want my mom to find someone new so she can be happy again. Sometimes I even say prayers that she will. But after that, I say a horrible, dark prayer. I pray that my mom never has another kid with the new someone because I don't want to lose both my parents.

When Dad got remarried, the things I imagined having in a family crumbled. I had to face the reality that my grand plans to re-create *The Parent Trap* weren't going to work. I wanted things to be a certain way and knew they couldn't. But I had dreams that maybe someday I could have my own family, and maybe I could make it all the things my family wasn't. And I had been starting to imagine Trevor as part of those dreams. Sometimes. When I was feeling extra mushy or we'd had a really good date. I know it was dumb of me. We're sixteen. I can't expect to meet someone who rescues my ideas on love and heals all my broken pieces. But I kind of thought I had.

Sunday, September 6

Trevor is finally going to get what he wants. At least, he thinks he is. I've broken radio silence to let him know that, yes, I have actually gotten his emails and texts and stupid, wonderful notes complete with sweet (albeit terrible) poetry. And yes, I guess I could come over and hang out today and talk.

What he doesn't know is that there is an ulterior motive for this visit. It's secret mission time. The goal: sneakily get access to Trevor's email and find The List. I will use spy tactics unlike any the world has ever seen. I really should have bought a wig. Of course, then Trevor would probably wonder why I was wearing a wig.

Peyton and Melanie Jane watch me climb over the fence behind the movie theater, because that's how you get to Trevor's. We had our moms drop us off, which means we have two hours to get this done because they think we're seeing the latest chick flick. I told the girls I didn't need their help, but they refused to let me go alone. Which is actually good because Peyton and I have been working on a separate devious plan that has nothing to do with the football team and everything to do with pumping Melanie Jane for information about a certain someone who couldn't be here today because she's at Jake's.

Melanie Jane can't get over the fence herself, so Peyton has to hoist her up. Her foot wobbles in Peyton's hands, and she clings to the top of the fence like a life preserver—she's surprisingly bad at this, considering standing on people and jumping around is 90 percent of what she does during football games. I help Mel-Jay down on the other side, and before she can regain stable footing, I hit her with the question.

"What happened with you and Ana?"

Peyton and I decided this was key—finding out what broke them before we try to glue them back together. We also decided asking Melanie Jane was by far the less terrifying option. Now, with Melanie Jane's startled eyes darting between us like laser beams, I wonder if we made the right choice.

"I used to have a crush on Chad MacAllistair," she finally says.

"Ew," I reply.

"Shut up." She shoots me a faux glare, but she no longer looks hard. My silliness has cracked whatever front she had up.

We trace our way through the woods together, following a dirt path that I know will come out on Trevor's street.

Melanie Jane spills. "I walked in on Ana and Chad hooking up at a party. She was my best friend. I didn't want to believe she could do that to me. But there was this video, do y'all remember that?"

I nod. "It was all over school."

"It was terrible," says Peyton.

"In the video . . . I mean, she really was all over him. I was so mad, like, how could she do this to me? But I kept thinking about that night and how she seemed so out of it, like maybe she didn't even want to be there.

"So, a few weeks after, I tried to talk to her. Find out what happened. But she wouldn't let me. I called, I texted, I was beating my brains out trying to get her to talk to me. But she cut me out just like I cut her out."

"Do you want to make up?" asks Peyton.

Melanie Jane lets out a sigh that is laced with missed chances. "Of course I do. She used to be my best friend. But I think it's too late. We tried it before, and it was all *cavoli riscaldati*."

We blink at her.

"Oh, sorry. It means reheated cabbage. It's Italian for what you get when you try to fix an unfixable relationship."

I bite my lip. "But what if it wasn't? Unfixable, I mean? Couldn't you just apologize and see what happens?"

She shrugs uncomfortably. I get it. Putting your heart out there like that is a huge risk.

"What if we talked to Ana first?" says Peyton.

Slow down there, champ. Talk? To Ana?

"I guess I could think about it," she finally says.

And then I stop them both because we've reached Trevor's house.

Melanie Jane blinks. "Trevor lives *here?*"

"Yes." I square my shoulders automatically. Trevor's house is like every redneck joke in one place. Dogs under the porch. Knee-high grass punctuated with broken-down cars and appliances. A goat bleating at us from the side yard.

Two little girls play house with a rust-covered dishwasher. Their hair is neatly braided, and their pretty gingham dresses swish when they run. Trevor's mom makes most of his sisters' clothes.

"I'm sorry," says Melanie Jane, and I can tell she feels terribly uncomfortable about what she just said. "So . . . are you going to kiss Trevor?"

I scoff. "This is a secret mission."

"Uh-huh. I still think you should kiss him."

I look to Peyton for support.

She shrugs. "I think you should kiss him too."

My jaw drops. "*Traitor.* I can't believe you two. I'm going to get to work on THE MISSION now before either of you get any other ideas."

I send The Boy I Am Not Going To Kiss an email just before I walk up to the house. It's a picture of a pink fairy armadillo. Trevor and I had this thing we used to do where we'd send each other pictures of the strangest, most ugly-cute animals we could find. It's weird, I know, but it's actually really fun to start your morning by waking up to a random picture of a baby wombat. The picture is supposed to help me out with the next phase of my plan, but I wasn't expecting to feel a pathetic wistfulness while Google-searching for animals. I really do miss him.

I reach my hand through the gashes in the screen and knock on the front door. Trevor opens it.

"Hey!" His face says seeing me here, on his front porch, is the happiest surprise in the universe.

I follow him up to his room. It smells like chocolate-chip cookies inside because his mom bakes them homemade almost every day. He takes the desk chair, and I hop onto his bed because it's the only other place to sit. I try not to think about the things that used to happen on it.

"Hey, have you checked your email recently?"

"Nope, why?" A small flush creeps up his neck, like he's trying not to think about the same things I'm trying not to think about. "Did you send me something?"

"Yep. Check it! Check it!" I bounce up and down a little, and the flush reaches his ears. Oops. No bouncing.

He turns to the old computer that was a hand-me-down from his grandfather, and logs in to his email. I don't catch the whole

password. It has an *e* and a 4. Not exactly helpful. But that's okay.
I have other plans.

Trevor snort-laughs. "What *is* this thing?"

"It's a pink fairy armadillo! Isn't it awesome?!"

"Yeah." He looks at it and starts laughing again. "Yeah, I love
it."

He isn't laughing now. His face is serious, and his eyes are on
mine, and he's saying love, and I want to throw away all my plans
to be strong and jump in his lap and say, "Yes, I'll be your secret
girlfriend. I miss you so much it hurts." But I don't.

What I say is, "I'm really thirsty. Do you mind getting me
some water?"

That's the next step of the plan. Get him to leave the room
once he's logged on to his email. I think it's going to work too,
until he clicks the little logout button before he gets up.

"Sure thing. I want some too."

Crap. Well, this isn't working out like I'd planned. I knew
I should have worn a wig. I probably should have had more of a
backup plan too, but I had this feeling I'd be able to slip in like a
secret agent and make something happen. I guess I could come
right out and ask him. He's not like Weston or one of those other
guys who might rat out Rey for telling me. Trevor's safe. I think
part of the reason I haven't asked him is because I'm hurt. Rey,
this guy I barely know, told me, but Trevor couldn't. I need to
know why and dread finding out at the same time.

He's back with our waters now. He sets one glass on his desk and holds the other out to me just as I'm saying, "I know about The List."

The water almost ends up on both of us.

"How'd you hear about that?"

"One of the guys, Rey, told me. You can't tell anyone."

"You know I wouldn't do that."

"I thought I knew a lot of things about you," I say. And then, because he looks so damn sad, "Sorry."

I gulp down half my water and wait for him to break the silence, but he's picking at the wooden slats of his chair and not making eye contact.

"Why couldn't you tell me?" I'm holding my breath before I even get the question out.

"I wanted to," he says to the chair. "I just— I didn't want to hurt your feelings. Plus, I wasn't sure how you'd take it. If anyone found out I told, I'd be dead."

"Yeah, but so would Rey."

Trevor shakes his head. "No. He wouldn't."

"That doesn't make any sense."

"It does if you understand how these guys work."

I'm mildly horrified at the idea of finding out how people like Chad MacAllistair work. I'm also DYING to know.

"Rey has more power on this team than I do. The coaches love him. He's an incredible player. I don't think it's possible to make the guy look bad. Me, I'm good. But I'm not that good. And besides, I'm offense. The defenders can hit me hard at practice and make it look like an accident. If offense tried the same thing on Rey, they'd probably hurt themselves." He takes a sip of his water and stops when he sees the look on my face. "They're not all bad guys, Liv, but no one will go against Chad. He's the golden boy. And he hates me."

I frown. "Shouldn't he have stopped messing with you by now? You did what he wanted."

"Yeah, well, I don't think Chad likes there to be any other stars on his offense. Nobody expected me to be this good, and that's making the buzz even bigger. I can almost see him seething over every pass I catch. Every bit of attention I take off him."

I wince. I hate what they've done to him. And what they've made him do to me. All because Chad MacAllistair has sick ideas about what he's entitled to.

"I want to see The List," I say.

"Sugar, I can't. I just told you why."

Being called "sugar" makes this hurt even more. I think Trevor senses that because he moves to sit beside me on the bed. He puts his arm around me, and when I don't protest, he rubs my back in gentle circles.

"I'm so sorry," he says. "For everything that happened. For all the things that are still happening. If I could think of a way to fix this that didn't involve screwing up my future, I'd do anything."

The familiar touch of his hand on my body. The gray of his eyes searing into mine. I'm tempted to tell him that I'm going to pay them back for both of us. But I have to keep my secrets too.

So I keep my mouth shut—in the spilling-secrets sense only. In reality, there isn't enough willpower inside me to stop me from telling him AND to keep me from kissing him. Not when his face is so close to mine and his lips are parted like that. It's like we're in slow motion, him running his hand up to the back of my neck, me leaning toward him. Thousands of seconds pass where I could stop this from happening. I ignore each and every one of them.

Our lips touch, featherlight, like they've forgotten they know each other. I can feel his smile against my mouth. I can't hold back anymore. I need this—the crush of his lips against mine, the cinnamon-sweet taste of him. His strong arms wrap around me, and I pull him closer. Pull him to a place where they can't touch us and no one and nothing matters more than the blissful, dizzy feeling of being together. I press him into the blankets, taking more more more. His hand slips up the back of my shirt, and I return to my senses.

"Trevor, I can't."

He sighs and hugs me to him, but he doesn't try anything else. "I know."

We stay that way for a long time, neither of us willing to let go.

The front door opens downstairs, and we tear apart. It feels like when you rip a piece of superglue off your finger and part of you goes with it. I tell him I better go. And I do. But I can't help wondering which parts of me I left stuck to him.

Wednesday, September 9
PEYTON

Why does it feel like a date? I didn't do anything special, like wear eyeliner or try to shrink my pores. We're just studying. Geometry. Which has to be the least sexy subject in the world. I mean, half the classics we read in Brit lit are chock-full of sex, and biology can be awkward too, especially when you have to say words like *spermatozoa* without giggling. But what does geometry have other than lame pickup lines like "I don't mean to be obtuse, but you're acute girl" and "Hey, baby, nice asymptote"?

"Hey, Peyton."

I know it's him before I turn around. Rey, as my tutor, that's what geometry has. He sits next to me at the cafeteria table—we both had our parents drop us off early so we could study together before school.

"Do you care if I eat breakfast?" he asks.

I shake my head. "Go for it. I already had a giant bowl of cereal at home."

"Me too," he says. And then he pulls out two bananas, a stack of bagels that have been cut, cream-cheesed, and rebagged, and a bottle of orange juice that looks like it's meant for a family.

"Wow, you eat a lot, huh?" Did I really just say that? He's going to think I'm an idiot. Oh, wait, he saw my last geometry quiz, so he probably already does.

He smiles. "During football season I have to."

And then he gets right to work, both on eating the bagels and teaching me about angles. The date feeling goes away, and I'm glad. We go over practice problems, and Rey is super patient, even when I ask questions I would feel way too dumb asking in class. He's also super patient with the four different girls who interrupt us to flirt with him. They mostly glare at me, but one of them smiles. I hope he ends up with that one.

"She seems really nice," I say after she leaves.

"Who, Victoria? Yeah. Yeah, she's cool."

Soon, we're finished with the practice problems, and we only have a few minutes left, so we end up talking about all kinds of random stuff while Rey drinks his OJ. I finally get up the nerve to ask him something I've been dying to know.

"Do you really have those tattoos?"

He laughs, and it's the warmest, happiest sound in the world. "You heard about that?"

"*Everyone* heard about that."

"Oh." And for a second he looks almost sad, but it passes before I can ask him about it. "Yeah, so I went to Samoa to visit my family this summer. My cousin, Tupe, he's a few years older than me, he was getting his *pe'a*—it's this tattoo that wraps around your whole body from your waist to your knees. It's kind of like a rite of passage. It takes a really long time, and it hurts like crazy, so I told him stories and stuff during a lot of it. That's as close as I came to getting a tattoo."

"So that's where the rumor comes from."

"Yeah. I want to get one, though. Someday. It's a really big deal in my family." He polishes off the last of the juice. "Mom says I have to wait until I'm done growing though. Hey, I wanted to ask you something."

"Yeah?" The first-date flutters come back with a vengeance. I feel there is a high probability of me running into things.

"You remember those kids I was talking about at FMF, right?"

"Sure, I was hoping to get involved with that."

His grin lights up the entire hallway—seriously, I think it could power a continent. "Right on. Well, I'm going to see them tomorrow after practice, and we were going to play football again. Some of the girls are into it, but I can tell some of them are really bored, and I was thinking since you're a dancer . . . ?"

"Totally! I would love to come do some dance stuff with them!"

"Okay. Well, cool."

"Yeah, cool."

He nods, that grin still shining on his face like a beacon. "Cool," he says again.

I feel suddenly and supremely shy, like I've been struck with a disease that makes me incapable of speech, and my hands are these huge awkward things that wave around of their own accord, never finding a place to rest. So, I settle for smiling, trying for a good closed-lip one that will make me look friendly but not constipated. But one look at his face, and my smile bursts at the seams, and it's broadcasting all of my secrets, and if I don't shut it down soon, he's going to know I spent three whole minutes of our study session thinking about orange juice–flavored kisses. Mercifully, the bell rings. We go our separate ways, Rey calling good luck to me as I walk the long hallway to geometry.

Karl falls into step beside me. "Peyton, can I talk to you? *Now.*"

I get a rush of anxiety—the kind that makes you feel cornered and queasy at the same time. "Um, sure."

"What were you talking to that guy about?"

"Nothing. He was just asking me if I wanted to help with teaching dance to some little kids."

"So, that's what you were talking about all morning in the cafeteria? *Dance?*"

"No, he helps me study for geometry."

"I should be the one helping you study for geometry."

It didn't click before, but now it does. "Were you watching me?"

Karl ignores my question. "I don't like the way he was looking at you. Is he your boyfriend?" The way he says it implies I'm not allowed to have one.

"No." I hurry to say it, almost like it's an apology, and then I remember it's absolutely none of Karl's business. I lift my chin the way I've seen Melanie Jane do. "I'd like him to be my boyfriend."

Karl narrows his eyes. "So, what, are you trying to make me jealous?"

"No, I . . . Look, you're not my boyfriend anymore. And you treated me so badly that I don't think it's good for me to have you in my life at all." I force my voice to stay calmer than I feel. "I don't think we should talk anymore."

"Wow. You must really like this guy, huh? What's his name?"

"I don't want to talk to you about him." I feel protective, as if by knowing about Rey, Karl could somehow infect that relationship too.

He sighs into his hands like he's exhausted. "I miss you, okay? I love you so much." He tucks my hair behind my ear, and his blue eyes sear into mine. "I know I've made mistakes, and I'm sorry. But we can work on things, I promise. We'll make it just like last year, like when it was just you and me. You'll see."

I cross my arms. "Look, I'm glad you're realizing this, but I can't get back together with someone who treats me like dirt and tries to control me."

"We've shared something that makes us inseparable for life. I had a good reason."

"No." I shake my head firmly. "There is never a good reason to talk that way to someone you love."

Karl steps backward in surprise. "Maybe I didn't treat you well, but I gave you all the respect you demanded."

"Wait, so now you're saying it's my fault you treated me badly? You're only confirming the fact that this is a good decision."

He opens his mouth to argue, but I raise a hand to stop him.

"We're not together anymore. That means I don't have to

argue with you if I don't want to."

Karl takes another shocked backward step. If he goes any farther, he'll trip over a newspaper stand.

"I have to go. I can't answer anymore if you call me."

I see him realize that I mean it. That we really are over. Permanently. The shock turns to hurt turns to desperation turns to him grabbing my arm like I'm a disobedient toddler.

"No one will ever be able to love you like me," he says into my ear. "You probably can't get the kind of guy you want anyway. Good guys want girls who are virgins."

"That's not true." I say it fast, like a reflex. Because that is my secret dark fear, and now that he's named it, it feels more real.

I walk away like it doesn't matter, but how could he know I worry about that? My mind drifts to this lesson we had in Sunday school last year on one of the days they split up the girls and boys. They brought in this rose and had us pass it around. "You can pull petals off, turn it upside down, smell it, whatever." When it got to me, I just sniffed it and passed it to the next girl. It smelled like how a rose was supposed to smell. I didn't really get where we were going with this. By the time the rose went around the entire circle, it wasn't looking so great. The Sunday school teacher placed it on the table, and then she brought in a box of new roses and put them in a pile beside it. She said we could each pick a rose to take home. Well, of course, every girl picked one of the fresh, pristine roses and not the sad lonely rose with the bruised petals falling every which way. Then our teacher talked all about how you're supposed to save your virginity until you're married and how nobody good is going to want you if you're used. And a part of me knows that's not really the way the world works. But another part of me thinks, *Why would a guy like Rey Lemalu, a guy who could have any girl in this school, want to pick the ugly flower?*

I'm still thinking of that Sunday school lesson and what Karl said—all through school, all through dance team practice, right up until it's time to go to Wednesday night church. Mom and I drive there together, and then she leaves for her class, and I should go to mine, but instead I plop down on a bench in the middle of the courtyard. And I start bawling. I cry until I run out of tears. Even then, my body keeps going through the motions of crying, like when you get really sick with the stomach flu and you dry-heave even though there's nothing left.

My eyes drift to two children playing on the balcony over the courtyard which reminds me of us hiding out in the hayloft in Big Tom's barn which makes me think of the vow which makes me realize I desperately do not want to be alone right now. I wipe my cheeks with the back of my fist and text Melanie Jane. The Montgomerys never miss a church service.

A few minutes later, she hops onto the bench next to me. "Hey, girl!"

"Hey," I reply, the word coming out shakier than I want it to.

"Are you okay?"

"N-n-nooo." A sob rises in my throat, but I manage to turn it into a hiccup. I hate crying in front of people.

"Oh, no. Peyton. Hey, it's going to be okay. If you want to talk about it now, that's fine. And if you don't, that's fine too. I'll just sit here."

I'm still working on not crying, so I don't say anything back. Melanie Jane has her hands clasped in front of her like she's restraining herself from doing any number of things. And then she does the best thing she could possibly do. She drops her hands and scoots closer to me so our shoulders touch. It was just six inches, but I feel like she crossed miles and years to pull me back from a precipice.

I try talking again. "Karl and I had a fight, and I told him I can't talk to him anymore. It was bad, I guess, but not that bad. I mean, I stood up to him, so I should be happy. I'm embarrassed I cried so much."

"Maybe you're crying about more than the fight," Melanie Jane says.

I nod. "I think I am." I try to organize my thoughts, while she waits, as promised. "I feel like an idiot. I wasn't ready to have sex, but I did it anyway, and then I realized Karl was toxic, and I'm upset I waited so long and then had sex with some guy who isn't the one and didn't even treat me that well."

"You're not with him now. That's something. A big something."

I shake my head. She makes it sound so simple. "But I lost my virginity. And my religion says . . . I mean . . . we're Southern

Baptist. I feel like Karl and I are bound for life. Like it was wrong to have sex with him and now it's wrong to break up with him because it's like we were married."

"Whoa." Melanie Jane grabs my shoulders and turns me so we're looking each other straight in the eye. "Peyton, you are not and never were married to Karl. Losing your virginity doesn't condemn you to a lifetime of misery."

I almost start crying again. I want so badly to believe her. I tell her the story about Sunday school and roses—I'm pretty sure she was there that day. She looks like she wants to kick something.

"Okay, first of all, that's a bunch of crap, and you should forget it right now. Side note: I'm a little disappointed that they used such a tired metaphor. And second of all, I want to know what the boys were doing in their class because you know for damn sure they weren't talking about saving their flowers."

I snort. "Maybe they taught them that girls who don't wait for marriage are worthless. It would make a lot of sense." The overwhelming feelings hit again. Hard. "I don't know what to do. A part of me still believes it—that no one will want me now."

"You can't talk like that. Anyone with a brain would want you. Look, choosing to wait until marriage makes me feel empowered. But if the same choice cripples you, then it wasn't the right one."

I sigh. "I wish I could be more like you."

She smiles. "Well, I wish I could be more like you. You leapt into love, and it didn't work out, but at least you went for it. And you'll leap again, and next time it'll be for someone who's worth it. And I'll probably miss out because I'm scared."

It's funny because I can't imagine her being scared of anything. "Maybe we should both make a promise that we won't be scared this time around."

She links her pinky with mine. "It's worth a shot."

RANBURNE PANTHER SCAVENGER HUNT

In Ranburne:

1. ~~Fill a condom up with water. Draw a face on it. Put it on Principal Corso's doormat, and ding-dong ditch. (One person)~~

2. ~~The egg-on-a-string trick. Hang an egg from a power line by a string and watch a car run into it. (Everyone)~~

3. ~~Paint the David Bowie statue at Old Lady Howard's corn maze. (Everyone)~~

4. ~~Chair race through Walmart. (Everyone)~~

5. ~~Get a picture of the team with the Ranburne Panther. (Everyone)~~

6. ~~Go to the Dawsonville football field. Find that stupid rock they touch before their games. Pee on it. (Everyone)~~

In Nashville:

7. ~~Visit the illustrious Delta Tau Beta fraternity at Vanderbilt. Have a beer with Panther alum TJ McNeil and take a picture of the legendary scar he got during a game-winning play against Dawsonville. (One person)~~

8. Go to LP Field and reenact the "Music City Miracle." (Everyone)

9. Go to Centennial Park and jump into the pond behind the Parthenon. (Everyone)

10. ~~Go to The Jackrabbit Saloon. Walk to the very middle of the dance floor and attempt to do the worm. (One person)~~

11. ~~Go up to a girl who is totally out of your league, get down on your knees, and ask her to marry you. (One person)~~

12. Go up to a fat girl and tell her "You're so beautiful . . . for a fat chick." Bonus points if she throws her drink on you. (One person)

13. ~~Hug a biker. Bonus points if he has a mullet. (One person)~~

14. Get a girl to give you her thong. (One person)

DARES REMAINING: 4

12:35 A.M.

MELANIE JANE

The cheerleader throng is in full party mode. I exchange side hugs with everybody, making a big show of hanging out.

"Hey, girl!" yells Aubrey. Whew. Someone started their night early.

"We didn't know if you were going to show!" says Chloe.

"Of course!" I try to mimic their excitement. "I wouldn't miss spending tonight with my girls."

I can't stay long though. We need to knock out the rest of these dares and get out of here. Hopefully, they'll be able to get a couple done without me. I sneak a glance at the friends I just abandoned, my gaze lingering on Ana. She looks up, and it's like she wants to say something to me, like the words are just waiting to pour out of her mouth, even though I'm on the other side of the bar. And I feel exactly the same way. It's like this whenever we're around each other lately. Like this Yaghan word, *Mamihlapinatapai*—the look that passes between two people when they're desperate to make something happen, but neither knows where to begin. Greg barrels past me like a drunken rhinoceros, and the connection is broken, and our twin wishes dissolve.

The guys must be feeling pretty cocky about how much of the hunt they've finished because they're mostly just hitting on chicks and hanging out with the older Varsity guys. Better do some recon just to be sure. I snake around the circle to see who's got the list. It's Trevor. That makes sense.

"Trevor!" I laugh, and push his shoulder and try to sound more like Aubrey. "Are y'all gonna make it or are you gonna be naked at Homecoming?"

He grins. "Just a few more things to go. I think I get to keep my birthday suit to myself."

I pretend to teeter on my heels so I can grab his arm and get a good look at the list. He's been checking it off like a good boy—only the last three items are left.

"Oops, here you go." He helps me stand straight again.

"Thanks." I smile sheepishly. "Stupid heels."

Yeah, right. With all my pageant practice, I could run across a lava field in stilettos.

"What's up, Trevor?" Chad comes up behind him and squeezes his shoulders in a way that would be friendly if his fingers weren't digging in like talons. "Did you forget that girls aren't supposed to see the list?"

"Oh, right." Trevor folds the list in clumsy creases and shoves it into his pocket.

"Now what are we going to do about your lack of respect?" There's a boyish grin on Chad's face, but his eyes are mean. "I'm thinking—"

Before he can dole out any kind of punishment, Greg starts puking into a trashcan. Big Tom yells at Mason, asking him why the hell he let Greg drink so much.

"Sorry," Trevor says after Chad leaves. He glances around the bar. "Hey, um, is Liv here? She texted me earlier."

"Yeah, she's here. I think she's dancing."

"Cool. Cool." He nods, and his eyes find her, and he's got the most heartbreaking look on his face. "Do you think she'd talk to me?"

I squeeze his shoulder. "I think so. You should at least try."

My phone buzzes in my purse. A text from Ana.

Michael's here! We're in the room with the darts.

"Gotta go. Be right back!" I call to everyone in the general area.

"You just got here!" Chloe yells after me.

I'm already power walking to the dart room though, scooping up Liv on my way. Ana's there playing darts. Alone.

"Where's Michael?"

"He went to get us some Cokes."

"Oh. Well, we need to hurry. The boys only have the last three dares to do, and they could do all of them here. We still have numbers twelve and fourteen, plus eight and nine that we have to drive to, and I did not pee on a rock for nothing!"

Ana puts a hand on each of my shoulders. "Okay, chill. We'll find a guy to wear a thong, and then we'll figure out what to do about dare number twelve."

"Okay." I take a few deep breaths and say it again because it makes me feel better. "Okay."

Just as my craziness levels are returning to normal, Michael arrives with the Cokes.

"Hey!" He hands them off so he can hug me without spillage. "You look gorgeous."

"Hey," I reply. "I need you to wear a thong."

Ana spits her Coke, and if Michael had taken a sip of his, I can tell he would be doing the same thing.

He recovers quickly. "I didn't think we had reached that phase in our relationship."

"We haven't. I mean, that's not something I would like normally. Or ever. I just—" I reach into my purse and pull out the ruffly thong. "I need you to wear this and dance around a little while Ana takes a picture. And I can't tell you why."

"Um." He looks at all three of us like we are the weirdest girls in the universe. "It's really important?"

"Vitally. It's vitally important," says Liv.

He shrugs. "Okay."

I pass him the thong. He holds it up to the light and grimaces before putting it on.

I'm stuck on what he said earlier about phases in our relationship. What phase are we at? He isn't my boyfriend. Why hasn't he asked me yet? Does that mean something's wrong? That this doesn't mean as much to him as it does to me? Usually, boys ask me inside of the first couple of weeks.

He coughs, and I realize the thong is in position. Pink lace ruffles cover his crotch, and thin pink bands circle around the back of his jeans.

"So . . . what kind of dance am I supposed to do?"

Liv and Ana are choking back giggles. The camera is at the ready.

"I don't know. Can you do that really fast butt-cheek-shaking thing that strippers do?"

Michael attempts it. It is every bit as amazing as you might expect.

"You're done. You're done." Liv laughs and gives him a huge hug. "Now take it off or people are going to start stuffing dollar bills in your pockets."

Michael removes the thong, and I fling my arms around his neck. "Thank you so much. You were wonderful."

"Anything for you," he says. "Even the modeling of questionable undergarments."

The music changes. The band is playing a slow song now.

"Hey, do you want to go dance?" he asks.

"Definitely. You go on ahead. I'll catch up in one second."

Ana turns off her camera as he walks away. "Where's Peyton? Do you think it's okay that she wasn't here?"

"Bathroom," says Liv just as I say, "I think so."

"It's a one-person dare. Plus, the rules just say we have to stay together. We're still all in the same bar." I don't take my eyes off Michael. "Do you think he likes me? Like, really likes me? He hasn't asked me to be his girlfriend yet."

Liv snorts. "Melanie Jane, the boy just danced around in a thong for you. He *likes* you." She pushes me toward the dance floor. "Now go kiss him."

He's waiting for me on the dance floor, a small smile on his face, and lights streaming down from overhead. I take his hand, and he wraps his other arm around my lower back. I wonder if this is weird for him, slow dancing to country twang in the middle of a bunch of guys in cowboy hats. They probably don't get much of that in Boston. We dance for the rest of the song, and he turns me until I'm dizzy. I get my wish that the next song will be a slow one too. I feel his eyes on me, and every hair on my arms stands up, like my body knows something's about to happen even though my mind doesn't.

"Hey, Melanie Jane?"

"Yes?"

He squeezes my hand in his. "Do you want to be my girlfriend?"

"Yes," I say almost before he finishes the question. "Yes, I would love to be your girlfriend."

It's the perfect way to ask. No awkward DTR talk. No "let's be exclusive." Just an honest, straightforward question. It's almost old-fashioned, and it is so Michael. He smiles at my answer, never letting go of my eyes. Jittery, giddy feelings flood my body, make me feel like I have fireworks living inside of me. My legs go wobbly in a way I can't blame on my heels. *I have a boyfriend.* Without an expiration date. I lean forward and kiss him impulsively, our noses pressing together, my fingers weaving into his soft hair to pull him closer. I don't stop until the song ends, and when it does, I can't help but blush.

"How do I always end up kissing you in the most public settings?"

"I don't know."

It's completely unlike me. I'm the girl who hides everything and thinks public displays of all kinds are unladylike. But somehow, being with Michael has a way of making me forget.

Out of nowhere, Michael's shoulder catches me in the jaw.

"Ow."

"Sorry," he says. "Somebody—"

But I cut him off because I see Weston behind him. "Weston?"

Weston smirks at Michael, who I now realize has a full drink dripping down the back of his pants. "My bad."

At this point, most of the guys at Ranburne High would start punching. Michael just holds up his hands. "It's fine. Maybe you could try staying away from me, okay?"

Weston narrows his eyes. "For now," he says before he goes back to his band of Neanderthals.

"What was that about? Has he been messing with you?"

Michael looks as uncomfortable as I've ever seen him. "Kind of. I mean, yeah. He's pissed we're together, so he and the other guys keep doing dumb stuff like tripping me in the hallway and whispering 'Jew-boy' when I make presentations in history class."

I am livid. *"What?"*

"It's fine. I can take care of myself."

"That's not the point."

I stomp in the direction of the football crew. Grab Weston's shoulder and whirl him around.

"Oh, hi," he says. Is it me or did his face go a little pale?

"Yeah. Hi." I punctuate each word like I'm trying to stab him with it. "I'm only going to say this once: you're going to leave my new boyfriend alone, and you're going to call off your dogs too. I'm not about to be the next Charlotte Fisher."

Weston is working up what I'm sure will be a real winner of a response when Trevor pulls him away from me. "Hey, man. Come over here. You're not pulling your weight, and I need you to go hug one of those bikers over there."

I find Michael at the bar near the bikers trying to stuff an entire stack of napkins down the back of his pants. "I'm sorry," I say. "Are you doing all right?"

He stops stuffing for a second. "I'm good. Actually, I was going to ask you about something before we got interrupted. Do you want to come over next weekend? My parents are going to be in Boston all week."

"Oh." And I don't know what kind of face I'm making, but it must be a bad one because he backtracks.

"Oh, no. I didn't mean *that*. I just thought it would be good to spend some time together. Away from people we go to school with."

"Oh," I say again, displaying my legendary powers of conversation. "That would actually be really nice. There's much less danger of getting your pants wet that way."

"Hey, is everything okay?" Chloe appears with Aubrey at her hip. I wonder if she heard us, and with the way she's smiling, I'm going to guess yes. "I saw what happened."

"I saw it too," says Rat Tail, startling all of us. "That boy did it on purpose. I would have punched him."

I laugh. "Me too." And then a glimmer of a wonderful, evil idea hits me. "He's an awful boy," I tell Rat Tail and his biker crew. "Do you know he broke up with me just because I don't want to lose my virginity until I'm married?"

The men are appalled. I guess some things are sacred, even to bikers.

"Yeah, he's horrible. And he *totally* deserves to get punched."

As we walk away, I am the one smiling. Weston is going to have to hug one of those mountain-sized men. And I just made sure it won't be easy.

8

Thursday, September 10

LIV

"It won't be easy."

"I know," says Peyton.

I check to make sure Coach Tanner isn't watching because I'd like to make it through at least one practice without getting my name screamed over the bullhorn. Then I whisper, "It might even be impossible."

"I know."

"But you still want to try?"

She smiles and begins the next stretch in our warm-up sequence. "Yep."

"I think you are secretly hiding a honey badger under all that sweetness."

"Ha." And then her seemingly endless supply of hope runs out. "But how are we supposed to do it? Ana seems so *angry*, and she won't ever talk about anything. How are we supposed to get two people to make up if one of them won't even admit there's a problem?"

"We lock them in a room with a bottle of tequila and don't let them out until they promise to be friends again?"

"Liv Lambros and Peyton Reed! Whatever it is you're talking about must be pretty important because it just earned you four laps after practice."

We groan in unison. But when Coach Tanner paces to the other end of the field to yell at somebody else, Peyton turns back to me.

"That's not really your plan, is it? Sometimes it's hard to tell with you."

I stick my tongue out at her. "Do you have a better one?"

"We could talk to Ana."

"Oh, sure. Well, if you want to do it the easy way." I walk my fingers out across the grass in front of me until my nose touches the ground and a pleasant kind of burning travels through my leg muscles. "Want to go to Jake's after practice and see if she's there?"

Peyton nods. "But we have to be careful, you know? Ana's so tense, we could mess things up worse. We need to be stealthy."

"I am nothing if not stealthy." And then I realize I have no idea where Coach Tanner is, which is a very dangerous thing.

"That's eight laps, ladies! Do I need to make it twelve?!"

The bullhorn blares right behind us. Peyton and I practically jump out of our skin.

"No, ma'am," we reply, and it's the last thing we say for the rest of practice because we'd rather not face death by aerobic exercise.

We trudge to Jake's when we're finished. After a grueling practice followed by a two-mile run punctuated with bullhorn heckling, we've definitely earned some ice cream. Thankfully, someone else is manning the counter, so we're able to corner Ana in a lounge that has a couch upholstered with the solar system.

"Hey," says Peyton. "I really like your shoes."

"Hey," I say. "When are you and Melanie Jane going to make up?"

Peyton elbows me. "Nice job, stealth."

I shrug. "I can't help it. And anyway, this way saves time. So?" I raise my eyebrows at Ana, who seems to be frozen in place.

"Um." The spell breaks, and she leans over to pick up some empty ice-cream cups. "I don't know what you're talking about."

"We know something's going on with you and her." Peyton leans too, trying to make eye contact, but Ana is having none of this friend-tervention. "We're not asking you to tell us—"

"Good. Because I'm not." Ana's voice is all hard edges. She throws the cups in a trash bag and sighs. "Sorry."

Peyton smiles. "It's okay. And I'm sorry if it seemed like we were trying to get in your business. We care about you. Both of you."

I hate seeing them like this. I can't keep it inside anymore. "You have to make up. You and Melanie Jane are two of my favorite people!"

"Melanie Jane was one of my favorite people too," says Ana.

I wince at her use of the word *was*. "Couldn't you both just apologize and go back to being friends again?"

Ana slumps into a chair, like even the act of standing is too much for her. "A lot of things happened between us. We can't undo them. We can't snap right back to being friends like none of it happened."

Peyton balances on the chair arm beside her and touches her shoulder. "But maybe you could have a different kind of friendship. If she tries to talk to you, just give her a chance, could you do that?"

Dude. I had no idea Peyton was the friendship whisperer. I'm feeling a sudden urge to apologize to Chloe Baskins for putting gum in her hair in second grade. The magic seems to be working on Ana too.

"Maybe," she says.

I sure hope she means it.

Thursday, September 10
ANA

appreciate what Peyton and Liv are trying to do, I really do, but they just don't get it. Melanie Jane and I will never be friends. Allies against a common enemy, yes, but friends, no. Because when everything happened, I gave her so many chances. I beat my brains out trying to get my friend to talk to me, and she pushed me away. And, okay, yes, she may have eventually tried calling me. And texting me. And driving by my house. And cornering me after class. And even crashing one of the boys' weekend-long Magic-playing fests. But she should have done it sooner. She should have been there for me when I needed her.

People like Liv and Peyton think having a big talk and letting it all out will make everything wonderful. Like, if I go tell all my secrets to Melanie Jane, our friendship will magically be repaired and we'll go riding off together on matching unicorns. But I've already tried the whole spilling-my-guts-to-a-third-party thing, and it most definitely did not result in any kind of helpful friendship mediation. If Melanie Jane and I talk directly, it'll probably only make things worse.

I should have learned my lesson after I told the counselor. Should have realized that in this town, at this school, no one was going to be on my side. But I hadn't heard from Melanie Jane all weekend, and she wasn't answering my calls. I was desperate to talk to her—she was my best friend, the only person I really wanted to tell. Plus, she was the last person to see me that night. Maybe she knew things that could help.

I saw her in the hallway after I left the counselor's office (well, after I left the bathroom where I had a sob fest after I left the counselor's office). The bell had rung a minute before. Classes were changing, and she was standing there in the hallway. I wanted to fall into her. Cry everything that happened into her shoulder. But something in her face stopped me. It was her mouth. It was so tense. And before I could think of what to do next, she was walking away.

On top of everything else, now my best friend was acting like she'd been replaced with a Cylon. None of it made any sense, and it set me crying all over again. I found my way to a back hallway. To the cement stairs outside the drama room. There was a good view of the pine forest that snuggles the left side of the school there, and the stairs were usually empty. Not today, though. Apparently, Chloe Baskins came here for her nicotine fix. It was too late. She'd already seen me.

"Don't let it—"

"Close," I finished. "I know."

The door locked behind you automatically if you didn't wedge a stick or piece of paper or something into the crack. My hand was on the door handle. A retreat seemed like the best possible idea.

"Hey, are you okay?" asked Chloe.

I froze. I couldn't very well walk away after she'd asked me a direct question, so I adjusted the stick she had tucked in the door and sat down beside her. The steps were hard, but it felt good to have something solid underneath me.

"Not really," I said.

She took a puff of her cigarette and blew a smoky breath at the pine trees. "Do you want to talk about it?"

I knew what kind of girl Chloe was. Debutante. Gossip. Annoyingly perfect, at least on the outside. But I also knew she was Melanie Jane's friend. And out here on the steps, hiding her cigarettes, she seemed like a different person. Like the kind of person you might actually want to talk to.

So, even though I shouldn't have, I did. I didn't tell her the whole story, just the skeleton. Enough for her to know what Chad did. That it wasn't my fault. And that I was worried about what Melanie Jane thought of me. She was a better listener than I expected.

"Do you think you could talk to Melanie Jane for me?" I asked, folding and bending my fingers into knots. I felt like I was one step away from having things get better, and I was desperate for any scrap of better I could get.

"Sure." She flicked her cigarette butt on the ground and dug her heel into it. "I'll do it today."

I should have known by her gentle smile and the delicate way she patted my shoulder. Chloe Baskins is not gentle. By the next day, half the school knew that I was trying to ruin the life of Chad MacAllistair, star receiver and all-around Boy Scout. That

Ranburne's chances at State might be torpedoed because some dumb slut did things while she was drunk and changed her mind the next morning. That was when everything really started to go to hell.

The missing purple panties showed up. I found them taped to my locker one morning, the words *Lying whore bitch* scrawled beside them in red. People were clustered all around, waiting to watch me find them. Faces twisted and mean like I was surrounded by fun-house mirrors instead of actual humans. I couldn't take them down, much as I wanted to. The people or the panties. Seeing them again dragged me back into the nightmare, so I ran away crying. I'm sure it was everything the vultures were hoping for. I hid out in the old tree house where the guys and I used to have campouts. I didn't want to explain to my mom why I was home from school. Grayson found me after. He had cleaned up my locker for me. He sat beside me for a long time, but we didn't speak. I was done telling people what happened.

A video surfaced. Me dancing with Chad. All blurry like it came from a drunk guy's phone. And the video, well, I'll admit it. It looked bad. I was dancing all over him and grinding. No wonder Melanie Jane wouldn't talk to me. No wonder people believed him. It didn't change the truth. I wanted to dance with him after he gave me that shot. Probably *because* he gave me that shot. But I didn't want any of the things that came after. Unfortunately, I was alone in this belief. So, I quit. I quit the cheerleading squad. I quit trying in school. I quit life for a while. At some time I can't pinpoint, the days started getting easier instead of harder.

Now I have a chance to do something about what happened. Stealing the football—I feel like it could be something bigger. It's why I'm not about to let anyone give up.

Things that haven't gotten us any closer to stealing the Football of '76:

- Melanie Jane's attempts to wheedle the trophy case key out of Coach Fuller
- Spying on the Varsity initiation ceremony (though, let's be honest, I did feel some shivers when we made that vow at the end)
- Flirting with boys at parties (I can't believe any of us thought that was going to work to begin with)

Getting that breakup list hasn't been going so well either. We know it exists, and we know it's in an email, but since none of us are hackers, all that knowledge adds up to jack squat. I'm starting to get worried. Without a clear plan, everyone is losing steam. Well, everyone except me. After I saw what they did to Grayson, I knew I couldn't let this thing die. Besides, if I don't think of a way to boost morale soon, Liv might do something crazy like try to seduce Chad.

So, as guilty as it makes me feel going to Toby again, that's what I've got to do. Today we're doing the one-minute version of *Game of Thrones*, episode 4, which means jousting, which means all the boys are acting like they're twelve years old. Isaiah screams, "The seed is strong!" over and over. Grayson's running around shirtless, but you can't see the marks they gave him anymore. Not on the outside anyway. I tuck stray wisps of black hair under a silver wig because we're supposed to film the Daenerys clip next. If I can ever get them to stop jousting, that is.

Grayson comes over and bumps me with his hip. "I still think I look way more like Princess Daenerys than you."

I fix him with a regal glare. "You dare to question the Mother of Dragons."

"Okay, okay," he laughs. "That was good. I'll give it to you. Maybe not Grayson-level good, but we can't all be me."

Now it's my turn to laugh. It's weird, though, laughing with Grayson when what I really want to do is ask him if he's okay. I haven't mentioned anything since the day I drove him home, but every time we're together now, it's like the air is full of unasked questions.

"Hey, Grayson . . . ?"

He looks at me, but I hadn't really figured out the stunning conclusion to that sentence.

"I'm okay," he says, throwing an arm around my neck and giving me a squeeze. "Thanks for asking."

Then he runs back into the jousting frenzy.

I have to wait for them to take a water break before I catch Toby alone. "Hey, Tobes, how's it going?"

He goes on about his new girlfriend for a while. I tell him

he should bring her around next time we're taping because she sounds pretty cool. After an appropriate amount of conversation, I ask what I really want to know: "Are you going out with the football team the night of the scavenger hunt?"

He frowns. "I told you, I don't get to do stuff like the scavenger hunt. Water boy, remember? Second-class citizen."

"Well, I thought you might still be hanging out with the older guys. Don't they usually party at some of the stops on the hunt? Like at one of those places where they line dance?"

"I don't know." He suddenly looks hopeful. "Yeah, maybe they'll ask me."

"Cool. So do you know where any of this year's stops will be?" I pretend like my complete focus is on my stage makeup, like the answer to my question is the least of my concerns.

"Why do you care?"

Oops. Maybe Grayson's right and my acting could use some improvement.

"I don't. Some girl in my first-period class *desperately* wants to go, and when I told her I might have a friend who could tell us, she about peed herself, so I felt like I had to ask you."

"Oh." Toby sits taller, pleased to think of himself as a football insider. "That's kind of cool. Well, I know they're pregaming at some fraternity at Vanderbilt. And then they're going to be at this country bar, The Jackrabbit Saloon, that lets teens in—that's where the cheerleaders and people are meeting them."

This I already know. Melanie Jane has been complaining

about how she's obligated to go, and she doesn't feel like dealing with Weston following her around like a puppy. Or stalker.

"Anywhere else?" I ask.

"Well, they always end it at this strip club out in Slocomb that doesn't card." He laughs. "Apparently, there's this stripper who's older than dirt that guards the football. I don't think your friend is going to want to go to that though."

I laugh too. "Yeah, probably not. I'll let her know about the bar thing though."

Toby has given me exactly what I needed. There is a window of opportunity when the Football of '76 is not in the trophy case or the ham-like hands of a football jock. I seriously doubt any girls from our high school would dare show up at that strip club. Any girls but us.

Saturday, September 12
MELANIE JANE

Another date with Michael, another day of sneaking down the driveway to his car so I don't have to tell my parents about him. I've heard that a frog will let you boil it to death in a pot of water. Not if you throw it right in the boiling pot—then it hops out. But if you put it in warm water, and then turn up the heat by degrees, it's like it doesn't realize what's happening, and it sits there until it's cooked. Sometimes, I worry that getting more comfortable around Michael means I'm the frog.

It's not that I don't still get the jitters around him—I do. Oh man, do I get them. But that reinforced concrete surrounding my heart? It's cracking. And so is my resolve. I go whole hours now forgetting the pain that comes with caring. Forgetting how dangerous it is to let someone near your fragile insides.

Tonight we're going to see a movie. Some kind of action-y superhero one. Totally safe. Plus, there isn't much choice when there's only one movie theater in town and it only has three screens. It's opening weekend, and I forget what that means until we walk into the main lobby, and everyone from our high school is either waiting in line for popcorn, or gossiping by the new release posters, or in the bathroom putting on makeup. It's not like I've been keeping Michael a secret—anyone with eyes can see us talking in the hall and stuff—but I haven't exactly told people about him either. A fact I become very aware of when we pass by a cluster of cheerleaders, and Chloe nudges Beth and whispers something into her ear.

We find our theater and watch the previews before the previews—the random, boring stuff when the lights are on and it's still okay to talk. Michael's hand finds mine as soon as we sit down, like it's the most normal thing, like that's where my hand is supposed to fit. I lean into him while I tell him about this Halloween project I'm helping out with for Friday Morning Fellowship. He's stroking the back of my hand, and the water in the pot is bubbling all around me, and I'm thinking maybe we're strong enough to survive my parents knowing about us. Maybe I'll tell them when I get home tonight.

"So, what religion are you?"

"Huh?" I realize he is asking me a question. "Oh. I'm a Christian. What about you?"

"I'm Jewish."

"You are?"

"Yeah, are you okay with that?"

"Of course I am."

Outside, I am smiling and calm. Inside, not so much. I don't care that he's Jewish. I secretly wished for a Jewish best friend growing up so she could teach me all the cool Yiddish words. But my family—we're Baptists. And not just on Christmas and Easter. It's every Sunday and every Wednesday and random other days of the week when my mom decides the less fortunate need more casseroles and baked goods. I was going to tell Mama and Daddy tonight, and oh my gosh, how am I going to tell Mama? She thinks our neighbors across the street are pagans, and they're *Catholics*. Just last week she was telling me how she thought she heard them sacrificing cats to Mary in their basement—because didn't you know that's what those Catholics do for fun?

The theater goes dark, and the future of our relationship right along with it. I am so screwed.

I have no idea what happens during the movie because my brain is chasing itself in circles. And it only gets worse when I realize I have half a dozen texts from the cheerleading squad asking who I'm on a date with.

Afterward, they jump me in the bathroom. Not the cut-a-bitch-take-your-Coach-bag kind of jumping. The cheerleader kind. It is much scarier.

"Hey, Mel-Jay, who's the new guy?" asks Chloe.

She and Beth appear in mirrors on either side of me like a planned ambush.

"He's just a guy. He's Michael." The girl in the mirror's cheeks turn pink, and I curse her for giving so much away.

Beth smirks. "Now we know why we've hardly seen you lately."

"Is he your *boyfriend*?" Chloe draws out the word like we're in seventh grade.

"No. Not yet, anyway. We've only been on, like, three dates."

Aubrey joins us at the sinks. "How come you didn't tell us

about him?" She says "us," but she means "me." Even if I didn't want to tell Chloe and Beth, why did I keep it from her?

"I'm sorry." And I mean it. She's a good friend. "It's just Weston and I just broke up, and he's being kind of weird and jealous."

"But he broke up with *you*," says Beth.

"I know, right?" I shake my head like his craziness is sooo beneath me. "So anyway, I'm trying to be chill about stuff with Michael so he doesn't completely flip out or something."

Deflecting the gossip mill onto Weston is definitely the best strategy. Especially since everything I'm saying is true.

Aubrey squeezes me to her by the shoulder. "Well, you're off the hook for the past couple of weekends since you've got a new guy, but you have to hang out with us on the scavenger hunt. No squelching."

"I promise," I say. I'm sure I'll have plenty of time after we get the football. Plus, having an alibi can only be a good thing. I hug her back and hope she gets the message: *I really am sorry I didn't tell you. You're not like the others, I promise.* "I better go, though. He's probably wondering where I am."

Michael waits by the water fountain, grinning when he sees me. "Did you fall in?"

I roll my eyes, but I'm smiling. "No. Some girls from the cheerleading squad wanted to talk to me."

We walk to his SUV, the stars overhead twinkling like they're exchanging messages in Morse code. He stops at the bumper instead of moving to the door. He runs his fingers over the waves in his brown hair. Once. Twice. I wonder why he's so—kissing! He's finally going to kiss me. Three dates is an eternity when it comes to waiting to be kissed and, as a lady, I never kiss first. I've had so much time to obsess and imagine. Will he be gentle and hesitant or will the waiting unleash a torrent of passion? Would he mind if I ran my fingers through his hair because it looks so very soft and I have been dying to do that? Ana told me they call that *cafuné* in Brazil. I don't care what it's called as long as I get to *cafuné* the crap out of him while he kisses me. The cautious side of me whispers that the kiss will turn me into a lovesick zombie—a sort of reverse Sleeping Beauty effect. I ignore her and take a step closer. Tilt my chin up ever so slightly. *It's okay. You don't have to be nervous. I want this.*

He opens his mouth, but nothing comes out. Aw. He's about to ask permission. That is adorable.

"Melanie Jane?"

"Yes?" I say in a voice that is not unlike one of those breathless damsels.

"Is it a problem that I'm Jewish? You've been different since I told you."

I think my mouth is hanging open. I shut it. Yep, it was definitely open. "No, it's not a problem at all." I rush to get the words out because the waiting looks like it's killing him by degrees. "I mean, it's not a problem for me, but . . . I haven't actually told my parents about you yet."

"Is that why you always tell me to wait at the bottom of the driveway?"

I nod. "My mom is such a control freak. My boyfriend from eighth grade wasn't good enough for her because his parents didn't own half of Nashville. I don't want to think about how she'll react to this. She's, like, the queen of the country club and volunteering at church and stuff."

"Yeah, I'm nervous about my mom too. She's the stereotypical Jewish mom." I look at him vacantly, and he smiles. "That means she's a control freak too. She wants me to marry a nice Jewish girl and have a billion grandchildren."

A wave of relief radiates through my body. "You know, it makes me feel better to hear that. Like, at least I'm not the only one. I know she cares about me, but she forces me to do all this stuff, and sometimes I feel like she's trying to live vicariously through me."

We swap stories about our crazy moms until I feel much better. I still have no idea how to tell my parents, but at least there are no longer ulcers forming in my stomach.

Michael shoots me a sly glance. "You looked so shocked when I asked you. I thought you were going to pass out or something."

"I wasn't—I just. That wasn't what I was expecting to happen." How do I always end up a stuttering mess around him?

"What were you expecting?" The sly smile is back, and suddenly he's standing so very close, and my skin tingles from all the places he could be touching but isn't yet. "This?"

His lips touch mine, and his hand slides behind my back, and I forget to analyze how good a kisser he is. I forget that we're standing in the middle of a parking lot with half the student body of Ranburne High. Forget to worry about telling my parents about us. I forget everything but the press of my body against his and this moment and his tongue parting my lips and the feeling that if he let go of me right now, I'd float away like a helium balloon. My fingers find the back of his neck and then his hair and, oh my gosh, it is every bit as soft as I thought it would be. I am totally the girl making out in public against the back of a car. It is completely unlike me, and I don't care. Being a lovesick zombie feels good.

A horn blares right next to me, and my heart nearly stops. Michael and I jump apart. A Ford Bronco with Weston riding shotgun peels past us, him glaring as one of his friends burns rubber out of the parking lot.

"Who's that?" asks Michael.

"He's no one," I say. "We used to date, but it's over now, so he's no one." I wrap my arms around him and pull him into another kiss because this moment isn't over until I say it is.

RANBURNE PANTHER SCAVENGER HUNT

In Ranburne:

1. ~~Fill a condom up with water. Draw a face on it. Put it on Principal Corso's doormat, and ding-dong ditch. (One person)~~

2. ~~The egg-on-a-string trick. Hang an egg from a power line by a string and watch a car run into it. (Everyone)~~

3. ~~Paint the David Bowie statue at Old Lady Howard's corn maze. (Everyone)~~

4. ~~Chair race through Walmart. (Everyone)~~

5. ~~Get a picture of the team with the Ranburne Panther. (Everyone)~~

6. ~~Go to the Dawsonville football field. Find that stupid rock they touch before their games. Pee on it. (Everyone)~~

In Nashville:

7. ~~Visit the illustrious Delta Tau Beta fraternity at Vanderbilt. Have a beer with Panther alum TJ McNeil and take a picture of the legendary scar he got during a game-winning play against Dawsonville. (One person)~~

8. Go to LP Field and reenact the "Music City Miracle." (Everyone)

9. Go to Centennial Park and jump into the pond behind the Parthenon. (Everyone)

10. ~~Go to The Jackrabbit Saloon. Walk to the very middle of the dance floor and attempt to do the worm. (One person)~~

11. ~~Go up to a girl who is totally out of your league, get down on your knees, and ask her to marry you. (One person)~~

12. Go up to a fat girl and tell her "You're so beautiful . . . for a fat chick." Bonus points if she throws her drink on you. (One person)

13. ~~Hug a biker. Bonus points if he has a mullet. (One person)~~

14. ~~Get a girl to give you her thong. (One person)~~

DARES REMAINING: 3

1:05 A.M.

LIV

Peyton, Ana, and I are at the edge of the dance floor, at a table made out of a barrel, watching Melanie Jane's drama unfold. Apparently, girls sitting still is the universal signal for every loser in the bar to come over and harass us because that is what happens. I am irritated with all of boy-kind.

An unsuspecting football player stumbles over and asks if any of us are wearing a thong he could have—they seem to be having trouble with that one.

"I'm doing this scavenger hunt thing," he explains.

He must not realize who I am. I don't have the patience for this.

"Sorry, sweetie. I don't wear underwear because I'm a huge whore, remember?" Not actually true. I have on undies, with a back and everything.

His eyes go huge as he backs away. Peyton and Ana raise their eyebrows at me. I don't usually lash out at people like that. I don't usually want to.

"Sorry," I say. "I'm just frustrated with getting hit on by weirdos. And with the football team in general."

I snag Ana's camera from across the table and start recording. Nothing in particular, at first. Some people dancing. A lady wearing cowgirl fringe and not in the ironic way. The table's centerpiece, which happens to be a jaunty raccoon eating Cracker Jacks. The camera somehow ends up zooming in on Trevor. All on its own, of course. I'm not so lame as to creepily film my ex-boyfriend. Just because he hasn't come over to talk to me, and I thought he would have by now, and who cares! Certainly not Trevor. And I don't want to talk to him anyway!

Some skeezy-looking guy has taken the empty barstool next to Ana and seems to be feeding her obscene pickup lines, so I sneakily angle the camera in that direction instead. She notices, and it's like I can see something click behind her eyes.

She turns toward the skeezy guy who is right in the middle of saying, "I'm hot. You're hot. It only makes sense that we should go dance together right now."

"You *are* really hot," Ana says like it's just dawned on her.

The guy freezes as if sudden movements will make her change her assessment, but then he gets this annoying, cocky grin. "You think I'm hot?"

Ana nods. "Super hot . . . for an asshole."

"BOOM!" I close the camera as he wanders off, mumbling something that sounds suspiciously like *bitch*. "That was the last bar one! And it was awesome! How did you think to do that?"

Ana flicks imaginary dirt off her shoulder. "Just naturally gifted."

"We better get Melanie Jane and go. We still have two more, and we have to drive to both of them, and I don't want the boys to beat us!"

I don't have to do any convincing. They can taste victory too. We rush over to where Melanie Jane is helping Michael clean up his pants.

"We have to leave. Now," says Ana.

It is clearly not a good time for Melanie Jane. "Right now?"

"Sorry, sweetie." I put my arm around her. "But we finished everything we needed to do here."

Her eyes spark. "Seriously?"

Peyton grins. "We're so close."

"Okay." Melanie Jane is back to business. She turns to Michael, an apology on her face. "I'm sorry, but I really have to go now. And I'm sorry about the thing with the thong." She cringes. "And also about your pants."

"It's okay," he says, holding her hands. "It was the most interesting night I've had in a long time. And you're definitely worth it."

Peyton, Ana, and I collectively sigh because damn. And then he pulls her into a kiss so fierce and hot I have to turn away for fear I will catch on fire. Someday, I'll get kissed like that again.

As if I've called him into my presence by thinking of passionate kisses, Trevor is suddenly standing beside me.

"You're not leaving, are you? I've been so busy with scavenger hunt stuff, but I really wanted to talk to you."

"Um." I estimate that I have at least two minutes until the

lovebirds next to me are finished. "Can you make it fast?"

"Oh. I guess so." He runs a nervous hand through his blond hair. Steers me away from the rest of the group. "It's just that the season doesn't have that many weeks left, and I miss you so much, and I was hoping, soon, maybe we could go on a date? Or I could just call you. Whatever you want."

He does care! Maybe it's not the thong-wearing, drinks-down-your-pants level of caring, but maybe it is. Maybe I won't know unless I give him another chance. I think about the email. It was clear he didn't want to hurt me, that he did love me. But he wasn't strong enough to keep fighting for me. Is he strong enough now?

Before I can give him an answer, Chad saunters over and slaps him on the back so hard he starts coughing.

"Hey, there, Trev. What have I told you about talking to this girl?"

Ugh. And speaking of the email, I can't see Chad without wanting to cause him bodily harm because of all the things he wrote.

"Oh, um . . ." Trevor's eyes dart back and forth between us, but I don't want to see who wins this tug-of-war.

Nothing has changed. They still own him. The seedling of hope sprouting in my chest dies.

"I'll see you later," I say sadly.

"No, Liv, wait!"

He chases after me, completely ignoring Chad's continued

heckling. I wonder how he'll pay for that later.

"I'm sorry. Just ignore him. It doesn't change what I said."

"Now's not a good time. Maybe later, okay?" His face says he wants to argue. Over his shoulder I see Weston attempt to drive-by hug one of the bikers. A chair is flipped. Punches are thrown. I point in their direction. "You should probably go see about your boy."

9

Friday, September 18

PEYTON

tap my pencil against my desk while Coach Mayes passes out the quiz sheets. I studied so hard, and I'm itching to get started before all that knowledge up and evaporates. The first question is an easy one, and I breeze through it. Every time a problem starts to trip me up, I just imagine Rey's calm voice explaining the angles.

It's going great until Coach Mayes steps out of the room. That's when Casey and Nate start whispering—first about what they think the answers are, and then about Angelica Davies's sudden change in cup size.

"I don't care how big they are," says Nate. "You can always see her nipples through her shirt."

Casey snorts. "And this is a bad thing, why?"

"Because they're always going in different directions, and it freaks me out. Like one'll be pointing north and the other'll be going southeast." Nate mimes multidirectional nipples with his fingers. "It's creepy."

I have to work extra hard to block out *that* mental picture, and even harder when Casey decides it would be a good idea to flick rolled-up balls of paper at me. I have to reread question six about eighty billion times—it'll be a miracle if I get it right. Somehow, I finish and even have time to check my work before Coach Mayes gets back and calls time.

"We're going to spend the rest of the day on the library computers. There are some interactive geometry games I want to show you guys."

Everyone races to get their stuff together because library time pretty much means free-for-all. I hang back.

"Hey, Coach?"

He shuffles the quizzes into a neat stack. "What's up?"

"I was wondering. Is there any way you could keep Casey from bugging me? Like, especially during quizzes and stuff? It makes it really hard to concentrate, you know?"

"I can take care of that. Sure thing. You don't need to go tattling on me again." He's grinning like it's a joke, but there is most definitely a flicker of annoyance in his eyes.

"All right." I feel good, but also a little uncomfortable. "Thanks, Coach."

I go to the library and find an open computer and start following the instructions on the handout. Casey plops down beside me and starts checking his email. I wait for the inevitable. It doesn't take long.

"Hey, Church Girl, I mean, Peyton. Hey, Peyton."

I resist banging my head against the keyboard in front of me, but seriously, if I have to sit through Casey talking to me for the rest of the class, someone is going to need to put me out of my misery. I look around for Coach, but he's on the other side of the room grading our quizzes.

"Hi, Casey," I say in the most bored, sarcastic voice I can manage, which for me isn't saying a whole lot.

"So, what do you think of—"

Smack! One of those little foam footballs beans Casey in the back of the head and ricochets around between the table and computers.

"What the hell?!"

We both turn around to see Nate and Brian duck behind one of the bookshelves laughing.

"Oh, you're gonna pay," Casey half yells because apparently, football players are exempt from using indoor voices in the library, along with everything else. He grabs the football and chases after them.

Saved.

I take a deep Casey-cleansing yoga breath, and stretch my neck from side to side. That's when I notice the screen of Casey's computer. His email account is still open. My fingers twitch against my keyboard. I could probably find The List. Right now. I'm sure it's still there. A guy who has—I glance at his screen again—1,486 unread emails probably didn't delete it. Just thinking about it makes my heart beat itself practically to death against my chest. What if he catches me? What then? I do this combination flip-my-hair-over-my-shoulder, turn-my-head-and-look-at-him move that I'm sure is the very opposite of stealth. He's still on the other side of the library, engaged in an all-out war with Brian and Nate. The football flies over five stacks of books and disappears, and the boys chase after it. This is my shot.

I slide into his chair and spend two blank seconds that feel like an eternity staring at his screen and freaking out because I have no idea what to do next. It's not like I can wrinkle my nose and the email will magically appear. I take a deep breath. A search. I can search for it. Yes, I've used email searches before. I can do this. A low giggle that is not altogether sane escapes me as I type LIV into the search window and click ENTER. It's searching! This is so exciting! I am totally a spy! I check over my shoulder again to make sure I won't be a dead spy, but the boys are still occupied. Pelting each other with a football and objects found around the library requires a lot of attention.

A few hits come up, including one with THE LIST as a subject line. Well, that was easy. I click on it, and skim for the part about

LIV. LIV LAMBROS. THIS SLUT HAS HAD SEX WITH MORE GUYS IN MORE PLACES—

I cringe. This is it, all right. I start to click FORWARD. No, wait! That leaves a trace! I open my own email and copy and paste the message into a new email instead. I feel like I'm taking forever. I hope no one's watching me. I type in LIV, and her email address comes up, but as I move the mouse over the SEND button, it's like my finger doesn't want to press it. *Should I really be sending this to her? The things in this email are horrible. What if she reads it and—*

"Hey, Peyton!"

Uh-oh. It's Casey. I hit SEND and then close both our emails, and not a moment too soon because he's right behind me.

"What are you doing?"

"Huh?" I blink up at him with wide, innocent eyes. "Oh, sorry, I thought you were done. I closed your email. My computer was being funny, so I wanted to check my email on yours."

I can't believe how calm my voice is. It's like listening to someone else talk who isn't freaking out. I hope he can't see my hands shaking.

"Oh, that's okay." Casey grins at me. "You can use anything of mine you want."

And then, I kid you not, he looks pointedly at his crotch. There is some kind of justice in it being his email that we finally used to get The List.

"Awesome," I say in a voice that clearly means it is anything but.

"Pack it up. Let's go," barks Coach Mayes over the not-at-all-quiet-anymore library.

Everyone gets their stuff, including Nate and Brian, who didn't sit in front of a computer for a single minute of the library visit, and who are getting away with it because life isn't fair. Coach Mayes catches Casey by the shoulder, and I'm so surprised, I trip, and Jimmy Ferraro runs into me.

I wait for Coach to say something about Casey bothering me during class, but instead he says, "I need to talk to you about one of your answers on today's quiz."

Oh. Oh, *wow*. Did he catch him having the same answers as Nate or something?

"I don't think you understood what I was asking with question number three. I just want to make sure you get it."

"Thanks, Coach."

Casey grins, and I get the feeling this has happened before.

Friday, September 18
LIV

When I check my phone between classes, there's an email from Peyton. Subject line: The List. Ohmygosh, is she serious?! I open it. She is! She totally got The List! I feel like doing a victory dance in the middle of the hallway. And then I read a couple of sentences, and my stomach drops. I can't read this at school. Not unless I want to look like I spent last night binge-watching *The Notebook*. So I spend the rest of the day taking out my phone and staring at the email I can't read. Opening it. Closing it. Reconvincing myself that saving it for later is the best policy.

And then, because it's a football bye week, I have to go to dance team practice even though it's a Friday. Peyton asks me if I've read it, and when I tell her no, she says I have to call her when I do. Before I do anything drastic. As if *I* would ever do anything drastic. Although, if I don't get to read this freaking email soon, I just might.

And it gets worse. Because when my mom picks me up, she announces we're all going to family dinner together at the restaurant on the way home. My phone is burning a hole in my pocket, but I have promised myself I am only reading this email in my bedroom, all alone, on my laptop, ideally with a metric ton of chocolate on hand. The seconds tick by with painful slowness while my brother and sister attempt to use silverware like civilized humans and my mom asks me questions about school and stuff. I have no idea what I tell her. All I can think about is getting home. *I AM NOT GOOD AT DELAYED GRATIFICATION, PEOPLE!*

By some kind of miracle, I finally get back to my bedroom and barricade my siblings out. I open the email, and also a square of extra dark with sea salt, just to be safe. And I read.

Gentlemen,

A new school year is upon us, and a new crop of Varsity players is chomping at the bit to get on the field. And you know what that means. It's time for The List.

We have certain standards here at Ranburne High, and while I'm sure you all thought you were hot shit when you were on JV, you're not. You turds don't know shit about shit, and you definitely don't know shit about women, which is why we have to help you out every year by making certain you're not dating fat, ugly losers. We just want you to live up to your potential, gentlemen. We do this because we care.

1. Abby Clayton. I'm pleased to see we only have one whale to spear this year. Greg, we have a rule on this team—no one is allowed to date a girl fatter than Coby's girlfriend. (He likes his girls thick, and she has an ass

kind of like Beyoncé's, so we let it slide.) Greg, your girlfriend does not have an ass like Beyoncé's. She has an ass that is 50 percent cottage cheese and 50 percent bacon grease, and every time she wears shorts I throw up in my mouth a little bit. Seriously, whenever I see her eating (which is often), I lose my appetite. Greg, you are embarrassing us all, so I'm only gonna say this once. Spear. The. Whale.

Everyone knows fat girls don't have feelings because their blubber insulates them, so just dump her and get it over with. If you give her a gallon of ice cream as a parting gift, she probably won't even care.

2. Natalie von Oterendorp. Jacob, let me be honest here. Your girlfriend's face looks like a Proactiv before-picture. Now if it were just that, I'd say buy a paper bag and be done with it, but it's not just that, Jacob. It's a lot of things. So many things I think you must be trying to piss me off on purpose. She's in the band. Her teeth need their own zip code. She wears Winnie-the-Pooh sweatshirts. For God's sake, the girl snorts when she laughs. You need to break up with her, stat, in case whatever she has is contagious. And speaking of contagious . . .

3. Liv Lambros. This slut has had sex with more guys in more places than Casey's mom in the '80s. (Sorry, Case,

your mom told me about her groupie days the last time she was drunk.) I wouldn't even get in a hot tub with her for fear of catching something the CDC has yet to identify. There's slutty-hot and there's slutty-gross, and this girl is GROSS. Trevor, you need to break up with this walking cesspool of venereal disease. Quickly. Like before your dick falls off.

4. Carrie Sullivan. There is nothing inherently wrong with Carrie. She's a freshman cheerleader. She's pretty. She wears those adorable little necklaces with the owls on them. She is also Big Tom's little sister. And given the size of Big Tom's neck, I have to ask, Mason, are you a fucking idiot? No, really, I'm going to need you to email me back with the number of hits you took to the head on JV last year because I think you might be brain-dead. Did you really think you could hit on Carrie at the field party last weekend without Big Tom finding out? Whenever a guy flirts with Carrie, she goes on and on about it at dinner, so if you do it again, Big Tom will know, and the only way you'll be eating dinner for the rest of your life is through a tube.

That goes for all you assholes. Stay away from Carrie Sullivan because I can't be held responsible for what Big Tom does to your face after.

Honorable Mentions

Danny—Your girlfriend is not a whale. Yet. But she's only a few cheeseburgers away, so if you like her, I suggest you put that fatty-in-waiting on a diet. Get her to go running with you. Make her eat a few salads. Hell, I don't care if she throws up her food in the bathroom as long as I don't have to watch her stomach get any bigger. Do this for me, buddy. I don't want to have to break out the spears.

Weston—You're dating one of the hottest sophomores in school. Congrats. But you really need to get laid already. And until you do, you can give us weekly updates on the progress you're making. Thursdays after practice will be "Weston's Adventures in Losing His Virginity" time, during which Weston will stand on a bench in the locker room and regale us with how much closer he has gotten to melting the icicles on Melanie Jane's snatch. Weston, I hope for your sake you have a blowtorch.

Hugs and kisses,

Your Team Captain

I don't get angry, and I don't cry. Not at first, anyway. Because what I've just read is so over-the-top that all I can do for the first few minutes is stare at my laptop with my mouth open. My tongue starts to dry out, so I close my mouth and stare some more. I start over at the beginning, the coating of shock beginning to crack and fall away in tiny pieces, and then I feel it. RAGE. And hurt. And a squishy feeling in my stomach because the whole thing is so disgusting.

I'm tempted to do about fifty things at once: forward the email to every girl in school, call Carrie and explain to her why she's never had a boyfriend, find Chad MacAllistair and punch him in the balls. But even as my mind reels with possibilities, I realize there's more. It's a whole chain of emails. I steel myself for whatever horror is coming next, but when I scroll down, the next email is from Trevor.

Hey, guys,

I think there's been some kind of mistake. My girlfriend's not a slut. So, I'm just going to keep dating her because I'm kind of in love with her :)

Trevor

He did stick up for me! He even told them he was in love with me! I'm happy for a second, but I know how this story ends, so I swallow it down and read on.

Trevor,

That is so adorable that you actually think you get a say in this. You don't. I'm really glad you sent that email, though, because it's always good to make an example early in the season. You're going to break up with that skank, and you're going to do it soon. I don't want this to get ugly.

Chad

There's a reply email from Trevor time-stamped just a few minutes later.

Yeah, I'm not breaking up with her. It's my choice. What can you really do? Not invite me to all your parties? Fine with me. I'll just be at home hanging out with my hot-ass girlfriend.

Trevor

The email after that is just one line from Big Tom's address:

You'll find out at practice today.

And then the practice must have happened because there are all these one-line emails starting around 6:00.

How are your nuts feeling, Trev?

Did we break anything?

Your face sure does look prettier with a bruise on it.

There's a lot more where that came from.

I remember a practice a few weeks ago when Trevor had hobbled to my mom's car covered in bruises. He didn't want to talk about it, and I just assumed he had had an off day and was embarrassed, but now that gash under his eye seems so much more sinister. The next email from Trevor is later that night:

Is this really what it's going to be like?

And then the reply email from Big Tom:

It's going to be a thousand times worse.

He goes on to outline how Trevor will never get passes during the games, and they're not afraid to completely screw up his season unless he does what they want.

There's one last email, from Chad this time, playing the good cop.

We really don't want to do this to you, man. Just break up with her and you'll see how great everything can be when we've got your back.

I wish Trevor had felt comfortable enough to tell me all this instead of suffering alone. Especially since everything that was happening to him was because of me. Because of *them*, I correct myself. Everything bad that happened to him and to me begins and ends with the football team.

And suddenly I know exactly what to do, and I'm not waiting around for anyone to help me or talk me out of it. I text Peyton before I go.

Getting that key from Chad. Tonight.

Friday, September 18
ANA

"What did the text say?" I ask for the fiftieth time.

I pull out of the driveway, Peyton in the backseat and Melanie Jane riding shotgun.

"It said she was going to get the key from Chad tonight." I can see Peyton frowning in the rearview mirror. "I have a bad feeling about this."

You don't know the half of it. I get to the end of the street. "Where am I driving?"

"Big Tom's," says Melanie Jane. "They're having a field party at the back of the property. It's only fifteen minutes away."

"I'll have us there in ten."

A field party could be a good thing. No bedrooms. Not that that'll stop him. I shake my head. Everything's going to be okay. I'm going to get to that party before anything bad happens. I have to. But why did she insist on going over there alone? I didn't have any time to warn her. I sent her a text that said, STAY AWAY FROM CHAD. I'LL EXPLAIN LATER. But she never replied. He's probably giving her a shot right now, and she's Liv, so she's probably throwing it back with a laugh. I drive faster.

"Watch it, okay?" says Melanie Jane as I whip through a yellow light, kissing my fingers and pressing them to the roof of the car as the light turns red. She's biting her lip and watching me with this weird, pinched look on her face.

I don't have room to worry about her, though. Just Liv. That horrible day comes flooding back, and I see myself giggling with Melanie Jane and teasing her about being so completely over the moon about Chad MacAllistair. She was begging me to talk to him. So I did.

I left our circle of friends and walked around Casey's house until I found him. He was mixing drinks at a makeshift bar by the pool table in Casey's basement.

"Hi, I'm Ana," I said.

He looked up from his collection of bottles and grinned. "I'm Chad. Can I get you a drink?"

"Nah. I'm okay for now." I watched him pour juices and alcohols into a pitcher—the colors swirled together like someone stirring a sunset. "What are you making?"

"Sex on the beach." He winked at me, but in the nice way, not the creepy way.

"Sex on the beach!" yelled Casey beside him, and girls materialized from nowhere to have their cups filled.

"What's in it?" I asked.

"Orange juice, cranberry juice, vodka. Little splash of peach schnapps. My own special Chad MacAllistair magic. You sure you don't want one?" His eyes crinkled when he smiled, and they were the color of celery. "Hey, you're on the freshman cheerleading squad, right?"

"Mmm-hmm."

"You any good?" He tugged at my fingers playfully, and I pulled them away.

"Yes!" I said indignantly. "Are you any good at football?"

He laughed and slung an arm around my shoulders like we were conspirators in a plot I didn't yet know about. "I'm the best, baby. You keep an eye out for number twenty-four when you're cheering, okay?" His hand stayed on my shoulder, fingers running down the strap of my tank top.

Uh-oh. He thought I was here for me. I needed to fix that and fast. "My best friend is on it too. Melanie Jane Montgomery. Do you know her?"

He shook his head.

"You will. She's probably the prettiest girl in school." I wasn't exaggerating. The girl is stunning.

"Well, in that case, you should go get her and bring her down here, right, Casey?" He elbowed Casey, who nodded a furious agreement. "But first, you need to take a shot with us."

"Sure. Let me just go get my friend. We can all take one together." I started to move away from the bar, but he grabbed my hand.

"Noooo. You can't go yet. Just take one shot with us first, and then you can go get her. Please?" He put on a sad puppy face. "I'm about to make my specialty."

I shifted my weight to my other foot, wavering, and Casey took the opportunity to start up a chant of "Shots! Shots! Shots!" A couple of other guys joined in.

"What do you say, freshman?" asked Chad with a grin that really was as charming as Melanie Jane said.

"Okay. One shot. Then I'm going to get Melanie Jane."

"Success!" yelled Casey as Chad mixed the shots for us.

His hands flew from bottle to bottle. Other people approached the bar—Casey's cries of "Shots!" had attracted a crowd. Chad pulled out extra shot glasses that were hidden away underneath, and I tried not to think about their cleanliness.

"Done!" he said, expertly pouring so you could almost follow the line of liquid across the row of glasses.

He snagged the one on the end and handed it to me with a little flourish before grabbing a glass of his own. Hands fought their way in from every direction to get the others. We clinked our glasses and toasted to winning State this year. Chad caught my eye, and we downed our shots together. I coughed, narrowly winning a battle with my gag reflex.

"Ew, that was horrible. What's in this? Furniture polish?" I was so disgusted I forgot to be polite.

He just laughed, apparently unfazed by the shot. No one else coughed either, and I felt very much like the freshman at the bar even though I'd had alcohol before and thought it had tasted kind of okay.

"Here." He handed me a glass of orange juice. I swished it around in my mouth and resisted the urge to gargle with it.

"Whew. I really better go get my friend now."

But before I could move, a guy fell right at my feet. Not in the romantic way—he'd been decked. The biggest guy I'd ever seen jumped on top of him and kept punching. Casey started yelling, "Fight!" He's big on the chanting, that one. I stood there in shock as they flailed around on the floor in front of me, backing into Chad when the violence moved a little too close.

"Don't worry," he said. "It's not a party until Big Tom punches someone."

After a few minutes, they wore each other out. A tiny girl with curly hair convinced Big Tom to come upstairs with her. Another couple of girls brought the other guy some ice. I felt like I was about to do something before the fight. But someone turned on music, and it was loud. And intoxicating.

"I'm going to dance," I yelled to no one in particular.

I flew to the other side of the room where some girls had already started dancing and let the music carry me away. I was always a decent dancer, but never like this. This was like one of Nicki Minaj's backup dancers had taken over my body. I worked my way over to a support beam and danced around it like a pole. *Poles sure do make it easier to dance in these heels. Why don't I dance on poles all the time?*

Every boy in the room was staring.

"Slut," I heard one girl mutter to a friend. *Whatever, she's just jealous.*

Chad appeared from behind the jealous girl. "Chad!" I squealed, and grabbed his hand like we were old friends. "Don't you love this song? I freaking love this song!" I pulled him toward me because he had to experience the wonder that was dancing to this song. Right now. This perfect, irresistible, adrenaline-filled moment. At some point, someone turned on a strobe light. The people around me blurred together in the flashes. I tripped and almost fell. Chad caught me, but only just.

"Whoa, Ana. Let's go upstairs and get you some water, okay?"

"Water?" I screwed up my face like I'd been mortally insulted.

He grinned. "Well, at least let's go sit down or something."

I leaned against the support beam for a second, eyes shut. It helped with the dizziness. Sitting down did seem like an awfully good idea. I nodded.

"Cool." He scooped an arm across my back and helped me up one flight of stairs and then another. I only fell down a few times. *How am I so drunk right now?* He squeezed me even tighter to him after the last stumble. "I got you." His breath tickled my ear, and I giggled.

Somehow, he got me to the top floor, to a door at the end of the hallway and an empty bedroom. He let go of me to shut the door. Standing up by myself seemed incredibly difficult. He had to grab my arm to keep me from face-planting.

"Are you okay?" he asked.

"I don't . . . feel right."

"Here," he whispered. "Come sit down. You'll feel better."

He eased me onto the bed, and I let myself fall back into the pillows. The comforter was soft and warm. I pressed myself against it, shivering. This was better. My eyelids felt like they were coated in lead paint instead of shimmery powder. Keeping them open was too much of an effort. My head bobbed to one side. It was so very cold.

His voice in my ear. "You're gorgeous. You know that?"

His lips against mine, his tongue forcing my mouth open. Even through the haze, that didn't seem like a good idea.

"Hey, Chad." *When did talking get so hard?*

"Shh. I'll take care of you."

His mouth on mine again. Hands tearing under my shirt, pulling at my bra, pawing at me.

"Hey." I tried again, but this time my voice sounded even weaker.

My arms were heavy and dead. Legs too. A tremendous weight pressing down on me. Like being buried in sand or snow. I tried to move something, anything, but it was like the nerves connecting my brain to my body had been cut. Except not all of them. The ones telling me he was taking off my panties worked fine. I tried to scream. Tried again, forcing air past straining vocal cords. I think it came out as a moan. And then I think my eyes rolled back in my head. Which was maybe the best thing that could have happened. Or the worst.

The next thing I remembered was Melanie Jane standing over me. Chad was gone.

"Mel-Jay?"

I didn't understand. I tried to push myself up with my elbows, but I couldn't support my own weight. The room was still spinning. My eyelids fluttered. Consciousness fading in and out. A flash of her carrying me downstairs. A glimmer of the inside of her car. She must have taken me home and put me in my bed because that's where I woke up the next morning.

There was a trash can positioned on the floor next to my head and a half-empty water bottle tucked into the covers with me. I felt like I had been hit by a truck, and I couldn't find my underwear. From somewhere, the smell of vomit. Had I thrown up? I didn't remember throwing up, but my room smelled exactly the way my mouth tasted. How could this have happened? I only had one shot. And that's when it got worse. The pieces of the night before started to knit themselves together inside my head. I remembered more than I wanted. And also not enough. With each wave of details, I screamed the pain into my pillow. But they weren't telling me what I needed. I still didn't know. Did we have sex? I was sore, but did that mean—? I couldn't even think the words. It might make them true. I pulled my blanket over my head and tried to hide from my dangerous thoughts. I didn't get out of bed for the rest of the weekend.

"Is she here? Do you see her?" I jump out of the car with Peyton and Melanie Jane trailing behind me. "Split up so we have a better chance of finding her."

Melanie Jane puts a hand on my arm. "I'm sure everything's fine."

"No. No, it isn't. Not until we find her."

She opens her mouth like she wants to say something else but instead she just nods and heads toward the circle of truck beds in the middle of the field.

I peek in every car window—the ones outside the main circle—he'd have taken her somewhere secluded. Most of the cars are empty. Every once in a while I see half-naked bodies and flailing limbs. Luckily, Liv's hair is so blonde and so curly I almost never have to rap on the windows. It should make me feel better, but every time I spot a couple and realize it isn't them, my apprehension grows. What if he didn't take her to a car? What if they're in the woods somewhere? He could be doing anything to her right now, and we'll never be able to—

I get a tap on the shoulder and nearly have a heart attack. It's Peyton. And she's got Liv.

All the fear and dread and adrenaline I'm feeling crashes against a wall. I am made of skin and muscle again instead of electricity. I throw my arms around her and squeeze her so tight it probably hurts, but I don't care.

"You found her!"

I pull back to see Melanie Jane has joined us, but my focus is Liv.

"Are you okay? Did you drink anything he gave you?" I'm holding her hands and practically shaking them.

She gives me a puzzled look. "I'm fine. We were just talking when Peyton grabbed me and said there was something urgent she had to talk to me about."

She's fine. She's completely and totally fine. I crush her in another hug—I'm so relieved tears start melting out of my eyelids. Liv pats me on the back.

"I can take care of myself, you know. You guys didn't have to rescue me."

"Not with him. You have to promise me you'll never try this again. We don't need the key that badly." I lean back so I can look her straight in the eye. "Promise me."

She thinks I'm crazy. So do Peyton and Melanie Jane. They're all staring at me like I'm some kind of circus freak.

"I promise," says Liv, and the tension I'm feeling releases in one giant breath. "Did something happen with him?"

"Um." I wipe under my eyes with my fingers and hope my mascara isn't a mess. "I don't want to talk about it."

Peyton and Liv look to Melanie Jane like she's supposed to know how to fix me. She puts an arm around me like we're still best friends, and I don't flinch away. I let her lead me to a log at the edge of the tree line. And when we get there, I sit down and put my head in my hands and crumble into a sobbing, hiccupping mess.

"It seems like there's more to tonight than you're telling us," she says softly. "Is everything okay?"

She's looking at me so sincerely, and her eyes are red like she's about to start crying too, and even though she totally abandoned me and was partially responsible for ruining my life, I think about telling her. Because for a second, she isn't Melanie Jane Montgomery, Head Bitch in Charge of the Sophomore Class. For a second, it's last year, and she's my best friend, and I know if I tell her she'll listen and hug me and help me figure out the torrent inside me. But then I imagine her face when I tell her I don't know if Chad had sex with me that night. And I remember that it's not last year.

"Yes." I can't meet her eyes. "I mean, I guess it isn't really, but I just can't talk about it, okay?"

She waits like she's hoping I'll say something else, and when I don't, she hugs me, my first hug from her in a year. Having her arms wrapped around me is both strange and familiar. It's also kind of nice.

"Okay. But I'm here." She hesitates. "And I'm sorry."

She stands there watching me, her eyes so intense, like if she stares hard enough, she'll beam everything she's thinking right into my head and I'll understand her. I've tried to do that with people so many times over the last year. Which shows you how well it works.

She walks back to the others, and I follow behind her.

"I'm fine, you guys. Really. I just wanted to make sure Liv was okay, and she is, so everything's fine. Better than fine. I think I know how we're going to get that football."

There's a second of awkward silence where I can see them shift from wanting something more to being willing to let it go.

"Good." Liv pulls a few sheets of paper from her purse and slaps them into my hands. "Because I want that football more than ever."

We make our way back to my car and read The List huddled around my trunk under the glow of a flashlight. My dad makes me keep one in there as part of an emergency kit. The reading is accompanied by ranting and swearing and several instances of holding Melanie Jane back so she doesn't haul off and punch Weston. Or Chad. Or the first football player she runs into.

"Okay, well, what are we going to do?" she asks, her cheeks still flaming. "What's your big plan, Ana? Because I really need it to work this time."

"The scavenger hunt," I say. "During the scavenger hunt, the football is out of its case for the whole night. And . . ."—I pause to heighten the suspense—"the person who's guarding it is a woman."

"What?"

"No way."

"They'd never let anyone without a penis touch that thing."

"They would if she's a stripper," I say.

"You're not serious," says Melanie Jane.

"Oh, I am. The scavenger hunt ends every year at some middle-of-nowhere strip club between Ranburne and Nashville. They drop it off with this stripper at the start of the hunt, and it stays there while they're out running amok. If we go there after they leave, it'll be all alone and ready for the taking." I flash them a triumphant grin.

"Well, not all alone," says Liv. "The stripper will have it."

I shrug. "So, we'll ask her for it."

"Do you really think she'd give it to us?" asks Peyton.

"Sure. I mean, girl power and solidarity and all that. I know we can convince her."

"It's worth a shot," says Melanie Jane. "In fact, it's probably our last shot."

She's right, but that only makes me more determined. "Then we better make it count."

RANBURNE PANTHER SCAVENGER HUNT

In Ranburne:

1. ~~Fill a condom up with water. Draw a face on it. Put it on Principal Corso's doormat, and ding-dong ditch. (One person)~~

2. ~~The egg-on-a-string trick. Hang an egg from a power line by a string and watch a car run into it. (Everyone)~~

3. ~~Paint the David Bowie statue at Old Lady Howard's corn maze. (Everyone)~~

4. ~~Chair race through Walmart. (Everyone)~~

5. ~~Get a picture of the team with the Ranburne Panther. (Everyone)~~

6. ~~Go to the Dawsonville football field. Find that stupid rock they touch before their games. Pee on it. (Everyone)~~

In Nashville:

7. ~~Visit the illustrious Delta Tau Beta fraternity at Vanderbilt. Have a beer with Panther alum TJ McNeil and take a picture of the legendary scar he got during a game-winning play against Dawsonville. (One person)~~

8. Go to LP Field and reenact the "Music City Miracle." (Everyone)

9. Go to Centennial Park and jump into the pond behind the Parthenon. (Everyone)

10. ~~Go to The Jackrabbit Saloon. Walk to the very middle of the dance floor and attempt to do the worm. (One person)~~

11. ~~Go up to a girl who is totally out of your league, get down on your knees, and ask her to marry you. (One person)~~

12. ~~Go up to a fat girl and tell her "You're so beautiful . . . for a fat chick." Bonus points if she throws her drink on you. (One person)~~

13. ~~Hug a biker. Bonus points if he has a mullet. (One person)~~

14. ~~Get a girl to give you her thong. (One person)~~

DARES REMAINING: 2

1:30 A.M.

LIV

By the time we pass by the front of The Jackrabbit Saloon in Ana's car, Weston is being ejected by a bouncer and appears to have at least one black eye.

Melanie Jane claps her hands gleefully. "That'll slow them down."

"We still have two things left, though." Ana turns right at the light and floors it. "They could easily beat us."

I pull up the YouTube video of the Music City Miracle again so we'll know how to properly re-create it. Turns out it's some super important football play the Tennessee Titans made, like, a million years ago. I've got the play memorized. I know what our parts will be. We're all set. Until we get to the parking lot at LP Field and realize none of us thought to buy a football.

We decide Melanie Jane's Kate Spade clutch is the next best thing. We get to work reenacting the play (we can't actually get inside and run around on the Titans' field, but there's a nice stretch of grass between the stadium and the Cumberland River) while Ana videotapes.

Melanie Jane covers her eyes as I hold the clutch in front of me. "I can't believe I'm about to let you punt Kate Spade."

"Pay attention. You're going to have to catch that," says Ana. "We need to get this in one take."

My foot hits the bag, and it goes tumbling end over end through the air. Melanie Jane's eyes snap open, and she taps into punt-returner powers I never knew she had.

"Don't let it touch the ground," she shrieks like it's an American flag or something.

She rushes to get in position under the falling clutch, and in what really is a feat of miraculous proportions, she catches it. She slings it to Peyton, as per the video. Peyton catches it too—she's probably terrified of what Mel-Jay will do to her if she doesn't. Then, she sprints to the end of the grass and does a victory dance that I seriously doubt you would ever catch a Titan doing.

Ana rushes us back to her car and on to our last dare. The excitement in the car could power Nashville. We're so close. We can do this. Last. One.

Centennial Park closed hours ago, but we sneak in with our flashlights. We're power walking, then jogging, then full-on running by the time we pass the Parthenon. It's a full-scale replica of the one in Athens and the site of many a field trip. Lightning bugs flick on and off around us. At any given time, one of us is bursting into giggles, almost like we're playing a game of hot potato with our laughter.

The heat and moisture press at us from all sides. My clothes stick to my skin in patches.

"This is absolutely disgusting," Melanie Jane says. "I feel like I'm running through a cloud."

I pull my hair off the back of my neck. "It's going to feel so good to jump in that water."

"Do you think this is illegal?" Peyton almost whispers it, like if someone overhears, a SWAT team will jump out of the bushes and handcuff us.

"It's a public place," says Ana. "But it's after hours. So maybe. All the more reason to hurry."

"If we skinny-dip, it's public indecency." I grin, and Melanie Jane shakes her head.

"I'm not taking off my clothes."

When we see the pond, Peyton and Melanie stop, but Ana and I are already drifting toward it as if invisible fishing lines are reeling us closer. I kick off my sandals and break into a sprint, leaving pieces of clothing in my wake like a trail of bread crumbs inviting the rest of them to follow me. I leap through the air with a loud "Woo-hoo!" and make a huge splash. The water is so cool, I half expect to see steam rise from my hot skin with a hiss.

"You have to come in. This is exhilarating!" I call.

Melanie Jane grimaces. "Really? Because that water looks disgusting."

Ana reaches the water next, stripping off her clothes with military precision and using them as a pile for the camera to rest on as it captures our awesomeness. She keeps on her black bra and matching bikini-style bottoms and throws her hands in the air as she jumps in beside me. Melanie Jane removes her shoes a few yards away from the pond. We look up, interested to see if they're getting in.

"We don't have much time, and I'm not losing to Chad MacAllistair. I will drag the two of you in if I need to." Ana says it like she's joking, but I saw her face when she said his name. I didn't think it was possible to squeeze so much pure ferocity into five syllables.

When Melanie Jane starts to remove her skirt, Ana yells triumphantly, and I wolf whistle. She mumbles something about not being able to believe she's doing this, but I can see her smiling. She folds her skirt and top with perfect creases and daintily places them on top of her shoes, I'm assuming so they don't touch the ground. Then she sashays to the edge of the water and gracefully hops in with pointed toes and an almost imperceptible splash. I frolic around and try, unsuccessfully, to engage Ana in a splash fight.

"Peyton, are you coming in?" she asks.

"It really does feel amazing," chimes in Melanie Jane. "As long as you ignore the smell."

Peyton hovers at the edge of the pond like a skittish cat. "What if we get caught?"

I pause mid-flail. "By who? There's no one around. Don't worry."

"Just jump in and jump right back out." Ana wades over to the edge where Peyton is standing. "It'll only take a second, and then we'll be done with everything."

She hesitates and looks in every direction.

"C'mon," I say. "You can keep your clothes on if that's what you're worried about. You can even do the thing where you inch in by degrees. We won't judge."

A faux tough look settles on her face. "No. If I'm doing this, I'm doing it right."

After a moment where she appears to be having a silent argument with herself, she strips down to her underwear and jumps in after us.

I fling handfuls of water into the air like I'm throwing confetti. "Woo-hoo! We did it! We are the champions of the universe! We are golden goddesses of success! We are untouchable and amazing and 2,000 percent BADASS!"

The other girls laugh, but Ana frowns. "I just hope it's enough."

10

Saturday, September 26

A N A

I know more than I've ever wanted to about Chad MacAllistair. That he looks both ways before eating his boogers. That he thinks butt scratching is an Olympic sport, and he's going for the gold. That he will not, for the love of all that is holy, leave his freaking house and pick up the Football of '76 already. We have been staking him out for two hours, but it feels like several lifetimes. Even Liv looks dejected—she gave up cataloguing his questionable hygiene practices using my video camera and her best Animal Planet reporter voice forty-five minutes ago. Melanie Jane's binoculars sit on the floorboard of my car. We don't really need to watch him through his window. We just need to know when he leaves the house.

Which is apparently going to be *never*.

Liv cracks first. "I can't take this anymore!" she almost yells, effectively spiking everyone's blood pressure. "I am literally going to die of boredom. We're playing the questions game."

"What's that?" asks Peyton.

"It's where someone asks a question, and everyone else has to answer honestly." No one argues. It's not like we have anything better to do. "I'll start. If you could hook up with anyone—regular person, movie star, whatever, who would it be?"

"Austin Butler," says Melanie Jane without missing a beat. "He is six feet tall, and he is yummy."

Peyton turns pink. "Taylor Lautner. Or maybe that British diver. Chris Mears? Somebody with lots of muscles."

"I'd pick Hunter Hayes. I'm a sucker for musicians," says Liv. "What about you, Ana?"

I consider my options. "Anyone at all?"

"Anyone at all," says Liv.

That settles it. "Legolas."

Peyton giggles. "I think you mean Orlando Bloom."

"No, I'm pretty sure she means Legolas," says Melanie Jane.

I nod. "Yes. Only as Legolas."

"They are the same person," says Liv.

And then I have to explain to her how they aren't at all the same because long, blond hair and bow skills and *elf ears*, hello!

We get through almost an entire round before Chad's front door opens and we all have to duck.

Liv peeks up from the backseat. "There he is! Follow him! Follow him!"

"Try to keep at least a couple of cars in between you," says Melanie Jane. "And don't turn on your lights."

I raise my eyebrows. "It's daytime, champ."

"Oh, yeah."

We tail him to school, but that's where things get tricky. The parking lot is almost empty because it's a Saturday, and I can't risk him recognizing my car. We have to wait around the corner near the entrance for several agonizing minutes and hope when we see his car again that the football is inside it. We follow him to the highway, and he heads in the direction of Nashville. A very good sign. I try to keep a couple of cars between us while also keeping him in viewing range and ignoring "helpful" advice from the peanut gallery.

He eventually turns off at an exit that seems to have a truck stop and not much else. We pass by eighteen-wheelers, buildings with peeling paint and rust stains, dirt roads leading to nowhere. Even the trees out here look sad. Finally, at the top of a hill, shining like a beacon, is a tired neon sign that says CATCALLS. Chad pulls into the parking lot. I turn into the Wendy's next door, the only establishment nearby. Because nothing says strippers like a junior bacon cheeseburger. I park by the Dumpster and wait.

"He has it! He has the football! I can see it under his arm!" yells Liv.

Peyton claps a hand over her mouth and tackles her in the backseat, the two of them erupting in giggles. Melanie Jane and I exchange a glance that says "children."

Liv whips out the camera again and begins narrating. "Chad MacAllistair has just entered Catcalls with the Football of '76. Will he return? Will he stop to get a lap dance first? Will Liv's undeniable craving for a Frosty keep her from finishing this video?"

It only takes her a couple of minutes to get bored and turn off the camera.

"My turn for questions!" She taps a finger to her face like she's pondering one of life's great mysteries. "I know! Let's have the virgin talk. Who's had sex before?"

"I'm waiting till I'm married," says Melanie Jane primly. You can almost hear the judgment in every word.

Peyton fidgets in the backseat. "I had sex for the first time a few months ago."

I glance at her in the rearview mirror. Her eyes are on the floor. Liv wants to say something to her, I can tell, but she seems to change her mind.

"I've had sex with Trevor," she says. "And only Trevor."

She glares at the door of the strip club like she's trying to laser beam Chad with her eyes from the outside.

I can't answer this question. I don't know. I'll never know. I feel like someone tore away a piece of me without my permission. Does that mean I'm not a virgin? Maybe if I sit very quietly and don't make any sudden movements—

"Ana didn't answer! Spill! Spill!" Liv's squeals from the backseat are gleeful. She has no idea what this question is doing to me.

I open my mouth, but nothing comes out. What am I supposed to say? Maybe? I can't say that because then I'd have to explain why I don't know, and I can't do that right now. I could just say no. Refuse to give any details. Yeah, that's what I'll do. It's just a one-syllable word, only two letters, but I can't make myself say it.

"She's a virgin too," says Melanie Jane in a voice that says end of discussion.

"Um, okay, cool," says Liv. And half a second later, "Oh! There he goes!"

All talk of virginity is forgotten. I mouth the word *thanks* at Melanie Jane.

Chad doesn't have the football with him this time. We all know what that means, and we're pinging with excitement as we watch him drive away. I make everyone wait ten extra minutes, during which I think Liv will spontaneously combust, before we exit the car. Peyton stares up at the building like it will eat her alive. Melanie Jane's nose wrinkles like she can smell something the rest of us can't.

I throw out an arm between them and the front door. "Hold up. This isn't going to work. You." I nod to Peyton. "You look terrified. They're strippers, not vampires. And you." I turn to Melanie Jane. "If you go in there with your face twisted up all judgey-like, they're going to throw us out on our asses without helping us at all. Maybe Liv and I should go in by ourselves."

"What? No way. We're in this together. We all go." Melanie Jane's green eyes are hard, and I know from experience she won't budge.

I sigh. "Fine. But try to smile or something—isn't that what they teach you in pageants? And for heaven's sake, let me do the talking."

The girls adjust their faces, though to be honest, Peyton still looks pretty damn scared, and we enter the cement building with the painted-out windows. It's so dark inside, we have to stop to let our eyes adjust. Clusters of chairs and tables and two stages with poles start to take shape through the dim lighting and haze of smoke. A few men in trucker hats watch a half-naked woman gyrate to Def Leppard. I begin to think the strategic lighting is a good idea. Not being able to see the years of carpet stains is a good thing. Not being able to see their faces is even better. There's an all-day breakfast buffet. The bacon and eggs look and smell surprisingly good, and I've always been a big fan of brunch, but something about the combination of naked sweaty bodies and French toast seems unwise.

I squint across the room at the older woman wiping down the bar. I don't mean old like playing bridge in the nursing home, but she's definitely over forty. Which means she's like 250 in stripper years. I think she's who we're here to see. I lead the way across the room. A man at the back takes apart our bodies with his eyes, and I wish I had on a parka. The woman eyes us as we stop in front of the bar.

"Are you here for an audition?" Her washrag never stops moving. "You don't look old enough."

"We're not," I say. "We're actually here for something else."

I take in the lines around her tired eyes, the leathery skin of her arms. It's impossible to say how old she is. Whether time or sun damage or life or too many cigarettes has done this to her. I wonder if men were partly responsible. I wonder if that means she'll help us.

"We're looking for a football. We think a guy we go to school with just dropped one off."

I feel like a complete and total fool until she says, "Maybe he did."

"We'd—well, the thing is he—we were hoping—" I'm having trouble saying this in a way that sounds normal.

"We'd like you to give it to us," blurts Liv.

The rag stops. "Why would I do that?"

Melanie Jane steps up to the bar. To her credit, any trace of judgment has vanished from her face. "Because the football team is a bunch of jerks."

The girls fall all over each other, spouting off a list of injustices a mile long.

"They deserve to have to walk on that field naked at

Homecoming. We just want a little revenge," says Melanie Jane.

She seems very proud of herself. And the other girls were really very convincing. They wait, certain she'll pull the football from under the bar at any second and hand it over.

"No," she says.

They step backward in disbelief.

"The Ranburne team's been coming here for years. I ain't gonna risk all that business to help y'all out, even if that boy that just came in here is a snotty little pissant."

The other girls are fading into the background. Muttering thanks and turning around and giving up.

I lean across the bar, lowering my voice to where it's almost a whisper. "Ma'am, what's your name?"

Surprise flickers on her face. "Destiny."

"Destiny, that boy did something to me last year. Something you can't erase." I swallow down the tears building in the back of my throat. "And he didn't give me a choice. Do you know what it's like to have someone use you up and then discard you like a tissue?"

Her weathered eyes soften. She knows.

"Please." I'm begging, and I don't care. "I need this."

She watches me for a moment before letting out the longest, saddest sigh I've ever heard. I swear I can read her whole life in that sigh the way fortune-tellers read palms. "Tell you what." She reaches under the bar and pulls out not a football but a sheet of paper. "I've been paid to give the football to whoever finishes that list, so if you can finish it before they do, you can have it."

I stare at the paper in front of me. The Ranburne Panther Scavenger Hunt. The other girls crowd around me now.

"We do everything on the list . . . and you'll give it to us? You'll give us the football?" asks Liv.

"*If* you beat the boys," she says. She goes back to wiping down the bar like it makes no difference to her either way.

"Oh, don't worry. We'll beat them." I clench the list tight in my fingers, and there is fire in my eyes.

She smiles for the first time since we entered the club. "I think you just might."

RANBURNE PANTHER SCAVENGER HUNT

In Ranburne:

1. ~~Fill a condom up with water. Draw a face on it. Put it on Principal Corso's doormat, and ding-dong ditch. (One person)~~

2. ~~The egg-on-a-string trick. Hang an egg from a power line by a string and watch a car run into it. (Everyone)~~

3. ~~Paint the David Bowie statue at Old Lady Howard's corn maze. (Everyone)~~

4. ~~Chair race through Walmart. (Everyone)~~

5. ~~Get a picture of the team with the Ranburne Panther. (Everyone)~~

6. ~~Go to the Dawsonville football field. Find that stupid rock they touch before their games. Pee on it. (Everyone)~~

In Nashville:

7. ~~Visit the illustrious Delta Tau Beta fraternity at Vanderbilt. Have a beer with Panther alum TJ McNeil and take a picture of the legendary scar he got during a game-winning play against Dawsonville. (One person)~~

8. ~~Go to LP Field and reenact the "Music City Miracle." (Everyone)~~

9. ~~Go to Centennial Park and jump into the pond behind the Parthenon. (Everyone)~~

10. ~~Go to The Jackrabbit Saloon. Walk to the very middle of the dance floor and attempt to do the worm. (One person)~~

11. ~~Go up to a girl who is totally out of your league, get down on your knees, and ask her to marry you. (One person)~~

12. ~~Go up to a fat girl and tell her "You're so beautiful . . . for a fat chick." Bonus points if she throws her drink on you. (One person)~~

13. ~~Hug a biker. Bonus points if he has a mullet. (One person)~~

14. ~~Get a girl to give you her thong. (One person)~~

DARES REMAINING: 0

2:25 A.M.

ANA

Melanie Jane is frantic. "Ana, slow down! You're going to get us killed!"

I ignore her. "We can't let them beat us! We're so close!"

I feel like I've downed about eight *cafezinhos*. Are the guys right behind us? Are they already there? We spent too much damn time splashing around in that water. And stuck in Nashville nightlife traffic. Now that we're back on the highway, I fly. I don't bother finding a real parking space when we reach Catcalls. I don't bother checking for football players. Let the other girls worry about that. I race to the bar to meet Destiny, weaving in between dirty old men because things have really picked up since we were here earlier. Destiny is still there, but now she's serving up drinks rapid fire.

"Did we beat them?" I'm panting and clutching the bar like a life raft. "Did we?"

She finishes the complicated drink she's pouring with excruciating slowness. The lines of her face tell me nothing. That can't be a good sign. She sets the bottle down, and only then do I see the hint of a smile. "You might have."

"Woo!" I yell, causing every person in the club to stare at me. Oops. If there are any football players in here, I am screwed.

Melanie Jane elbows me. "Way to be discreet."

I feel the blood drain out of my face. "Are there—?"

"Nope," says Liv. "We already checked."

Whew. I have a moment of relief, and then we are falling all over ourselves trying to show her the camera and list all at once.

"Whoa," she hisses, her voice sharp. "Not here." She gestures for us to follow her to a back room. Not the one where the strippers get ready. This one is more like a large closet filled with boxes of alcohol. "I don't want anyone in there telling Ranburne I gave away their football. I'll give it to you here, and you'll sneak out the back. If you've done everything on that list."

We show her our pictures and video, and she checks them off. I think she's impressed with some of our changes. When she gets to the video of us in the pond, she nods.

"Everything seems to be here." She pulls an old paper sack from behind a box of Jack Daniel's. "I'd say you earned this."

She drops the bag in my lap. "I gotta get back to the bar. Make sure to go out that way." She points to the glowing, red exit sign.

I open the bag with trembling fingers. It doesn't look like much—just a dirty old football. But when I think of the weeks of planning, and everything we did tonight . . . When I think of what it will mean to the Panther football players . . . The girls crowd in from all sides, laying their hands on the football as I hoist it over my head. Maybe it could be more.

We have done it. We have beaten the football team. We head to my house for our celebratory sleepover, stopping at Waffle

House on the way because victory celebrations aren't complete without carbs. Then we camp out on the floor of my bedroom. I'm trying to laugh and chatter with the other girls, but it's hard. I thought this would feel different. Better. Instead, I feel like not a whole lot has changed. I tell the girls I'm going to get some water, but instead go to my backyard and curl up in our hammock.

It isn't long before Melanie Jane finds me. "Can I sit with you?" she asks.

"Sure."

I scoot around so I'm sitting sideways in the hammock instead of longways. She crawls in beside me, nearly flipping us in the process. After a few tense seconds, during which I think we might sustain head injuries, we're able to dangle our legs over the side and stare up at the stars.

"You don't seem very happy," she finally says.

I sigh. "It isn't enough to make them walk onto the field at Homecoming naked or have the shame of losing the game ball of '76."

"Well, damn, what do you want to do, light it on fire during halftime?"

I picture Melanie Jane blowtorching the football on the fifty-yard line as generations of Panthers look on in horror. I can't help but smile. It doesn't last though.

"No, I mean, it isn't enough to punish just this set of guys. Yeah, it'll suck for them and pay them back for what they've done to us, but it won't change anything. What about the next set of guys? And their next set of victims? How do we change that?" I try to figure out the words for how I'm feeling. "I don't know what I was expecting. It's like getting revenge on Chad doesn't mean as much since I never got any answers."

She turns to look at me, and the hammock shifts dangerously. "What are you talking about?"

Telling ruins everything. "Nothing."

"I don't think I believe you." Melanie Jane has these eyes that cut right to the truth. I feel like they're giving me an autopsy right now. I also feel like, this time, letting her see my insides might be okay.

I start at the beginning and tell her everything that happened. I don't leave anything out. To her credit, she doesn't cry or hug me or do any other kind of sappy thing that people do when they feel sorry for you. She doesn't interrupt me either. Not until I get to the part where everything went dark.

"So, I don't even know if I'm a virgin." I scratch a scab off my arm. "I guess he had sex with me because that's what everyone says."

"He didn't," says Melanie Jane.

I clench my teeth. "Yeah. That's what the school counselor said too. She didn't want me to ruin his chances at a scholarship."

"No, I mean, I was there."

If I was a different kind of person, there would be a swell of hope in my chest right now. I remember she took me home, after, but I thought—"What did you see?"

"I saw"—she can't even say it—"what you told me about. But he still had on all his clothes, and his pants were zipped and everything. I freaked out. And he ran away."

"I'm still a virgin?" The hope is real this time but fragile. It's not like being a virgin is the most important thing. It's not like I have these grand plans about it like Melanie Jane. But it's my body to decide what to do with and when. And I thought that choice had been taken away. "He didn't—"

"He would have," she says, squeezing the threads of the hammock like they're to blame. "I'm sorry. I didn't know enough to understand that you didn't want to be there. I didn't start to figure that out until later." She looks so defeated. "Why didn't you tell me?"

She doesn't mean it as an accusation, but that's how I take it. "Right. Like you would have listened."

"I know. I was a total bitch to you. But if I knew—I mean, if you had told me—it would have made all the difference."

I think about what I've learned tonight. "Yeah. It would have."

Neither of us says anything for a while. Her hand reaches out to hold mine. But in a fierce way. Like our locked fingers have taken a stand against the entire world.

"What if we *could* do something?" she says to the sky. "To change things."

"Like what?"

"I might have some ideas."

11

Monday, September 28

PEYTON

"Did you hear what happened?"

"Somebody *stole* the Football of '76."

"Do they know who did it?"

"I don't think so. The football team's crapping their pants right now."

Excited whispers follow me around school on Monday. They don't know they're about me. But they are. It's more than the usual flurry over a good piece of gossip though. The air is laced with revolution. The football team may be idolized by our town, but that's the problem with being gods. It makes everyone else a mortal.

It's all anyone is talking about when I get to geometry. Coach Mayes can't make us calm down, but a school announcement during the first five minutes of class shuts everybody up. Coach Fuller's face appears on the television.

"As I'm sure most of you have heard, the game ball of '76 was stolen this weekend. We here at Ranburne know this is more than just a football. It's Panther tradition, an important piece of history. We are asking that anyone with any knowledge of the theft come to my office or Principal Corso's office. We need to get that football back before Friday's Homecoming game. It can be left at the office—we won't ask questions. It is our hope that those involved will understand the seriousness of what they've done and that we will be able to put an end to this tragedy."

Tragedy? *Really?* I think that's going a bit far. You wouldn't know it looking at the football players though. By their somber faces, you'd think our town had been the victims of a terrorist attack.

"I don't know what we're going to do." Weston hides his face in his hands.

"You're gonna walk onto the football field naked on Friday unless you find it, that's what you're going to do," says Casey.

"It's more than that." Nate sits on his desk with the manner of a politician delivering a speech. "What if we never get it back?"

A girl comes up and touches his shoulder. "How did it happen?" She's all soft words and big eyes, the way girls are when they ask a guy how he broke his arm as a way of flirting.

Nate nods at Weston. "Some other guys did the scavenger hunt list first."

Casey narrows his eyes. "Stupid stripper couldn't tell the difference."

I badly want to say something, but before I get a chance, phones buzz around the room. Right on schedule. An email from an anonymous account has just been sent to every player on the Ranburne football team. We even created the account and the email at the Ranburne Public Library so it couldn't be traced back to us (us = best spies ever).

"Did you just get one too?"

"Yeah, what does yours say?"

"Mine's just a link."

"Mine too."

The whole class, even Coach Mayes, huddles around the guys as Nate clicks the link.

"It's a video," he says.

Even though I know what's on it, I can't help but crane my neck so I can see the screen of Nate's phone. Everyone gasps as four figures dressed all in black with grim-reaper hoods appear.

"They've got the football!" yells Casey.

He doesn't miss a thing, that one.

We made the video at Ana's after we drove two hours to an out-of-the-way Party City to get the costumes. We put on extra clothes underneath to make us bigger and wore our dads' work gloves. Sparkly nail polish is kind of a giveaway. Melanie Jane's the one holding the football. Ana's holding a set of white card stock signs beside her. The first one is blank. She flips it to the back.

We have the Football of '76.

Flip.

You can stop peeing your pants. We're going to give it back.

People snicker all around me.

Flip.

There are some things we need to tell you first.

Flip.

Check back tomorrow if you want to know more about your Ranburne Panthers. Same time. Same site.

The video goes black.

The classroom explodes. People are excited, shocked, impressed. A few of them are angry.

"I'm going to find out who those guys are. And I'm going to murder them," says Casey.

"How do you know it's guys?" It slips out before I can help myself.

He gives me a look that clearly says he doesn't think a girl could have pulled it off.

Coach Mayes moves back to the front of the room. "All right. All right. We *do* have class today. I finished grading your quizzes."

There's a chorus of groans, but only for a second. The video is all anyone can talk about. Best of all, sympathy for the football team is nearly nonexistent. Now that people know they're getting the football back, they just want to see what happens next. I can't wait to see what school is like for the rest of the day. I am buzzing on the inside. Man, did we look cool.

Coach hands me my quiz, and the buzz dims a little. The B+ at the top of my paper is judging me. A lot of the guys deserve this. Rey doesn't.

We finally get started on today's topic: triangles. Casey sits behind me, and I sigh. One of the best features of my new desk was that it was no longer two seats in front of Casey's.

"Hey. Hey, Peyton. I'm glad you came out this weekend. It was good seeing you at The Jackrabbit."

"Um, thanks." I turn back to the board and try to soak up everything I can about congruent and incongruent and equilateral and isosceles.

"Why were you talking to Rey, though? Do you know him?" Casey isn't even being that quiet. Coach Mayes has to be able to hear him.

"Yeah, he helps me with geometry," I whisper. *Kind of like the opposite of what you do.*

"Oh, okay, cool."

Coach writes another proof on the board, and I groan. Proofs are the devil.

"Hey, Peyton, check this out. Me and some of the other guys made it."

He shoves his phone in front of me. It's a video of the dance team performing at halftime during the first football game. Pink Panther Hotties—that's what the caption says. I can't help but smile. We look amazing. I can't believe how in sync we are. Then the video zooms in on each individual dancer, giving a score and some kind of gross assessment, like MARLEY SHELTON. 10 OF 10. CHECK OUT THAT ASS. Or CADENCE FIRTH. 4 OF 10. GIRL NEEDS A DIET. A few seconds later, the girl dancing in the video is me. PEYTON REED. 9 OF 10. WOULD BANG.

Casey nudges me. "What do you think?"

Normally, I would wait till the end of class or not say anything at all, but I am getting so dang tired of this, I wouldn't care if the whole school was watching.

I raise my hand, only it feels like I'm raising a red flag. "Coach, can you ask Casey to put his phone away?"

Coach Mayes sighs through his nose in a way that makes me think of a bull. His eyes move from me to Casey, that familiar annoyance flashing on his face, but just for a moment. Then he just looks tired.

"Peyton, why don't you move to that desk over there so you can concentrate."

That sentence says it all. In his eyes, I am the one at fault. The alternative would mean acknowledging that Casey has done something wrong. But, no. I'm a whiner, a narc, a tattletale, a prissy little girl who can't keep her mouth shut. It doesn't matter that he was distracting me when I desperately need quiet in order to learn. It doesn't matter that the things Casey said could be considered, no, *are* harassment. I will never be as important as Casey Martin.

I get up from my desk. Gather my things. And I walk right past the desk Coach Mayes pointed to. He doesn't realize until I get all the way to the door.

"Where are you going?"

I'm tempted to make a U-turn and sit down. But I won't let myself cower. I am brave. I am strong. I fearlessly sprinkle glitter on statues and perform the worm in front of hundreds of people. I can stand up to my teacher.

"I'm leaving," I say firmly. Like that says it all.

Coach can't seem to say anything back, even though his mouth is open. People are staring. Maybe they think I'm crazy. Maybe they think I'm right. I don't wait to find out, and I definitely don't wait to see what happens once Coach Mayes regains the use of his vocal cords. I step outside and shut the door behind me.

Ohmygosh, ohmygosh, ohmygosh, I can't believe I did that. I force myself down the hallway, legs shaking like they might give out at any moment. I go straight past the principal's office because that probably isn't the safest place for me today. Instead, I head to the counselor for students P–Z and sit down in the chair across from him.

"Hi, Peyton, what can I do for you?"

I don't know what kind of face I'm making, but I have a feeling it's the face of someone who doesn't get told no. "I need to be transferred to a new geometry class."

Tuesday, September 29
LIV

We are unstoppable. Everyone is checking their phones, the computers in class, anything to get to the next installment in the most exciting thing that has ever happened at our boring little high school. At 9:30, we give the people what they want. The List goes live. The entire email exchange, starting with the list of girls and including every email between Trevor and the other guys after that, is up on the internet for everyone to see.

The first-period teachers must hate us. They can't get anything done. The hallways are a frenzy after class. The truth can have that effect on people. Abby Clayton screams at her ex-boyfriend in a shrill language that may or may not be English. Natalie von Oterendorp cries while a circle of band girls hugs her and keeps Jacob from getting anywhere near her with his apologies. And Carrie Sullivan—holy spitfire. I always thought Big Tom was the scary one, but now he's cowering in front of this pink-tights-wearing slip of a girl. Watching her club him over the head with her history book has got to be the best thing I've seen all day.

I expect some backlash over being labeled a slut on The List, and I get it from a few guys. But most people are being so cool about it. It's like making The List is a badge of honor not shame. It means you were important enough to get the football team's notice. Girls keep coming up to me and saying, "It's so horrible." And, "I can't believe they did that to you." Guys too. I've gotten more hugs in one day than I have all year. And I do love a good hug.

It only gets better at lunch. I'm sitting with Marley and Peyton and some other girls from the dance team, like usual. All anyone wants to know about is how it feels being on The List, so I tell them between sips of Diet Coke. A few minutes in, Marley nudges me with this huge smile. Trevor is coming our way. Of all the guys on the team, Trevor is coming off the best right now. Especially with Ranburne's female population. His emails after The List have all the girls buzzing.

Marley stands as he reaches our table, blocking him from seeing me. "Is it okay?" she asks me.

I give her—and Trevor—a half smile. "Yeah, he can pass."

She sits back down as Trevor says, "Thanks."

"I need to talk to you," he tells me. And before I can process what's happening, he climbs up onto the lunch table and says in a voice that reaches every corner of the cafeteria. "And I need everyone to hear this."

When Jimmy Ferraro drops his fork six tables away, you can hear it. That's how quiet the student body is right now. Every last neck is craned in Trevor's direction. Some people have even whipped out their phones.

"My girlfriend is not a slut." A couple of guys at the table next to me snicker, but I hardly notice because I am still stuck on the word *girlfriend*. "She didn't do tons of stuff with tons of guys, but you know what, even if she did, who cares? It's not like that would make her bad or stupid or any different from half the guys on the football team." He's been delivering his speech to the general public, but now he turns, and it's like he's talking only to me. "My girlfriend is wonderful. And strong and impulsive and hilarious and sexy as hell. She cares about me more than I deserve." He hangs his head while the girls hang on his every word. "And I've been a dick to her."

He faces the crowd again, and his voice is a roar. "I have been letting a handful of guys dictate my life and I am done with it." He throws his hands in the air like he's throwing off chains, and the whole cafeteria cheers. "I'm going to do anything I can to make it up to her." His voice goes soft. "If she'll let me."

Everyone watches to see what I'll say. Trevor holds out his hand, and I'm reminded of that scene in *Aladdin* where he wants Jasmine to get on the magic carpet and he says, "Do you trust me?" And I do trust him. I give him my hand and climb onto the table with him, a move that makes the masses incredibly happy.

"I love you, Liv Lambros," he says, and I don't doubt him for a second.

"I love you too."

And then I grab his face and kiss him, and I don't have to hold anything back because I'm scared of what I mean to him or worried he's about to get snatched away. Cheers crowd the air around us, and hope floods my heart, and Trevor's kisses fill the empty parts of my soul until I think I might burst. A few seconds later, one of the lunch ladies jerks us down by our elbows because mealtime disruption and the importance of nutrition and all that. I don't mind. I've got Trevor back.

Wednesday, September 30
ANA

Today's post? A montage of video clips from the football team's initiation ceremony. I have it set to post automatically at 9:30 because the last thing we need is for someone to see one of us posting it during class and figure out who we are. I can't wait to see how people react to this one. The past two days have been more than I ever could have hoped for. I drive to school with Grayson beside me in the passenger seat. The past two days have been good for him too. We sing at the top of our lungs to bad pop music and drink tiny cups of *cafezinho*— I've totally got him hooked on it. It's strong and sweet and kind of the best thing ever. I've been making it for my parents since I was a kid: boil the coffee in water with a ton of sugar, leave a miniature cup on my dad's nightstand so he emerges from his bedroom a caring father instead of a minotaur.

My phone beeps as I pull into my parking spot. There's a text from Toby.

Maybe you should think about staying home from school today.

What is he talking about? This has been the best week of school I've had since, well, since before. There's no way I'm missing a second of it.

When I walk through the double doors that face the parking lot, I don't understand. Glaring and muttering and whispering behind cupped hands. People parting when I pass like I'm carrying a contagious disease. If I didn't know better, I'd think my car was a time machine programmed to drop me off in last year. The drones stare at me like I'm an animal. I can't read anything on their faces. Can't figure out what's happening to me right now.

And then he steps from the crowd to block my path. Chad MacAllistair. We are having a good-versus-evil battle, a final showdown in the hallway. Everyone waits to see who the winner will be so they'll know which side to pick.

"Everyone knows it's you." His voice is the scary, angry brand of calm. "They're gonna suspend you. Maybe even arrest you." He steps up close, and I cringe away before he can touch me. "Oh. And everyone thinks what you did is really lame."

Before I can respond, he's gone, and there's an announcement over the intercom.

"Ana Cardoso to the principal's office. Ana Cardoso, please come to the principal's office."

The masses watch me with hollow eyes as I head down the hallway to my doom. Clearly, I am the loser here.

When I get to Principal Corso's office, Coach Fuller is already there, angry as hell and panting and jumping around like a bull. I guess we know who will be playing the role of bad cop today. I take the chair across from them. And wait. When Corso sees I'm not about to offer up anything willingly, he lets Fuller attack.

Where is the football?

Who else was helping me?

Do I know I'm a stupid little girl and they're going to have my ass for this?

I give away nothing. I'm sure the other girls didn't either, and I don't want to be the weak link. Whenever I feel myself cracking, I focus on the abundance of chest hair protruding from the neck of Principal Corso's button-down shirt. The man is a missed haircut away from becoming Chewbacca.

He finally throws up a hand to silence Coach Fuller.

"You're suspended for the rest of the week," he says, bushy eyebrows coming together in a way that inspires fear in the hearts of Ranburne students. I try to argue that they don't have any proof, but they claim a "reliable source" turned me in, and it's enough to warrant a suspension pending further investigation. "We're calling your parents, and if that football isn't back by Friday, we're involving the police. You'll need to leave the school grounds now."

I manage not to cry until after I'm safely in my car. I'm shaking so much, I can barely drive home. Can they really do all the things they were threatening? It's just a football. And we're returning it. I didn't think we'd get in this much trouble. I didn't think we'd get caught either. How did they find out?

My dad's car is in the driveway when I get home. Which means he came home from work. This is definitely a bad sign. When I open the front door, Falkor isn't waiting to slobber attack me. Another bad sign. He's hunched by the doorway to the living room, sniffing at the air as if anger is something that can be smelled, and giving me a look that clearly says, "You are screwed."

My parents unleash a wave of fury on me the instant I enter the room. Holy crap, if my parents are this mad, I can't imagine what Melanie Jane must be facing right now. My father rants at me in broken English laced with Portuguese and calls me by my full name, Juliana Fernanda Oliveira Cardoso, which means things are level-5 serious.

"Why?" He's going to wear a hole in the carpet where he's pacing back and forth in front of the couch. "Why would my good, smart daughter do something like this?"

I swallow. "Do you really want to know?"

"Yes." They both say at once.

So, I tell them about last year. Or, rather, I tell the coffee table about last year. If I don't look at them while I say it, maybe they'll still love me. Telling Melanie Jane this weekend was good practice. It's like it got my truth muscles working. When I'm done, I guess I expect hugs and tears and stuff. My dad walks out of the room without saying anything. And then there are tears (from me) and hugs (from my mom).

"He just needs some time," she says.

I nod, but I don't understand. I go up to my room and pull the curtains shut and wish I could block out my feelings along with the light. Falkor climbs into bed with me and curls against my side with a sad doggy sigh. I wrap my arm around my demon familiar and bury my face in his fur and try not to think about how sad it is that my dog is giving me more support than my father. At some point, I guess I fall asleep because I wake up later to someone rapping on my window. I open the curtains to see Toby standing outside, so I open the window too.

"Your parents said you're grounded."

"Yeah, that makes sense."

He scratches his cheek. Turns his head from side to side like he's worried someone will overhear. "I'm really sorry about everything that happened."

Poor Tobes. You'd think he was the one who called me out in the middle of the hallway. "Aw, thanks. It'll be okay." Maybe. Hopefully. Someday. Or never. Never is also a possibility.

"No, I mean, I'm *really* sorry. I think Chad was the one who told Coach Fuller and the principal. Chad was talking about how he saw you at the bar, and why would you ever come there. And I remembered all the questions you had been asking me about the football and the scavenger hunt and stuff, and it all made sense. So, I told him." His voice goes so quiet I almost don't hear the last part, and it takes me a second to process.

"You told him?" Toby, my Toby, told *Chad* of all people? "Do you know how bad this is? How could you do that? You completely betrayed me."

He stares at me through the screen, his eyes turning red at the corners. "You betrayed me first, Ana."

His words cut me straight through the heart because they're

completely true. I did hurt him first. I used him, more than once, and I gave myself a free pass because I felt like it was worth it. Now I'm thinking it wasn't.

"I'll see you later, okay?" Toby walks away through my back-yard and disappears between the hedges.

I want to yell out his name, but I'm scared of how much it will hurt if he doesn't come back.

A few minutes later, my phone beeps in my pocket. My heart does a backflip. Toby? Oh. It's just Liv.

> We're in the tree house. Grayson said you might be able to meet us. Can you get out?

I almost cry when I read the text. It feels that good to have someone waiting for me. I can't believe the other girls were able to sneak past their parents and come all the way over here. They must really care about me. I slip out to the backyard, telling my mom first that I'm going to the tree house to think. She's used to me doing this, so she gives me a hug and lets me go. When I climb the wooden rungs to the top, the girls are all there, as promised.

Liv squeezes me in a hug before I can catch my balance. "Are you okay?"

"As good as I can be, I guess." I find an open space to sit. It's kind of a tight squeeze in here with four grown-up-sized people. "What about you guys? Are you okay?"

They pass confused glances back and forth. "What do you

mean?" asks Melanie Jane.

"We got caught." Our lives as we know them are going up in flames. How are they all so calm?

Peyton shakes her head slowly. "You got caught. We're still not sure how."

"It was Toby," I say. "He told Chad."

"What?!" Melanie Jane looks like she's about to fly out of the tree house on a broom. Possibly with a legion of flying monkeys with which to attack Toby. "I'll kill that little dork."

I put a hand on her arm. "It's okay. We're kind of even."

"They never called the rest of us to the principal's office." Liv shifts her legs into a butterfly stretch. "We kept waiting."

"Of course not. I didn't tell on you guys."

"That was really cool of you," she says, and the other girls nod.

"Yeah. I mean, we're in this together. Things are bad for me right now, but they don't have to be bad for everyone."

They breathe a collective sigh of relief.

"Oh, good," says Liv. "Because I don't think I'd have a chance of getting a scholarship with something like this on my record."

"Miss Nashville is right around the corner," chimes in Melanie Jane.

"I'd hate for Rey to know I was a part of this," says Peyton.

"Sure," I reply, feeling suddenly alone in this very cramped tree house. "I can take the fall by myself. It's not a problem."

I falter on the end of my sentence. Melanie Jane is picking

at her cuticles. Liv seems very interested in her split ends. Peyton is the only one of them who has the decency to look at me, and even she seems like she's about to burst into tears. And just like that I am dragged back into the darkness that consumed me for most of last year. Was this the only reason they came over? Did they care about how I was doing at all? I thought the whole point of this was for us to band together, but I guess I was wrong.

"I should probably go."

I crawl out of the tree house before they can stop me. Back into my house. Back into my bed. Back under the covers pulled up over my face. My parents hate me. Toby hates me. The kids at school never liked me to begin with. My girls have abandoned me. I have no one.

Thursday, October 1
MELANIE JANE

There is no vlog today. Though that doesn't stop people from checking at 9:30. And 9:31 and 9:32 and 9:40 and then at 11:00 just in case. The excitement of Monday and Tuesday is gone. All anyone can talk about today is that bitch Ana Cardoso.

"It just makes me sad, you know?" Chloe slides into the desk next to me in Spanish. "They're *such* great guys, and they totally don't deserve this. Ana Cardoso is a stupid bitch drama queen who likes to make other people's lives miserable. It's really lame."

I narrow my eyes. "You didn't think it was lame Tuesday before you found out it was Ana."

Chloe looks me up and down like she doesn't even know who I am anymore. "What's your deal, Mel-Jay? This is Ana we're talking about. Besides, that video she posted yesterday was way over the line. You can't just out someone's secret ceremonies. That's just wrong."

I shrug because if I open my mouth again, bad things are guaranteed to come out.

Ana is screwed, and I am drowning in guilt. Liv and Peyton too. We talked about it for over an hour after Ana left last night. Keeping our secret seemed like the best idea at the time, but now I'm not so sure.

Chloe snort-giggles next to me. "OMG. Have you seen this?"

She pushes her phone in front of me. It's a photo of Ana looking totally wasted, horns and a mustache edited onto the picture later. It's posted on some kind of website. I scroll down to find dozens, maybe even hundreds, of comments.

Ana Cardoso is a stupid skanky narc who needs to learn to keep her mouth shut.

She just wants to make everyone else as miserable as her.

She's a liar.

Slut.

Bitch.

And after the comments, there's another post. A video. The caption above it reads, WHAT ANA CARDOSO LIKES TO DO FOR FUN.

"Oh! That's the best part. Here." She clicks PLAY. "It's hilarious."

I feel like I'm going to be sick. This is the video from the night Chad tried to rape Ana. To anyone who doesn't know Ana was on drugs, all the dancing around probably would seem pretty funny. To me, it is disgusting. A thought hits me like a sucker punch: I wonder if Ana's seen it. Is she watching it right this minute? Is it dragging her back into that nightmare? Making her feel like she'll never be able to outrun it no matter what she does?

The video settles it. We *have* to confess. Take some of the attention off Ana. Give back the football and try to get through the next 2.5 years with our heads down. The more I think about it, the better I feel. It's going to suck, really badly, but telling is the right thing to do. And I think I know how I want to do it.

I give Chloe's phone back and pull out my own where Señor Barbas can't see it. I text Michael.

> Me: I know we were planning on Saturday, but can I come over tonight?
> Michael: Sure.
> Me: Awesome. And can Liv and Peyton come too? It's really important.
> Michael: Yeah. Is everything okay?
> Me: I think it will be. Also, do you have any video equipment?

There's a delay. He must think I'm so weird. Chloe is leaning over her desk trying to read my screen, so I scoot it farther under my Spanish book. Michael texts back.

> Michael: Yes, but you have to know, after the thong incident, getting texts like this from you is very scary :)

Yep. Definitely thinks I'm weird. Fantastic.

> Me: You're the best! I'll come over after cheer practice! And don't be scared :)

"I'm so glad we're doing this," says Peyton. "I've been feeling awful."

"Me too," says Liv.

We get right to work making a new vlog post. It feels weird doing this without Ana, but I'm hoping she'll forgive us when she sees it. Michael films for us—he's pretty amazing about rolling with whatever crazy thing I throw at him. We kind of had to tell him what was going on, but he had figured it out for himself after watching all of our shenanigans this weekend. Before I know it, we've wrapped, and the post is set to go live tomorrow, and Michael and I are alone in his bedroom. There is nothing left to do but make out. It is obvious. And it is creating an awkward silence.

Michael scratches the back of his neck. "Just so you know, I really wasn't inviting you over here as a sex thing."

"Good." I sit on his bed and swing my feet back and forth just a little. "Because we're not having sex."

I scrutinize his face for the wrong reaction, but he seems pretty okay with what I just said. "Are you a virgin?"

"Yep."

Some girls are embarrassed about being virgins. They get all shy and flushed every time they have to tell a boy because they're worried about what he'll think. Well, not me because I know what those girls don't. Every time I've ever told a boy I liked that I was a virgin, they had unilaterally the same response: they thought it was "so cool" or "very cool" or "really cool" or sometimes just plain "cool," but *cool* was always the word of choice to describe having retained one's virginity.

The problem is, even though they said it was "so cool," that's not what they meant. What guys mean when you tell them you are a virgin, and they tell you it's "so cool," is that it is "so cool that you have never had sex with anyone else as long as you are planning on letting me eventually have sex with you." Which is not, in my opinion, cool at all.

"I thought so," he says. And I must be giving him some kind of evil eye because he rushes to explain. "You said something about it at the bar. About Weston dumping you?"

Oh. Right.

"Is it tough?" he asks. "Waiting?"

"Sometimes." *It probably will be with you.* "What about you? Are you a virgin?"

"No. She was my girlfriend. Before I moved from Boston." He sits beside me. "Are you okay with that?"

"Yeah." *It only puts a ton of pressure on me.* "I have to ask you something else. Do you have any STDs or anything?"

"Nope. Do you?"

"No."

We both laugh awkwardly.

"Well, now that I've totally killed the mood . . ."

He grabs my hand. "No, you didn't. And now we can have fun without having to worry about anything. So. You just let me know if I ever do anything you don't want me to. I never want you to be uncomfortable, and I don't really know how this works."

"Okay."

I have no idea what I do or don't want him to do. This would be a whole lot easier if I had created a complicated formula taking into account the number of weeks we've been dating and how much I like him and doling out precise allotments of physical affection. Not that I normally do that. Okay, fine, I totally always do that. But not this time. Not with Michael. That boy is my exception. I'll have to be careful not to unleash years of pent-up sexual desire onto him all at once.

I kiss him until we're gasping for air, and we do things, wonderful things, and I have feelings I didn't know were possible. We don't do Everything, but I never realized how much the things we do could mean. It's euphoria—this freewheeling, flying, falling-in-love-for-the-first-time feeling. The Norwegians call it *forelsket*. And then we're wound up together in his sheets, my head resting against his shoulder. He opens one eye when I snuggle closer.

"Hi," he says.

"Hi."

We stare at each other, our eyes passing secrets back and forth about the last hour. He touches my cheek with the back of his fingers.

"I love you, Melanie Jane."

"I love you too."

Did we really just say that? This early? Oh, yes, my brain has definitely been washed. And dried. And maybe ironed with starch too. Before I can get a really good internal freak-out going, my phone vibrates on Michael's floor. I lean over and pick it up. And nearly swallow my tongue because on my screen in serious black letters is a text from my mother.

We need to talk about your boyfriend.

We need to talk about your boyfriend. Quite possibly the seven most chilling words in the English language. I turn them over and over in my head, like a pancake that just won't cook, as I climb the stairs of my house to find out my fate. My mother waits for me in the living room.

"Hey, Mama." I pause for the storm I know will follow.

"Melanie Jane, hello there. I was wondering when you might show up," she says sweetly. I am not fooled. I know what's underneath that sweetness.

"I saw your text."

"Yes, Chloe called the house tonight to ask where you were, but she figured you might be at your boyfriend's." Here we go. "Imagine my surprise. I didn't even know you had a boyfriend."

I am in panic mode. I do the only thing I can. I lie.

"Mama, he's not my boyfriend."

"So, you've spent the past five hours with a boy who isn't your boyfriend?"

Ooo. I walked right into that one.

"Okay, he is my boyfriend."

"So you just lied to me. I guess I shouldn't be surprised. You've obviously been lying to me for Lord knows how long."

Uh-oh. We've been talking for less than a minute, and she's already bringing the Lord into the conversation. I decide to try a new tactic.

"I'm sorry," I say.

Mama sighs. "Well, why didn't you just tell me you had a boyfriend?"

Because you're the most judgmental person I know. Because I knew the minute I told you I could expect calls from every living family member asking about my new boyfriend. Because you'd somehow find a way to ruin our relationship.

I hang my head. "I don't know."

"If you and this boy are serious, we'd really like to meet him."

I think about my mother meeting Michael. My stomach nearly turns itself inside out.

"No," I say softly.

"Excuse me?"

"You can't meet him."

"Why? What's wrong with him?"

Ugh. She is like a dog with a piece of meat. "That's exactly why you can't meet him," I snap. "You have to pick everyone apart. Find every little flaw. No one could ever live up to your standards. I know I've never been able to."

I shut my mouth fast, but it's too late. The words are already out there. There is silence, and my heart is doing backflips, and then:

"I just want what's best for you. I didn't realize that made me a terrible mother."

"No, Mama, I don't think—"

She cuts me off. "You have *wounded* my spirit. I can't talk to you any more right now." And then as if she feels it's inappropriate for a Southern woman to have such an emotional outburst, she adds, "I have a lot of work to do for the Junior League fashion show. I'll see you later," before whipping out of the room.

I could hear the lump in her throat. I know she ran out to avoid crying in front of me. I stare at the now-empty doorway and burst into tears myself.

Daddy finds me about an hour later, still tucked into the same chair in the living room.

"Hey, Mel Belle."

"Hey, Daddy. How bad is it?"

"Well. Remember that time you cut up your pageant dress to make a butterfly net?"

I gulp. "Yes. Mama's face turned four shades of purple."

"Well, this time isn't like that time. Your Mama's not angry. She's hurt." He clears his throat. "So am I."

The fact that my actions might have affected my dad hits me all at once. I'd been so worried about Mama, it never occurred to me he might have feelings. When I try to speak again, my breath catches.

"You are?"

"We used to be so close, but we've hardly talked since school started." He sighs, and it breaks my heart. "Why didn't you tell me? You always tell me everything, and I always help you work it out. That's what we do. And now I guess you have someone new to tell your problems to. I feel like you don't need me anymore."

My tears spill over again. "I'm so sorry. You aren't replaced. The only reason I didn't tell you is because I didn't want Mama finding out." I sniffle into a tissue. "I'm realizing that trying to keep him a secret was a huge mistake."

He sits on the arm of the chair and rubs my back. "Aw, princess, I wasn't trying to make you cry. Hey, how 'bout you tell me about him now?"

I sniffle some more and wipe my cheeks.

"What do you want to know?"

"Anything," he says. "I don't even know his name. What is it?"

"Michael." Even though I'm crying, my voice takes on a dreamy quality.

"Sounds pretty serious."

"It is."

"Well, what's he like?"

"He's in all the hard classes just like me, so he's really smart. And he's funny and kind and soo cute, and I sound like a girl in a romantic comedy, don't I?"

Daddy laughs. "Nah. He sounds great. Why couldn't you tell your mama all that?"

"Well, because he's also Jewish, and a Yankee, and quite

probably a Democrat."

"Oh." He pauses. "Have fun telling that to your mother."

"Daddy!"

"I'm kidding," he says. "You should just tell her. All of it."

"I will. I just have to figure out how."

Friday, October 2

I sneak down to the kitchen the next morning. Mama is at the table eating an egg white omelet, but she doesn't seem angry. Daddy slides another omelet onto a plate, and jerks his head in her direction. Message received. I accept the plate and sit across from her. And then I eat half my omelet in silence because I'm a chicken. I finally work up the courage to speak.

"Hey, Mama. I'm sorry for saying those things to you."

"No. I'm sorry." She reaches across the table and takes my hand. "I'm sorry they're true. I would never want you to feel like you're not good enough for me. You are a strong, phenomenal woman, and I'm proud of you every day. I've spent all this time pushing you because I wanted you to have more opportunities than me. I wanted life to be easier for you."

"Um, you drive a BMW, and our house has three fireplaces." It slips out before I can stop it.

She laughs, and there's a trace of bitterness in it. "My life isn't a Cinderella story." She chews at the inside of her lip. "I didn't want to tell you this because I want you to love your dad's parents, but they never let me forget that I'm not rich and I'm not white. It got better with each one of you kids that I had, but you should have seen them when your father and I were engaged."

Mama has turned my whole world upside down. My grandfather is a lovable, red-cheeked old man who belly laughs at my jokes and sneaks hip flasks of Scotch into my pageant competitions. And even though my grandmother is prissy and has a collection of wigs that smell like Chanel No. 5, she's always slipping me wads of cash when my parents aren't looking and telling me how dah-lin' I am.

"Grammy and Pop-Pop were mean to you?"

"They were." The hurt in her eyes is so fresh. It must have been terrible. "I don't want you to be mad at them. I just want you to understand me."

"That's all I want. I want you to understand me too."

"Well, tell me about you," she says.

"Huh?"

"I told you something you didn't know about me, so now tell me something about you."

"Oh. Well, I really like learning other languages."

She smiles. "I know that. I'm not completely oblivious."

"Right." I smile too, and our matching dimples line up across the table. "I like pageants. You kind of pushed me into those, but I really do love competing. I don't like all the pretending though—and I can't stand my pageant coach. I wish I could feel more like I'm being me at pageants. Even if it means I lose."

"I think we could arrange a new coach," she says.

"Cool. And I like Michael. And . . . you can meet him. I want you to meet him. But you have to be nice."

She places a hand over her heart, but in the joking way. "When am I ever not nice? Don't answer that. I'll be nice."

The clock on the stove says I need to leave for school now.

"Mama?"

"Yes?"

"I want us to have more talks like this."

Her eyes go softer than I've ever seen them. "Me too."

When I walk around the table and hug her before I leave, she hangs on for an extra second. At least things with Mama are good because when that vlog goes live today, my life as I know it will be over.

Friday, October 2
ANA

I am more alone than ever. Yesterday, I had no visitors. (To be fair, Grayson tried, but my parents sent him away.) Today, I languish under my covers with my stuffed animal dragon, Nostradamus, and attempt to eat my weight in *Romeu e Julieta*. Nostradamus doesn't judge. Neither does Falkor as long as I slip him hush money bites at regular intervals. I gulp down my last bite of sliced guava paste on white cheese and consider whether going to the kitchen to get more requires too much effort. The lack of human contact is making me spiral into despair—especially since all I've been doing is watching people trash me on social media. My phone buzzes. An update to tell me another person hates my guts? Excellent. I check it, but instead it's a text from Melanie Jane.

Look for a vlog today at the usual time.

A new vlog? We didn't make another one. Crap. It's almost 9:30 right now. I hurry and open my laptop—it'll look so much better there than through the cracked screen of my phone, and I need to see this. I go to the website. Wait for what feels like hours but in reality is about two minutes. There it is! The new vlog! I click PLAY.

There are three grim reapers on my screen, one of them

holding the football and another holding cards. The film quality is actually pretty good. I can't believe they were able to do this without me. I start to get excited, and then I remember I'm mad at them. Grim Reaper Number One flips the first card.

Ana Cardoso didn't act alone.

Flip.

It took four of us (FOUR GIRLS!) to beat the football team.

Flip.

And now we're going to tell you why we did it.

In smaller font, at the bottom of the card, are the words *Please forgive us, Ana.*

I lean forward, desperate to see what comes next, but instead of flipping another card, the reaper takes off her hood. Holy shit.

Curly blonde hair tumbles out. The girl underneath smiles.

"I'm Liv Lambros, alleged whore. I know a lot of you are pissed about what happened, but we had reasons for doing what we did. I had just gotten dumped by the love of my life, and it was because the football team made him do it. You guys have seen the emails. You know what happened to him when he tried to stand up to them. I don't want what happened to me and Trevor to happen to anyone else. And I don't want any other girls to feel how I felt when they called me a slut and a whore. You guys know you don't deserve that, right? No matter what you've done and who you've done it with."

Grim Reaper Number Two removes her hood next. Peyton.

"Hi." She clears her throat and raises her voice. "I'm Peyton

Reed. I don't think it's right that the football team gets special treatment in class when some of us are working really hard. And I don't think they should get away with saying whatever they want to the girls at our school. No matter what we're wearing. So, yeah, that's why I helped. And I'm sorry because some of the guys on the team are really sweet and don't deserve this, and some of the guys who aren't on the team *totally suck*." She pauses and looks straight at the camera, and I can tell she's imagining Rey's eyes. "I'm sorry if I hurt any of the good guys."

Grim Reaper Number Three, aka Melanie Jane, rips off her mask like that's about all she can take. I picture people gasping all around school. A cheerleader! And Ana Cardoso's nemesis too!

"I'm sorry too," she says in a voice that is anything but. "I'm sorry my loser ex-boyfriend felt the need to dump me because of my belief system. I'm sorry he and his friends felt the need to harass my new boyfriend who is better than him in every way. *Especially* at kissing. And I am sooo sorry that we spied on your dorky little ceremony and sent your cut list to the entire school and beat you at your own scavenger hunt by doing all the dares better and faster than you, even though we only had four people. Whew. I am just so sorry. But things needed to change. And someone needed to do it."

Best. Rant. Ever. I think she might be finished, and then:

"Oh. And the Football of '76 is in a box in Coach Fuller's office as we speak, so you can all just get ahold of yourselves."

The video goes black. That was the best thing I've ever seen. Holy amazing. I can't wait to tell them how awesome they all are. Because, naturally, after a performance like that, I have to forgive them. There's something else I have to do too. But we'll take care of that this weekend.

Saturday, October 3

You don't have to do this, you know," says Melanie Jane from behind the camera.

"I know," I say. "I want to, though. I need to."

I pull the black grim reaper hood over my head, and give her the thumbs-up sign. She starts rolling.

I take the hood back off.

"I'm Ana Cardoso. I don't even know why I'm bothering to tell you because you already know who I am and you already know I was part of this whole football team revenge thing. But I need you to know why. A lot of you have ideas about me. That I'm a slut and a liar and a life ruiner. And I need everyone to know the truth."

Don't cry. Don't. Take a deep breath. You can do this. I tell the camera what happened. The abridged version, not the gory details, but enough to know that Chad MacAllistair is not the shining prince they believe him to be. I also tell all about what it feels like being on date-rape drugs because I want every girl watching this to understand and get help if the same thing happens to her. I have to pause a couple of times when the memories feel like living things, dark winged demons slashing through the musty garage air. I nod when I'm finished, and Melanie Jane stops the camera.

I have done it. I have ripped out my own heart and videotaped the darkest parts of it. I'm about to put it on display for everyone to judge. I don't know what I'll do if people see it and still take his side. I try not to think about that. I try to focus on the one girl, more than one if I'm lucky, that could have her life changed by what I've done. Then, I collapse on the floor of my garage and burst into tears. Melanie Jane sits down beside me and pulls me into a fierce hug and whispers, "You are the bravest person I know, and I love you."

Saturday, October 17

At first it's such a disappointment. Everything is exactly the same. I don't know what I was expecting. That we'd walk into class and people would start clapping? Yeah. Something cheesy like that.

But then things begin to happen, like ripples in a pond. Trevor and Liv holding hands together without any backlash. A school board meeting about the football team's policy on hazing. And every now and then, someone will pull me aside. A freshman girl to say she thinks I'm brave. Grayson to tell me he hasn't been picked on all week. These are not small things. But I want more. I want football players to be treated like everybody else, and for the guys at this school to realize that rape culture isn't something feminists invented so they could have something new to be pissed about, and so many other things I don't even have words for yet. And most of all, I want to make sure no other girls have to go through anything like what any of us went through. That's why we're here at Jake's tonight.

The four of us are holed up in the room where it all started, crowded around the coffee table. I work on another entry in the scrapbook we're making—the book we hope will change everything. We've spent the night carefully cataloguing our secrets for any girls who come after us. Melanie Jane leans over me with a glue stick, not bothering to hide her finger as she slathers a border of glue around what I just wrote. Because if every page isn't coated in a metric ton of glitter, the message will surely be lost. Liv is demanding to go next, in between stealing bites of Peyton's ice cream. All of us are talking over each other, but in the good way. Melanie Jane says they have a word for it in Denmark: *hygge*. The cozy, intimate feeling that wraps around you like a hug when you're surrounded by your best friends and doing things like eating ice cream and laughing.

"You're going to come over to my house and get ready for the concert with me, right?" Liv asks Peyton.

Peyton passes me a cup of gel pens. "Of course. I'm so excited,

I've been listening to her new song on repeat. I still can't believe you convinced Rey and Trevor to go to a Lilah Montgomery concert, and—dude! Stop stealing my ice cream!"

"Did I tell y'all Principal Corso is coming after us again?" Melanie Jane adjusts the green beaded necklace she's wearing. I picked it up at an antique shop, and I made her borrow it because it totally matches her eyes.

I don't even try to suppress my smirk. "Haven't they realized yet that going against you doesn't work out for them?"

She grins. "Right? They keep making empty threats, and I keep leaving the website up. Oh. But I did have to listen to this hour-long lecture from my dad on how"—she makes air quotes—"once you put something on the internet, it can't be undone."

Liv puts an arm around her. "And we appreciate the hardship you went through."

I laugh, but her dad is kind of right. The police opened an official investigation because of what I said about Chad in my vlog. Another girl came forward. My dad ungrounded me and clutched me to him like a rag doll and cried that he was so sorry he couldn't protect me. He said he would move heaven and earth to make sure that boy paid for what he did. I haven't decided how I feel about the investigation yet, but I know who will help me figure it out.

I finish my entry and close the scrapbook before handing it to Liv. The words THE REVENGE PLAYBOOK shine out at me from the front cover, filling me with hope. We aren't the same people we were in August. I don't know what's going to happen next week, or next year, or even tomorrow. All I know is that we're here, together, today. And that's enough.

ACKNOWLEDGMENTS

A confession: I may have field-tested some of those dares in college. No, I won't tell you which ones. In completely unrelated news, doing the worm is a lot harder than it looks. Those nights of friendship and frenzy sparked the idea for this book, so thank you to all my scavenger hunt girls—you know who you are. ☺

I loved writing the friendships in this book, and I'm so lucky to have some of the best girlfriends in the whole world. Laura, Katie, Anya, Bethany, Mahoney, Holly, Rachel, Anna, Callie, Lisa, Jeanne, Sara, Kalynda, Bekah, and so many others. Thank you for making some of the best (and also most embarrassing) memories with me, and for being the kind of friends where, even after years apart, we fall right back into laughing, dancing, and doing pretend *America's Next Top Model* photo shoots. I love you, and I will hold your hair always and forever. Special mention goes to:

Nini—my scavenger hunt coqueen

Nicole—for telling me all about dance-y things and for being you

Becca—for believing in dragons and in me

Phae—I hope Liv is one-tenth as fun and energetic as you

To my unbelievable beta readers, I send you statues of David Bowie sprinkled in glitter. Jamie Blair, Rachel Simon, Dana Alison Levy, Erin Brambilla, Kate Boorman, and Emery Lord, thank you for making this book better, for your neverending encouragement, and for helping me figure out that pesky last scene!

Thanks to Kim Laver (aka mom) and Bethany Griffin for answering my IEP questions.

To all my buddies at OneFour KidLit, the AbsoluteWrite forums, my Atlanta writer dinner crew, and Little Shop of Stories. And to the LB's for being one part sorority, two parts sekrit writing lair, and three parts kraken. I'm already counting down the days till the next retreat.

To my agent, Susan Hawk, and my editor, Jen Klonsky, thank you both for putting up with the sleep deprived, spacey version of me this year and for being two of the most fun people to work with in all of publishing. I'm so lucky I get to work with you both!

Susan, thank you for being on top of all the things, all the time, and for always making me laugh on the phone.

Jen, thank you for working so hard on this book and turning it around so fast. I'm surprised you didn't sustain an editing-related injury. ☺ When I go through this book and think about all the things that wouldn't be there without you—the structure, the email, all kinds of friendship-y feels—I am blown away.

Huge thanks to Catherine Wallace (side note: Every time I get a package with your name on it, I do a happy dance). To Michelle Taormina, Alexandra Alexo, Lillian Sun, Karen Sherman, Christina Colangelo, Kara Brammer, Stephanie Hoover, Susan Katz, Kate Jackson, Andrea Pappenheimer and her whole team, and to anyone else at Harper who worked on my book in any way. You guys are the greatest.

To my family, for all the love and support this year, and

especially Mom, Mica, Bekah, Dennis, and Maxie for taking care of my brave, strong girl so I had time to write about brave, strong girls.

To Ansley and Xander, there aren't words to describe how happy you make me. And Xander, thank you so much for holding off on making your appearance until after I turned in this book. I will definitely keep this in mind when I'm deciding whether to show the naked baby pictures to your future prom date.

And to Zack Allen. Thank you for countless conversations on Brazilian food and language and culture. Ana wouldn't have been the same character without you. Also, thanks for being my person.

Sometimes a girl has to kiss a lot of frogs. . .

No matter how many boys Claire kisses, she can't seem to find someone who's right for her, or wouldn't rather date her best friend, Megan. Until Claire meets Luke. Only problem: Megan is falling for Luke too.

With true love and best friendship on the line, Claire suddenly has everything to lose. And what she learns—about her crush, her friends, and most of all herself—makes the choices even harder.